Finding Paradise

Finding Paradise

a novel

Michele Ashman Bell

Covenant Communications, Inc.

Covenant

Cover image by Philip Coblentz © Brand X Pictures/GettyImages

Cover design copyrighted 2004 by Covenant Communications, Inc.

Published by Covenant Communications, Inc.
American Fork, Utah

Printed in Canada
First Printing: May 2004

10 09 08 07 06 05 04   10 9 8 7 6 5 4 3 2 1

ISBN 1-59156-502-2

This book is dedicated to Gary—my hero, my best friend, my husband. It could never be paradise without you.

Chapter One

Aqua waves from the Caribbean Sea lapped at the shoreline, splashing warm, salty kisses against Morgan's ankles. She stopped to dig her toe into the white sand to loosen a seashell. Stooping down to pick up the shell, Morgan paused as a gull cried overhead, its wings spread wide in the warm, tropical breeze. It was more than picturesque, and for a fleeting moment she longed to capture it on a canvas. Slowly she moved on, leaving the artist inside her behind in that moment.

Ahead of her, a couple basking in the golden sunshine whispered and laughed together, stealing kisses and sipping on icy cold drinks with colorful paper umbrellas in them.

Morgan turned her head toward the ocean, focusing her gaze on a man dangling from a parachute while being pulled by a speedboat. He floated and dipped over the gem-colored water as onlookers clapped and snapped pictures.

Feeling like a fish out of water, Morgan decided to go back to her room and take a long, hot bubble bath. She'd arrived in Cancún earlier that day and came to realize very quickly that the lavish resort was not the best place for a single woman to hang out, especially around Valentine's Day. She was surrounded by couples enjoying the romantic atmosphere and families enjoying a vacation full of sun and fun.

Crouching down to gather one last seashell, she was surprised when a volleyball rolled in front of her and stopped. She picked up the ball and stood to find herself looking into a pair of blue eyes.

The man smiled—his broad, white-toothed grin lighting up his whole face. Morgan admired his tousled black curls and bronzed skin, and couldn't help smiling back.

He held his hands toward her. She stared at them for a moment before realizing why they were outstretched toward her. "Oh! This must be yours." She handed him the ball.

"Thanks," he said. "You want to play?"

She gave a brief glance at the group of bikini-clad beauties and muscular guys waiting for him to return with the ball and became painfully aware of her pale skin and less-than-buff body. "Oh, no," she stumbled over her words. "I was just on my way back to my room."

"Okay," he said with a wink. "Maybe another time."

He turned and batted the ball back to the group, then joined his friends and the game continued.

Morgan hurried away, feeling a flush of color rise to her cheeks. Part of her wished she had accepted his invitation to play volleyball, but the timid-librarian side of her won, as it usually did.

While Morgan wished her friend Samantha had planned a more traditional wedding rather than getting married on a powdery white beach in Cancún, Mexico, she figured there wasn't much she could do about her "square peg in a round hole" situation at the resort. Samantha was determined to get married on Monday—Valentine's Day, the most romantic day of the year—on the beach.

This is for Samantha. Just make the best of it, Morgan told herself. *Then you can go home right after the ceremony.* She'd planned on staying the rest of the week, like most of the guests attending the wedding. She thought she'd hang out with Samantha's little sister, Veronica—Ronny for short. But Veronica had a boyfriend who'd tagged along, and that meant Morgan was on her own. Of course, she'd received invitations to join Samantha's parents for dinner and to go on tours with them to see Mayan ruins, but that wasn't the way Morgan had planned on spending her vacation. It was her first vacation since starting at the library three years ago, fresh out of college.

The Gran Caribe Real was a sprawling, five-star resort and hotel with a luscious pool, five highly rated restaurants, and a view of the ocean from nearly every room. Morgan had been hesitant at first to agree to attend Samantha's wedding, but Samantha had insisted and helped Morgan realize that she deserved a vacation. And besides,

Samantha claimed, she couldn't go through such an important day without her best friend.

The two girls had been friends since junior high school and were as close as sisters. Samantha was LDS, like Morgan, but had stopped going to church soon after their high school graduation. Even though Samantha's parents were LDS, neither of them acknowledged any association with the Church. Samantha's interest and activity in church and Young Women had stemmed only from her friendship with Morgan and the efforts of loving leaders.

After high school, Samantha's full-time job required she work on Sunday. Morgan saw her friend less and less at church until finally Samantha quit going altogether. It broke Morgan's heart because she knew Samantha had a testimony deep down inside. Meeting and dating Trevor seemed to be the final step in Samantha's complete separation from activity in the Church. Samantha was still a sweet, wonderful person, but apparently she no longer saw the need for religion in her life. Yet Morgan vowed never to give up on her friend, especially when she was the only link Samantha had to the Church.

"Morgan," a voice from overhead called.

Morgan looked up to see Samantha waving wildly at her as she hung over the balcony four stories above.

"Come up!" Samantha yelled. "I need your help."

Moments later, Morgan arrived at Samantha's hotel room, where it looked as though a clothing store had exploded. Swimsuits were strewn from the balcony to the bathroom. Sarongs, cover-ups, lingerie, and all sorts of beachwear littered the floors and the beds.

"If you're expecting me to hang up all this stuff, I'm leaving," Morgan said. The two had shopped together enough for Morgan to know that it was usually Samantha inside the dressing room trying on clothes while Morgan sat outside watching the fashion show and hanging up the rejects.

"No, silly," Samantha replied. "I was sure about this dress," she said, holding up the white chiffon dress she'd planned on wearing for the wedding ceremony, "but I saw this dress downstairs in the window and fell in love with it." She held up another dress. "Plus I saw a few other things I liked."

"A few!" Morgan exclaimed. "Is there anything left in the shop?"

Samantha gave her an unamused look. "Come on, Morgan, help me. The wedding's tomorrow. I have to decide. You've got such great taste, and you know me better than anyone. Which one of these says, 'Samantha'?"

Morgan looked at the two dresses. The spaghetti-strap chiffon dress was airy and simple, light enough for the beach, and elegant enough for a wedding. The other one—a strapless, clingy number with sequins and a slit up the thigh on one side—was indeed an eye-catcher, but a little too glamorous and gaudy. Neither of them was modest enough, in Morgan's opinion.

"The strapless one says, 'Samantha,'" Morgan told her honestly. "But I like the other one the best."

"Well, that doesn't help much," Samantha complained.

"I can't choose for you, Sammy," Morgan said. "Why don't you try each of them on?"

Out of habit, while Samantha tried on the dresses, Morgan began hanging clothes back on their hangers. She'd gotten quite good at it over the years.

Samantha stepped out of the bathroom in the strapless dress. She looked stunning, but the bare shoulders and low-cut neckline just weren't flattering.

"I think Trevor would really like this one," Samantha said, turning from side to side in front of the full-length mirror.

Morgan grimaced. *Trevor.* Try as she might, she'd never grown to like her friend's fiancé. Sure, he was handsome and charming. And cute, if you liked bleached-blond hair in gelled spikes, tattoos, and pierced ears. He was just too rough and too crude for Morgan. But Samantha adored the ground he walked on.

Morgan noticed Samantha pulling the bodice up several times, and holding herself stiffly as if trying not to exhale too freely for fear the whole thing would slide to the floor.

"Try on the other one," Morgan suggested.

Continuing to hang up clothes, Morgan had one bed nearly cleared off when Samantha stepped out of the bathroom again.

Samantha walked to the mirror, the dress floating gracefully with each footstep.

"Compared to the other, this one is too plain," she decided.

Morgan walked over to her friend. She stood behind Samantha and took her long, curly blonde hair and twisted it on top of her head, letting several tendrils fall on each side of her face.

"This dress couldn't be more perfect," she said. "It looks beautiful on you, plus you don't look as worried in this one."

"Worried?"

"You know," Morgan clarified, "like you're afraid to breathe for fear it will fall off."

Samantha had to agree that the other dress did concern her a bit.

"You want people looking at you, not the dress," Morgan told her. "This one looks like it was made just for you, for this occasion." Morgan didn't tell her that ever since Samantha had begun dating Trevor, her appearance had changed from the wholesome beauty she'd always had to the hard, biker-chic look she now sported. Samantha had changed her silky, light brown hair to a bleached, permed style. Her creamy skin was constantly tanned, and she'd had several cosmetic surgeries to enhance her shape. She knew Samantha was still the same inside, but Morgan had noticed that Trevor's influence was even having an effect on her that way too. Samantha had never been a drinker nor a late-night partier, but Trevor's lifestyle involved those activities, and Samantha had learned that if she wanted to be with him, that's what she had to do.

Samantha smiled and took one last look in the mirror. "You're right. It really is beautiful."

"You'll make a beautiful bride."

"Thanks, Morgan. I'm so glad you came. It wouldn't be the same without you." Samantha gave her a hug. "Have you been having fun? Where had you come from when I saw you?"

"Just down to the beach."

"How's the water?"

"Warm and clear," Morgan replied. "The weather is really beautiful outside."

"Have you decided yet which tours you want to go on?"

Morgan busied herself hanging up a pair of white linen capris and didn't answer.

"Morgan, you're not still planning on going home early, are you?" Samantha scolded. "I won't let you! This vacation is long overdue for you. You need to learn to loosen up, have fun, experience life. You spend too much time with books and sitting behind a desk."

"I know, I know," Morgan replied. But Samantha didn't understand that even though Morgan agreed, a vacation alone was really no vacation at all. What fun was going to fascinating sites or experiencing new and interesting things if you couldn't share it with someone? And with Manny to consider, the last thing she wanted to do was try to meet guys while she was there.

She wasn't sure exactly how to define her relationship with Manny. They dated fairly regularly, but they were also free to see others. Manny had been the most popular boy in high school—handsome, athletic, and a born leader. Out of all the girls he could have had, Morgan was a little surprised she was the one he'd dated his senior year. But his family moved out of state after high school, and then he'd gone on his mission. After that, they'd drifted apart.

When he showed up in Sacramento again, it had been fun and exciting and Morgan had thought that maybe there was a reason he was back in her life. But now, after months of dating, she didn't think their relationship was going anywhere. They just didn't click. But in all honesty, at twenty-seven years of age she was afraid that if she lost him, she might never find anyone else. Sure, things weren't perfect in their relationship, but there was a sense of security that came from being with Manny. With him, she knew what she was getting.

"Hello?" Samantha said. "Earth to Morgan."

Morgan blinked and looked at her friend. "Sorry. Did you say something?"

Samantha rolled her eyes and shook her head. "Listen to me, Morgan. You are beautiful and intelligent. Go out and have some fun. Meet some new people. Who knows? Maybe you'll find someone special."

"But—"

"I know, I know, you and Manny are dating, but you two aren't really serious. It would be silly for you to not have fun while you're here. I have one suggestion, though."

Morgan knew that Samantha was Samantha, straightforward and honest—painfully honest. Though Morgan had grown used to her friend's frank opinions, she didn't always appreciate them.

"Yes?" Morgan prompted, wanting to get the advice over with.

"You need to tone down your goody-two-shoes image. I think you scare guys away."

Morgan wasn't offended by Samantha's statement—she'd heard it from her before. But she was curious about it. Why should she have to change who she was to get a guy? What was the sense in that? Shouldn't a person love her for who she was, not for who she pretended to be?

"Then I guess it will have to take a pretty special guy to fall in love with me, won't it? Someone who doesn't scare easily."

Samantha's expression softened, and she nodded. "I'm sorry. You're right. And I think you deserve someone very special."

"And he'll be someone worth waiting for, won't he?"

Samantha nodded again, then turned back to the mirror. "So, this is the dress I'm going to be married in. Can you believe it? I'm getting married tomorrow."

The telephone on the nightstand trilled loudly. Samantha rushed to answer it.

Morgan continued hanging up clothes while Samantha spoke briefly.

"That was Trevor. He's going to grab a bite to eat with Justin and the rest of the guys," she said after she hung up the phone.

"Which one is Justin?"

"Trevor's best man."

Trevor and all his college buddies were still very close, even though they'd been out of college for several years. In Morgan's opinion, Trevor seemed to place as much emphasis on his relationship with his friends as he did on his relationship with Samantha. She hoped it wouldn't lead to problems in their marriage down the road.

"I think out of all of his buddies, he thinks the most of Justin. He's a really great guy," Samantha continued.

"That's nice," Morgan said, clipping a soft, coral-colored sun dress onto a hanger.

"You should meet Justin. I think you'd like him."

Morgan shot her friend a warning look. She'd already advised all her family and friends that she was not going out on any more blind dates. For some reason, everyone who knew her thought they knew just what kind of guy she was looking for. But after all the setups she'd endured, she had finally told everyone that she was taking a break.

"I know, I know. I'm not trying to set you up. I just think you'd enjoy being around him. He's a lot of fun."

"I'm fine," Morgan assured Samantha. "I don't need someone around to help me have fun while I'm here. I can do that on my own."

"I hate the thought of you being alone, though. Especially here in Cancún. I didn't know Ronny was bringing her boyfriend. I'm sorry."

"Hey, I'm fine. Don't worry about me," Morgan insisted.

"But I don't want you to leave without at least seeing some of the ruins. My parents are going to Chichén Itzá. You should go with them."

Morgan looked at her friend's pleading expression. "I'll think about it."

"And would you promise me just one more thing?"

Morgan wasn't about to agree to anything until she'd heard the proposition.

"Promise me you'll at least try to get to know Justin."

Morgan opened her mouth to remind Samantha about her agreement not to play matchmaker, but Samantha stopped her. "I know, I know. I'm not trying to hook you two up, but he's special to me and Trevor, and so are you. It would be nice if you two were friends."

Figuring she had nothing to lose and that there was no commitment involved, Morgan agreed.

Samantha smiled. "Good. Now, help me take these back to the store and we'll go grab a bite to eat. I'm starving."

Chapter Two

Morgan stood before the mirror in her room and turned from side to side, wondering if she looked all right in the light blue dress she and Samantha had picked out for her to wear at the wedding. It was lovely, with short, feathery chiffon sleeves, a square neckline, and long, flowing layers, but she wasn't used to such frilly, feminine clothes. Her clothes usually bordered on the practical side—sensible shoes, comfortable pants and sweaters, or plain and simple skirts and tops. While the library didn't necessarily have a dress code, it just didn't seem the place for frilly and flirty outfits like this.

She wondered for a moment what would have happened had she followed her dream to become an art teacher. She'd always loved art and had planned to get a degree in art and a teaching certificate to teach at the high-school level, but it just hadn't worked out that way. Her minor was in art, but she'd graduated with a more practical major in history in anticipation of her current job.

Now she regretted it.

She often thought about going back to school and pursuing her dream of teaching art, but she never got around to doing it. Maybe it was the thought of all the work it would involve. Maybe it was the prospect of going back to school at her age. The library was safe and secure. Wasn't there something to be said for that?

Earlier that day, Morgan had spent the morning with Samantha and Veronica, getting her hair done. Her golden-blonde hair was now piled onto her head in tiny barrel rolls with braids and ringlets pinned and placed in various spots, then adorned with glittery, gem-studded bobby pins. She'd never felt so fancy and dressed up in her life, even when she went to her high school prom.

She slipped on a pair of strappy sandals, even though for the ceremony she'd be barefoot in the sand. Everyone would be barefoot. She was to walk down the aisle after Veronica, who would scatter a trail of rose petals on the beach.

She glanced out the window. The view from her room was directly above the beach where the wedding would take place. White folding chairs were placed in rows, facing the ocean. Tall, white stands held flickering lanterns, which swayed in the ocean breeze. An archway draped with tropical flowers crowned the spot where Samantha and Trevor would exchange their vows.

With her stomach in a knot, Morgan took one last look in the mirror, grabbed her tiny beaded purse containing lip gloss, Tic Tacs, her room key, and tissues, and left her room. It was time for the ceremony.

ॐ ॐ ॐ

Giving Samantha's hand one last squeeze for good luck, Morgan began her walk down the aisle. The sun hung low over the calm, shimmering ocean. Sunset. Samantha and Trevor wanted to exchange vows exactly as the sun was setting.

Holding her head high and keeping a smile on her face, Morgan took slow, measured steps toward the archway ahead of her. She caught Trevor's eye and grinned wider. He had been teasing her before the ceremony about how she didn't look like the Morgan he knew, saying that she must be Morgan's secret sister, who was a model from New York. Morgan appreciated his compliments. Obviously he thought she looked nice all dressed up like she was, but she also wished he knew when to stop. He'd teased her until she was bright red with embarrassment.

But now, he was just his regular old self, looking handsome in a white linen shirt and white slacks. His spiked blond hair looked even whiter against his freshly tanned skin.

She was almost to the front when her gaze slipped to Trevor's best man and she looked into a pair of familiar blue eyes. The person looking back at her seemed to register the same recognition. This time, instead of wearing swim trunks and carrying a volleyball, he was dressed in white linen trousers with a crisp cotton shirt that rippled in the soft Caribbean breeze.

He gave her a friendly smile, his eyebrows arching below glossy black curls.

Feeling a warm flush creep up her neck to her face, Morgan quickly looked away and took her spot next to Veronica.

Then everyone watched anxiously for Samantha to come down the aisle.

Samantha had chosen to wear the clinging, strapless gown she'd found in the boutique at the resort. She looked glamorous, but not quite right for a romantic wedding on the beach.

Yet after seeing the look of approval on Trevor's face, Morgan knew that Samantha had chosen the dress to please him.

For a moment, a horrible thought flashed across Morgan's mind. She found herself wondering if Samantha and Trevor would make it as a married couple. She envisioned him making all the decisions and Samantha waiting on him hand and foot, carrying out his every order. With all her heart, Morgan prayed they'd be happy together.

Samantha took her place next to Trevor. They gazed into each other's eyes, a look of love passing between them. As the rays of the setting sun cast a magical glow around them, the ceremony began.

Samantha's mother sniffed into a hankie as the man marrying the couple spoke about the marriage union and the importance of always showing love and kindness to each other. He reminded them never to go to bed angry and to put each other's needs before their own. Then he read them their vows, which they repeated in turn. Morgan listened intently as Samantha and Trevor spoke each word with love and sincerity. But there was something lacking in their promises to each other. There was no mention of eternal togetherness, no progression as a couple. Everything they built during their marriage on this earth would eventually end with death.

Tears filled Morgan's eyes, but they weren't tears of joy. Samantha and Trevor were good people, and they deserved an eternity of happiness. But their fairy tale ended with "happily ever after," and Morgan knew she wanted hers to be happily *forever* after. She wanted to marry someone who shared her goals and beliefs, who had the same values and saw the same purpose in life.

She wiped away her tears, hoping that this union would be blessed with happiness but knowing that, as with any marriage, there would be trials. The gospel could help them face those trials. She hoped that somehow Samantha would realize this and share her knowledge with Trevor. She just wondered what it would take to get them to realize it.

❧ ❧ ❧

Surrounded by columns of white and silver balloons, with a small local band playing festive Caribbean music, the wedding party expressed congratulations to the bride and groom before taking their seats at a banquet table in honor of the marriage.

Everyone grew quiet when they heard the clear, bell-like tapping of a knife on a crystal goblet. Morgan watched as Trevor's best man, Justin, stood and raised his glass to the bride and groom. "It's my honor, as best man, to say a few words to the newlyweds," he said. "First, to my best friend, Trevor, my congratulations. And to his beautiful bride, Sammy, my condolences." The group of family and friends laughed.

"In all seriousness, though," he continued, "getting married is the most important decision you'll ever make in your life. There is no greater commitment than that between husband and wife. May the love you feel in your hearts tonight give you a lifetime of joy, trust, and fulfillment, that your marriage will grow and deepen through the years. Trevor, you've just gained a wife and a devoted companion. Sammy, you've gained a husband who will cherish you and take care of you, along with four of the most obnoxious friends a guy could ever have. May the four of us be as lucky someday as our buddy Trevor is tonight."

Glasses were lifted, Justin's words were toasted, and the dinner began. Morgan did more observing than eating as the meal was served. She had to admit that part of her was jealous of Samantha. She, too, wanted romance and excitement in her life, but she knew there was much more to a relationship—and especially a marriage—than romance. This also caused her to worry about Samantha. Without the strong bond and commitment from a temple marriage, where common goals and eternal covenants existed, Samantha's marriage would be sorely tested. Samantha was giving everything to Trevor, but Morgan feared that even though Trevor loved Samantha, he saw her as merely an extension of the life he already led. Morgan hoped she was wrong. With all her heart, she prayed her fears would never come true.

She watched Justin out of the corner of her eye. He and his friends laughed loudly, their voices nearly drowning out the music. Wine and drinks flowed freely, and she found herself uncomfortable with the group. She'd never spent much time with people who celebrated with booze, and she didn't like seeing the tipsy, ridiculous side of them.

She thought of Manny back home. He was much more reserved and quiet than any of the men at the wedding, always one to keep his emotions in check and his life in control. He wasn't one for surprises or spontaneity. In fact, he was sometimes so dependable and practical that he bordered on boring, but if the choice were between someone like Trevor and someone like Manny, she'd take Manny.

Still, she found herself wishing that Manny would lighten up and have more fun.

"So, my dear," Samantha's grandmother said as she reached across the table and took Morgan's hand in hers, "tell me how things are going in your life."

Morgan recognized the question as one that really meant, "Are you ever going to get married?" She knew that to tell about her job, her church calling as Primary chorister in her ward, and the time she spent volunteering at the center for the elderly wasn't what Samantha's grandmother wanted to hear.

"Things are good," she answered vaguely, knowing it was the quickest way to end the discussion. "Nothing new, really."

"You're still at the library, dear?"

Morgan nodded.

Tsk-tsking in a grandmotherly sort of way, Samantha's grandmother shook her head slowly and patted Morgan's hand.

Morgan *wanted* to tell her to save her pity and assure her that she was blessed and had a wonderful life. She made a reasonable income, and she had security and a nice savings account in the bank. But in most people's minds, that didn't add up to having a man in her life, which seemed to be the summation of success and true happiness. At twenty-seven, she knew she was old enough to get married, but she certainly wasn't old enough to be considered a loser and a spinster.

"Well, you still have time," Samantha's grandmother said. "I just don't understand how such a pretty thing like yourself is still single. I imagine you don't meet many eligible men at the library, though, do you?"

"Not many," Morgan said, suddenly feeling the need to excuse herself. "Oh, there's Samantha! I haven't had a chance to congratulate her. Would you excuse me?"

Without even waiting for a reply, Morgan shot out of her chair and headed for the table where Samantha sat alone while Trevor visited with his friends at their side of the table.

"Hey," Morgan said, sitting in Trevor's seat.

"Hi," Samantha said warmly. The two girls hugged. "So, what did you think?"

"It was beautiful. You look really happy."

"I am," Samantha said. "Trevor is everything I've ever wanted in a man. I feel so lucky."

"I think he's the lucky one," Morgan said.

Samantha smiled. "You sure look pretty tonight. All of Trevor's friends have asked about you. Particularly Justin."

"Justin?" Morgan said, surprised by Samantha's comment.

"Isn't he a doll?"

"He seems kind of full of himself—a little too overbearing and overconfident for me."

"Yeah, he kind of is, but he's so cute."

"I've tried cute, and that's not enough for me. It's almost as if the cuter they are outside, the less substance there is inside."

"I think Justin would surprise you."

"Maybe, but he's not my type, and I'm not looking for a relationship right now."

"Because of Manny?"

"No, of course not. You know Manny and I are free to date whoever we want."

"Well, then, have a little fun while you're here. Who knows? Someday, if you're lucky, you'll find someone as wonderful as Trevor." Samantha cast a dreamy glance toward her new husband, who was laughing with his buddies as they raised their glasses.

I hope I do a whole lot better than that, Morgan thought.

ॐ ॐ ॐ

After deciding to give Cancún one more day, Morgan thought that the least she could do was come home with some sort of tan. She grabbed her beach bag full of suntan lotion, magazines, and a towel, and headed for the pool. Even at eleven in the morning, there was barely a free lounge chair to be found.

Finally she found one out of the way near a cluster of palm trees. Directly in front of her was the bar, which served drinks to guests in the pool, who sat on little stools immersed in the clear water on one side of the bar. The other side was under a thatch-roofed cabana.

She'd barely gotten her towel spread out on the chair when a young waiter approached. "Could I get you a drink, miss?"

She ordered a soft drink and relaxed back into the chair, letting her body soak up some sun before putting on suntan lotion. She'd slept well the night before, but there was something about the sun and the beach that made her muscles completely relax. As she reclined back in the chair, she allowed her cares and worries to drift away on the soft Caribbean breeze.

The music and the laughter of people splashing in the pool sounded as though they were in the distance. Morgan felt herself completely unwind.

She dozed for several minutes until the waiter returned with her drink.

"Can I get you anything else?" he asked. "Something from the kitchen?"

She had forgotten that her hotel reservation was all-inclusive, which meant she could eat and drink freely at any of the establishments on the property.

"I'd love some fruit. Do you have any?"

"Oh, yes, miss, we have fruit. I'll bring you some."

"Thank you," she said. She watched the waiter walk away and decided she liked having someone wait on her for a change.

A burst of laughter near the bar caught her attention. She looked over to see Trevor's buddies ordering drinks. Eyeing Justin, she watched him take a sip of his fruity drink, then laugh out loud at something one of the guys said.

A couple of girls walked by, and Morgan watched as the men turned, their gazes following the bathing beauties to their lounge chairs. Justin, however, was talking to the bartender and getting another drink. The guys shared a comment among themselves, then burst out laughing.

Disgusted, Morgan took a long drink of the ice-cold Sprite with a wedge of lime, then stretched out on the lounge chair and sighed lazily. She was the type who didn't know how it felt to be bored. Spare time was a luxury for her. She hardly watched TV, and she rarely entertained, since she had plenty of other activities to keep her days busy and full.

She put her drink on the table and glanced up, catching her breath as she saw Justin watching her.

Did he even recognize her?

She didn't have to wonder long. He gave her a smile and waved.

Her first inclination was to turn away, but she didn't want to be rude. She waved back, then acted as though there was something important she needed in her bag. She found a magazine and settled back to read, focusing her attention on an ad for getting stains out of laundry.

Just then, a shadow passed over her, and she expected to see the waiter show up with her plate of fruit. She looked up and saw Justin instead.

"Hi," he said with a friendly grin.

"Hi," she answered, wondering what he was doing.

"Mind if I sit down?" He pulled a lounge chair next to her and sat down. "So, you're Samantha's friend?"

She nodded. "I'm Morgan Rose."

He extended his hand toward her. "I'm Justin Connery. We never got a chance to meet last night. You must have left right after dinner."

He'd noticed?

"I think I had a touch of jet lag," she replied.

"How long have you known Samantha?"

"Since junior high," she told him.

He nodded. "I met Trevor in college. That's where all of us met, in fact. We all played football at San Diego State."

"Are you from there?"

"No, I'm from the Bay Area originally. Now I live in Manhattan, and my parents live on Long Island."

Now it was her turn to nod.

"So," he continued, "what about you?"

Just then, the waiter arrived with her plate of fruit. Justin glanced at the appetizing array and ordered one for himself. Then, as soon as the words were out of his mouth, he turned to Morgan. "That is, if you don't mind me eating with you."

Morgan certainly didn't want to be rude and say no, and besides, if the truth were known, it was kind of nice having someone to talk to. He did seem pleasant enough.

"I'd also like to order some drinks, please," he told the waiter. "Morgan, have you tried their strawberry daiquiris? They're out of this world."

"Oh, I don't drink alcohol," she told him.

"Could we get two virgin strawberry daiquiris?" Justin asked the waiter.

The waiter nodded and hurried away.

Justin turned his head to look at his shoulders. "Does it look to you like I'm getting sunburned?"

"Your shoulders do look a little pink. So do your cheeks," Morgan confessed.

"I'd better see if any of the guys have sunscreen," he said.

"I've got some you can use," she offered. She rifled through her bag and handed him a tube.

"Looks like you've thought of everything," he said, applying the lotion. "So, you were just about to tell me about yourself."

Morgan didn't feel like telling him about her life. First of all, he was practically a stranger, and second of all, her life was boring.

She hesitated a moment longer, trying to decide what to say, when he piped up again. "Wait, I know. Let me ask you three questions. From how you answer, I'll bet I can tell you about yourself."

Morgan's eyebrows lifted with amusement. "You think so, huh?"

"Try me."

"Okay, what's your first question?" Morgan stabbed a piece of juicy cantaloupe with her fork and nibbled on the corner.

"Where did you grow up?"

Morgan swallowed. "Well, I was born in Salt Lake City, Utah, and lived there until I was ten. Then my father got a different job, and our family moved to Sacramento. I've lived there ever since."

"Okay," he said, appearing to process the information. "Where do you fit in your family?"

"I'm the third out of four children. The two oldest are boys, and I had a younger sister, but she died."

"How did she die, if you don't mind me asking?"

Morgan hesitated. Somehow she felt safe enough to talk openly. "In a car accident. She was hit by a drunk driver the day after she got her driver's license."

His eyes filled with sadness. "Wow, that must be hard for your family. I'm sorry."

"Thanks. It's still hard, even though it's been over five years."

He looked at her, studying her face, his own reflecting sincere sympathy. "I guess you really understand the saying, 'That which doesn't kill you makes you stronger.'"

She shrugged. "I don't feel very strong. You just do what you have to do to get through it." It was true that time helped heal the wound, but Morgan doubted that enough time would ever pass to make her quit missing her sister. And she knew that her parents would never be the same. Her dad seemed to handle it better than her mom. He was still his fun, joking self, but her mother seemed to find little joy in life anymore.

"Do you mind if I ask my last question?" he asked. "Or maybe you'd rather we stop."

"No, not at all," she said. "I'm fine, really." It hadn't always been easy to talk about her sister's death, but she felt surprisingly calm telling Justin about it.

He looked her straight in the eye. "You're sure?"

She gave him a smile. "I'm positive. Ask me anything."

"Where do you work?"

She chuckled. She'd been expecting a much more personal question. "At the county library," she answered.

"Hmm. Not what I thought you'd say."

"Really? What did you think I did for a living?"

"Something creative and artistic."

His answer surprised her. "What made you think that?"

"I don't know. I think it's the way I've seen you study things."

She laughed again but secretly wondered what he was talking about.

"I watched you on the beach the other day. You seemed to be memorizing details, studying movement, observing people. And at the wedding dinner, you seemed fascinated by everything going on around you."

Morgan was surprised at the accuracy of his statement. "I studied art in college. I wanted to be a high school art teacher."

"How did you end up at the library?"

"It was a much easier and quicker means to an end. I guess, though, in all honesty, I gave up. A degree in art required much more work than history. But don't get me wrong, I love what I do."

"That's good. And I guess that's what's most important—that you love what you do."

She agreed, though she had always wondered if she would have loved teaching art more. She rarely spent time painting these days, even though she thought about it all the time. She missed it. It was as if something inside her soul wasn't being fed.

Justin brought up the back of his chair to a straighter position and smiled as the waiter approached them.

After they received their drinks and his food, he handed Morgan her strawberry daiquiri and assured her, "You're going to love this."

Morgan hesitated to taste it just in case the waiter hadn't followed their order correctly to leave out the alcohol, but since Justin was watching her, she took a small sip from her straw. The icy, berry-flavored mixture slid deliciously down the back of her throat.

Without pause, she took another drink. "Wow," she couldn't help saying. "This is good."

With a triumphant smile, he took a sip from his own drink. "I'm glad you like it."

She took one more drink, then looked at him with anticipation, curious to know what kind of conclusion he'd drawn from the questions she'd answered.

With a teasing lift of one eyebrow, Justin returned her gaze, still saying nothing.

"Well?" Morgan asked.

"Well, what?"

"Aren't you going to give me your analysis?"

He chuckled. "You're anxious to know what I think?"

"It's more like I'm curious to know how close to the truth you can guess."

"Okay." He took one last drink and set down his glass. "For starters, I'd say you're intellectual but that you have a very quick wit. You love to laugh, but to most people you seem reserved, maybe even shy. Which you're not," he stated matter-of-factly. "You just don't like to draw attention to yourself."

Morgan listened without expression.

"No, let me rephrase that. You don't *need* to draw attention to yourself."

"What's the difference?" she asked, trying not to act surprised by the accuracy of his appraisal of her.

"The difference is you are self-assured and confident in who you are. You don't need the validation of others to prove your worth."

She again tried not to react to his comment, but she realized that he had managed to state in words something she'd always felt in her heart. Many people thought of her as shy and quiet, but in truth, she just didn't feel a need to get others' attention by being loud and overbearing. It wasn't her style.

"Having two older brothers, I'd guess you're pretty tough, and I'll bet you're good at sports, too. You play the piano well, and you probably love books and reading. You're also very punctual."

Morgan's mouth dropped open. Except for the piano part—and especially for the punctual part—he was exactly right.

"Actually, I play the flute," she told him.

He nodded. "Okay, I probably should have said musical instrument, but with those long fingers of yours, you would have been a fantastic piano player."

She couldn't hide the disappointment she felt.

"I'm sorry, did I say something to upset you?"

She shook her head. "No. It's just that I did take piano lessons until our family moved to Sacramento. Then we couldn't afford them anymore. My mother played the flute and taught me how, but I always wanted to play the piano," she told him. "Always."

"It's never too late, you know," he said. "I mean, there's still a lot of things I haven't gotten around to doing yet but plan to do someday. Same with your art. Why don't you go back to school and get another degree? You'd be a great art teacher."

Morgan looked at him with admiration. "I should. I'll think about it."

He shrugged and attended to his platter of fruit.

"So how do you do it?"

"Do what?" He speared a chunk of pineapple and poked it into his mouth with gusto. "This pineapple is incredible," he said, his words garbled by the fruit.

Morgan nodded in agreement. She'd sampled all the different fruits on her plate, and all of them were delicious.

"How do you figure out so much about a person from those three questions?"

"I studied psychology in college. I love figuring out people. It's not really that hard."

"Are you a psychiatrist?" Morgan wasn't sure she liked having a conversation with him if he was. She didn't want to find out about any more of her problems than she currently dealt with.

"No, actually, I'm in international business, but it's amazing how much psychology is a part of my job."

"So, is it my turn?"

"Your turn?" he replied, his expression puzzled.

"Yes. Do I get to ask those same three questions of you?"

He appeared to be surprised by her request. "I'm usually the one asking the questions."

"It's only fair," she said.

"I guess it is."

"Okay, then. You already said you're from the Bay Area, so we'll start with your family. Where do you fit in your family?"

Justin didn't have a chance to answer before one of his buddies came running over to them, his Hawaiian-print trunks hanging low on his hips. "Dude, our boat arrived. We gotta go," he said, raking his hand through a mop of sun-bleached blond hair.

"Morgan, this is Derek," Justin introduced them.

"Hey." Derek nodded at her briefly, then turned to Justin again. "The guys are waiting."

"Guess I have to go," Justin said apologetically. "We chartered a boat to take us scuba diving. Do you dive?" he asked.

"Sorry," she answered. She didn't even know how to snorkel.

Derek took off to join his friends, turning once more to remind Justin to hurry.

"Maybe we could get together later," Justin suggested. "Are you going to the karaoke party?"

As much as she liked to sing, Morgan would never be caught dead singing disco songs in front of a group of strangers. "I wasn't planning on it."

"You should come. It's a ton of fun," he urged, taking one last bite of pineapple.

"I'll think about it. I may be going home tomorrow, though."

"Home? Didn't you just get here two days ago?"

Morgan nodded.

"You can't go home yet, then. Have you even been on any of the tours?"

"No."

"You should stay," Justin urged as his friends hollered for him. "Listen, I have to go, but promise me you won't leave tomorrow," he said.

Morgan remained silent, surprised by his insistence.

"Promise me, Morgan."

"Okay, I promise," Morgan replied, a little shocked at her own willingness.

"Good." He flashed her a charming smile. "I'll find you tonight at dinner."

With a quick turn, he bolted for the beach, the muscles in his shoulders, arms, and legs rippling as he ran.

Morgan took a deep breath, wondering what had just happened. Why in the world would a guy like him want anything to do with a girl like her?

Chapter Three

———————————— ❦ ————————————

That night before dinner, Morgan found herself paying extra attention to her hair and clothes. She told herself not to be silly, that Justin probably wouldn't even show up. Besides, even if he did, he wasn't her type, and they would probably never be anything more than friends.

Still, she spritzed a little of her favorite perfume onto her neck and checked her reflection one last time in the mirror. She'd gotten slightly more color than she'd planned today, but the healthy pink looked good against her emerald-green silk shirt and floral-print skirt. Her golden curls were clipped up onto her head with a few stray tendrils teasing at her neck. Long, glittery earrings sparkled at her ears, and a matching bracelet circled her wrist.

"Not bad for a librarian," she said, then opened the door, turned out the light, and headed for the restaurant.

❦ ❦ ❦

"Did you have a fun day, dear?" Samantha's mother asked. "You look like you got some sun."

"I hung out at the pool most of the time," Morgan told her. "But my mother told me not to come home without some vanilla, so I did a little shopping and sent a few postcards."

"I'm glad you reminded me," the woman said. "I want to take some vanilla back for my neighbors." She placed her napkin on her lap and smiled at Morgan. "I'm also glad you decided to join us tomorrow. This tour is supposed to be quite amazing. I think you'll enjoy it."

Morgan had allowed Mr. and Mrs. Blakely to talk her into going on a tour to some of the Mayan ruins. It was an all-day excursion and involved a long drive on a bus, but it sounded interesting.

Mrs. Blakely and Morgan placed their orders and nibbled on fresh rolls while they talked about the wedding. Samantha's parents thought Trevor was about the greatest person on earth, and Morgan wondered why she wasn't head-over-heels crazy about him like everyone else. There was just something about him that didn't sit right with her, but since she couldn't put her finger on it, she kept her feelings to herself, figuring it was just a personality conflict.

Morgan was buttering a piece of her roll when she noticed Mrs. Blakely sit up and grin from ear to ear.

"Good evening, Mr. and Mrs. Blakely," a voice from behind her said, one she immediately recognized.

"Justin, you've met Samantha's best friend, haven't you?" Mrs. Blakely said.

"Yes, we've met," Justin said. "How are you, Morgan?"

Before Morgan could answer, Mr. Blakely invited Justin to have a seat in the empty chair at their table.

Justin's gaze connected with Morgan's, and he gave her a knowing smile. He'd told her he would come and find her, and he had.

After seating himself, Justin visited for a moment with the Blakelys. Morgan noticed how politely he conversed, as well as how warm and sincere he was. It was obvious that the Blakelys adored him, and Morgan couldn't blame them. He was confident—there was no question about that—and he was very good with people, and that was a trait she admired, one she wished she had herself.

"So, what have you two got planned while you're here?" he asked the couple.

"Tomorrow we're taking a tour to the Chichén Itzá ruins. It's supposed to be quite an experience."

Justin nodded. "You'll enjoy it. Make sure you take swimming suits."

"Swimming suits!" Mrs. Blakely exclaimed. "What for?"

"The tour bus usually stops at Dzitnup to let you swim in the cavern there."

"I think they said something about a cavern, but I don't remember them telling us to bring swimming suits, do you, Morgan?"

"I think they mentioned it," she told them. "But only for people who were interested in swimming."

"You're going with them?" Justin asked.

"They talked me into it," she confessed with a shy smile.

"You don't even have to have an interest in history to be fascinated by the ruins," he said. "Make sure you climb to the top of El Castillo."

"What if I'm afraid of heights?" she asked.

"It's worth doing. The view on top stretches for miles and miles over thick, green jungle."

"Well, I for one am not going to be swimming in a stinky old cavern," Mrs. Blakely said.

"The water in this cavern is fresh and crystal clear and about a hundred and fifty feet deep. It's also very cold, but you should do it," Justin urged. "Besides, you'll warm right up once you get outside in the heat again."

Just then, the waiter returned with their order, and even though the Blakelys invited Justin to stay and eat with them, he declined their invitation, explaining that he was meeting friends at Gaviotas, the restaurant by the beach.

He stood to leave, and Morgan realized she wished he would stay with them. His conversation was much more lively than the Blakelys'. With them the conversation typically seemed to revolve around health issues or politics.

Watching him walk away, Morgan surprised herself by wishing he'd asked her to join him.

ॐ ॐ ॐ

Before bed that night, Morgan left her room to get some ice from the machine. The sound of music downstairs in the lobby caught her attention. Was that the karaoke party?

Unable to resist, she peeked down into the lobby, where, next to the bar, a group of people sat around a small stage and a big-screen TV.

A young girl belted out a Mariah Carey song, covering any flat notes with plenty of volume. The worst thing was that she insisted on singing all three verses of the song, which further convinced Morgan that she'd made the right choice to decline Justin's offer to join the party.

Still, the crowd clapped and cheered for the girl when she was done, and the girl returned to her seat with a triumphant smile. Morgan knew that there wasn't enough money in the free world to convince her to get up on that stage and sing, even though she'd been told she had a nice singing voice and had been in her high school concert choir.

She watched as a different girl and a guy got up and sang a country song she wasn't familiar with. They got a well-deserved round of applause from the audience.

In the pause that followed that performance, Morgan noticed Samantha and Trevor seated with the group of Trevor's friends, as well as several women she didn't recognize. And there in the middle of all of them was Justin.

The crowd erupted with cheers when Trevor, Justin, and three of their friends went onstage. Morgan felt tingles of excitement watching them get into position, ready for the music to start.

The Beach Boys song "California Girls" began, and the five men began. There were a couple of times when they messed up the words and weren't together, but they always managed to sing the chorus, "I wish they all could be California girls."

Morgan saw Samantha and the other girls in the audience jump up and clap when the guys ended their song. The guys got plenty of hugs and kisses before they sat back down. Morgan couldn't tell if Justin had been on the receiving end of one of those kisses, and she chided herself for even noticing or caring. What he did and who he was with didn't concern her.

Turning away, she took her bucket of ice and went to her room.

ළ ළ ළ

Bright and early the next morning, Morgan stood in line waiting to board the bus that would take them on their day's journey. The tour guide, Santos, was a rotund little man with a booming voice. He gave them instructions and information about the two-and-a-half-hour drive to the ruins, which would include a stop at a Mayan flea market and lunch at a Mayan restaurant.

The Blakelys sat together in the seat in front of Morgan, and within five minutes, Mr. Blakely was asleep. Morgan was glad she'd brought along a magazine to read. The ride was going to be a long one.

"Excuse me, is this seat taken?" a man standing in the aisle asked.

Morgan looked up and smiled. "What are you doing here?"

Justin smiled back at her. "It's been a few years since I've seen the ruins. I wanted to go back and see if they've changed."

Morgan laughed, unable to help the silly smile on her face. She was thrilled that he'd decided to come along with them. The Blakelys were equally thrilled, and Morgan thought maybe it wouldn't be such a bad trip after all.

The bus engine roared to life, and soon they were off, heading inland. Once they had left the city of Cancún, Morgan noticed the land was flat and covered with thick, green jungle growth.

As they began visiting with one another, Justin told Morgan about the time he'd come to Cancún with his parents and had visited the ruins. It was the summer after high school, and he'd wanted to spend his vacation at the beach, not wandering around old buildings. But when they got to the ruins, he had become fascinated with them.

Morgan gazed out the window, marveling at the miles of jungle. She felt Justin's eyes on her and turned to see him staring intently at her.

He smiled.

"What are you looking at?" she asked.

"You," he answered, causing her to blush. "You have a wonderful profile," he continued.

She reached up and touched her nose and chin. "I broke my nose in junior high playing soccer. That's why there's a little bump on it."

"I like the little bump."

She blushed a deeper shade of red and looked away. Why did she let him get to her? He was nothing more than a flirt and a socializer. She'd have to remember that.

Mrs. Blakely passed a bag of candy to them that she'd brought along. Morgan was surprised to find that cinnamon was Justin's favorite flavor too. While they shared a handful of cinnamon bears, Morgan decided that this was the perfect time to give Justin his own famous "three-question" analysis.

"So, Justin, let's start again. Tell me, where did you grow up?"

He smiled at her. "In Menlo Park, south of San Francisco. But we moved to New York just before my senior year in high school."

"Where do you fit in your family?"

"I'm an only child."

"And what do you do for a living?"

"I'm an international business consultant. I'm based in New York, but most of my clients are in São Paulo, Brazil. We import things like Brazilian tile, furniture, crystal, and shoes. I spend two or three months a year there."

"Wow!" she exclaimed. "That must be fascinating."

"I love what I do," he said.

She bit the head off another cinnamon bear, and the strong bite of cinnamon made her cough. Her eyes watered until Justin produced a bottle of water from his backpack.

After taking several gulps, Morgan finally managed to clear her throat.

"Thank you," she said, wiping at her eyes.

"Got a strong one, huh?"

"Straight cinnamon." She cleared her throat and took another sip, then handed him back his water bottle. "Sorry. It's nearly gone."

"That's okay. Keep it."

She looked at him for a long time, wondering what this guy was really all about. She had to admit to herself that her first impression of him was nothing like the great guy he really seemed to be. But that was her biggest question. Was he really as great as he "seemed" to be?

"So, how did you like our song last night?" he asked suddenly.

Her mouth dropped open. She shut it quickly and swallowed. "You saw me, huh?"

"Why didn't you come down and join us? It was a lot of fun."

She shrugged, feeling stupid that he'd caught her. "I don't know. I went to get some ice and heard the noise, so I stopped to see what was going on. I was surprised when you guys got up. You did a good job, though. I liked it."

"I would have dedicated it to you if I'd known you were going to be watching," he said. "You being a California girl and all."

"Yeah, I guess I am," she said. "Hard to believe, huh?"

"What do you mean?"

"I don't know. I never really got into the beach scene."

"You don't surf?"

"No."

"You can swim, though, right?"

"A little."

"Do you snorkel?"

"No."

"Have you been sailing or deep-sea fishing?"

She shook her head.

"Is this your first time out of the country?"

She nodded.

"Have you been to Disneyland?"

She looked down at her knees and didn't answer for a minute.

"Your parents never took your family to Disneyland?" he asked quietly, his tone shocked.

"We couldn't really afford it," she defended her parents. "We went camping a lot, though."

He nodded thoughtfully. "Can I ask you something?"

She wrinkled her forehead, answering with caution. "Yes."

"What's the craziest thing you've done or the most exotic place you've been?"

"Well . . ." She started scanning her memory for an answer to his question, but she came up short. "I've . . . well, I've . . ." She stopped, knowing that there was no memory to find. She'd never really done anything crazy or been anywhere exotic.

He continued to look at her, waiting.

"I guess coming on this trip," she said, recalling her mother's complete disapproval at her spending such an enormous amount of money to go to her friend's wedding.

"Okay," he said, sounding as though he were weighing her answer.

She felt herself grow defensive. "Not everyone has the means or the opportunity to travel and experience exciting and unusual things, you know. I mean, so I've never been to Disneyland. That doesn't make me a boring person."

"No, of course it doesn't," he was quick to answer. "I didn't mean that at all." He studied her face as he continued, "I guess the bigger question is, do you wish you had gone to Disneyland as a child or run through a graveyard at midnight on Friday the thirteenth or toilet-papered someone's house? Of course, maybe you did go toilet—"

She shook her head before he could finish. Her mother would have skinned her alive had she done something like that.

"I don't want you to take this wrong or be offended," he said, "but do you ever feel like you're missing out on life?"

Her mouth dropped open in sheer exasperation. Who was he to assume her life was boring, predictable, and uneventful? And even if it was, who was he to assume she didn't want it that way? She wasn't missing out on anything . . . was she?

"I'm sorry," he quickly apologized. "I was way out of line to say that."

She licked her lips and pursed them together, unsure of what to say.

"It's just that . . . you're a very attractive woman, Morgan. You're classy and refined, and I can tell you're a very caring and giving person."

She refused to let his words make her feel any better.

"You seemed kind of shy when we first met, but I get a sense that inside there's a fun-loving woman who could embrace all the wonderful things life has to offer. Someone just needs to give you a little nudge."

"And that person is you?"

He shrugged. "I enjoy being with you. I'd love to see the look on your face the first time you go snorkeling and see a sea turtle or feel the air beneath you as you parasail over the ocean, or drink in the view from the top of El Castillo."

"I can't do that. I'm seriously afraid of heights."

"Why?"

"I don't know. I just am," she said, the defensive tone returning to her voice. "Besides, I'm not like you, Justin. I'm not wild and crazy, and . . . I have different standards than you do. I don't party or go clubbing. It's just not my kind of scene. Drinking, smoking, and stuff like that don't appeal to me."

"And you think they appeal to me?"

Now it was her turn to shrug. "It seems like you and your friends do your fair share."

A hurt look crossed his face that she didn't understand. He looked away, remaining silent.

What had she said? He hadn't tried to hide his partying, so why in the world would her mentioning it offend him?

"I'm sorry if I said something wrong, Justin," she said. "I didn't mean to."

He looked back at her. "I know. Just remember, though, that you can't judge a book by its cover."

She lifted one eyebrow, amused by his comment. Isn't that what he'd just done with her?

"I think we should both remember that," she told him. "Maybe your three-question analysis isn't so accurate after all."

"Oh? Are you saying I'm wrong about you?"

"I've thought of some outrageous things I've done before," she stated perfunctorily.

"Really. Like what?"

"Okay, well . . ." she thought for a moment. "Oh, I know. In college, my roommates and I got a midnight craving for red licorice and Twinkies, so we went to the grocery store in our pajamas . . ."

Justin raised his eyebrows and waited for a moment. "And . . . ?"

"That's it. We were in our pajamas. And slippers. Mine had Tweety Bird on them."

"Tell me something else," he requested. "Just one more."

"Well, I do stuff all the time—like not putting my cart away in the parking lot at the grocery store. Sometimes I hook the front wheels over the curb and just leave it there. Or sometimes when I'm shopping and I change my mind about something, I don't always take it back to where it's supposed to go. Sometimes I just leave it somewhere else in the store. Of course, I don't do that very often. Usually when I'm in a hurry."

"Of course," he echoed. Then he took one of her hands. "Morgan, I want to show you the best time today. But you may have to let me give you a few nudges along the way. You know, pull you out of your comfort zone."

"But comfort zones are good," she said.

"You only grow outside the comfort zone, though. We all need to grow, don't we?"

She couldn't argue with that, but she wasn't about to commit to some harebrained, risk-taking adventure either.

The bus began to slow down, and the tour guide announced that they were near the cavern, their first stop.

"You brought your swimming suit?" he asked.

Morgan wanted to say she'd forgotten it, but that was a lie. However, she didn't really want to plunge into a freezing cold bottomless pit of water either.

"Morgan?"

"Yes, I brought it."

"Good. Because you're about to have your first experience outside your comfort zone."

"Which is called the 'discomfort zone,' right?"

He chuckled. "No. It's called the 'fun zone.' The 'real world zone.' The—"

"Okay, okay, I get the idea."

He grabbed her hand and gave it a big squeeze, his eyes full of excitement.

She smiled back weakly, wondering what she'd gotten herself into. Maybe just hanging out with the Blakelys wouldn't have been so bad after all.

Chapter Four

⸙

Standing at the first lookout, Morgan and Justin gazed at the enormous, cavelike underground opening. Below, like a pool of glass, was the clearest water Morgan had ever seen. Moss, vines, and feathery ferns grew along the walls of the cavern. Above them, a large hole allowed a column of sunlight in. Shaped like large icicles, stalactites hung above the pond along with dangling vines and exposed tree roots. Morgan also spied a giant stalagmite reaching upward out of the depths of the clear water. It was surreal, like another world—a mysterious, enchanting, underground world.

"What do you think?" Justin asked.

"It's amazing," she replied breathlessly. "I had no idea it would be so beautiful."

Justin smiled, a glint of sunlight reflecting in his eyes. "I knew you'd like it." Then, without warning, he grabbed her hand.

"Where are we going?"

"I think you know," he answered, his voice echoing through the stairway of chiseled stone steps leading down deeper into the ground.

Suddenly, a whoosh of hundreds of black, fluttering wings filled the air.

"Bats!" Morgan screamed and flew into Justin's arms.

He pulled her close and ducked his own head as the swarm of startled bats made their way up the stairwell to some other damp, dark place.

"Hey," Justin said, "you're trembling." He tightened his hold on her. "It's okay. They're gone."

"I need to get out of here," Morgan said, stepping back.

Justin held her hands, trying to reassure her. "Just one foot in the pool, that's all I ask."

"You'll push me in."

"I promise I won't. You have my word as an Eagle Scout." He gave her a salute.

"How do I know you were an Eagle Scout?"

"Have I ever lied to you?"

"Gee, in the two whole days I've known you, I hope not."

"You can trust me, Morgan."

Their eyes connected, and she knew he was sincere.

"One foot," she reminded him.

They kicked off their flip-flops and piled them next to their bags and towels, then approached the water tentatively. Morgan knew she wasn't going in if it was as cold as the slab of rock she was standing on.

Sticking her big toe in convinced her to not go any farther. Justin, however, waded in above his ankles. "It's not that bad," he coaxed. "Refreshing, really."

"Morgan, Justin!" Mrs. Blakely called from overhead. She and Mr. Blakely were standing at the top, looking down at the pool of water. She held up her camera.

"She wants a picture," Morgan said.

"Well, let's give her one," he replied.

Morgan let out a little scream as Justin scooped her up into his arms and held her while Mrs. Blakely snapped several pictures.

"Okay, she's done," Morgan said nervously. "You can put me down." She noticed that Justin had a teasing glint in his eye.

"Justin, please don't. Don't throw me into that water."

He smiled and set her gently on the ground.

"I told you I wouldn't," he reminded her.

Morgan suddenly had a wicked idea. "And I appreciate that, but . . . I never said I wouldn't push you in!" She gave him a shove, and he tumbled into the freezing water.

Morgan hurried out, pushing through the dozens of other people from their bus who were daring enough to brave a dip in the pool. She knew she had to get out of there or he would pull her in with him.

She shoved her feet into her flip-flops and grabbed her bag, then stopped. Guilt flooded over her. She'd never done anything like that, and she felt terrible.

She walked back to the pool. Children shrieked as they entered the water, giggling and splashing with glee as their parents hovered to keep a close watch. Some were even joining their children.

Justin was still in the water helping a young girl, about ten years old, climb up to a ledge so she could jump in. He turned and looked at Morgan for a moment, his expression difficult to read.

A surge of heat filled her veins, and she knew what she had to do. She kicked off her shoes again, and before clear reason kicked in, she dove into the water.

A frigid shock numbed her limbs. The water was so cold she wanted to gasp but knew she couldn't. She fought her way to the surface, emerging to finally fill her lungs and get a grip on her shivering frame.

Justin hadn't seen her dive in, so she swam over to him. He was just about to climb onto a ledge where other people were jumping off into the water.

"Wait for me," she called out.

He turned and saw her, his face registering shock.

"What are you doing?" he asked.

"Freezing."

He laughed. "Felt guilty, huh?"

"That's the only reason I'm in here turning blue."

He nodded. "I'll accept that." He gestured to the ledge. "You want to jump in with me?"

"Sure, why not? If the temperature of the water didn't kill me, I doubt this will."

He helped her onto the ledge. How she had ever allowed it, she wasn't sure. But then, this cave was full of wonders.

"Are you ready?" he asked.

She nodded, glad that he was by her side in case the shock of going back into the arctic water stopped her heart.

Holding hands, they counted to three, then jumped.

This time it didn't feel quite as cold. It certainly wasn't comfortable, but it was bearable. "Let's do it one more time," she said.

Justin's eyebrows rose with surprise, but he agreed and they swam together to the ledge. This time, they climbed to a higher spot and jumped.

Members of the tour clapped when they surfaced.

Morgan laughed, but she could barely control her shivering jaw. "You ready to get out?"

"If you are," she said, trying to be tough but praying he'd say yes.

He helped her to dry ground and quickly wrapped her in a towel. Watching for bats and ducking below the low ceiling, they climbed the stairs and emerged outside, where a warm sun welcomed them. After finding a spot on a bench, they sat together and soaked up the golden rays, letting the sun's heat warm their frozen limbs. Morgan combed her fingers through her hair, letting it dry as a gentle breeze rustled the trees.

She turned her head and noticed Justin watching her. Smiling shyly, she sat up straighter and stretched her legs out in front of her.

"I'm proud of you," he said.

"You are?"

"Yeah. I know that wasn't easy for you."

She shifted her position so she could look directly at him. "It was fun," she said, with a smile.

He grinned back. "For me too."

The tour guide soon called for the members of his group to return to the bus, and before long they were on to the flea market and lunch.

ð ð ð

At the flea market Morgan found more than enough souvenirs for friends and family back home. There were carved stone figurines, hand-tooled leather goods, and brightly woven rugs. She purchased a jade-green stone carving of the pyramid they were about to see at Chichén Itzá for her mother, a leather belt for her father, and a wallet for Manny. Until she started shopping for souvenirs, she hadn't thought of Manny the whole day. Now, her thoughts turned to him in comparison to Justin. Manny would never have pressured her to jump into the water at the cavern like Justin had. In fact, he probably wouldn't have gotten in himself. If anyone liked his comfort zone, it was Manny. Justin, on the other hand, seemed to be more comfortable outside his comfort zone. And Morgan found his energy and enthusiasm contagious.

The flea market provided a wonderful taste of the local culture. After looking at their woven rugs and clothing, silver jewelry, and stone carvings, Morgan could tell the Mayan people, still living in small, poor villages, were nonetheless expert craftsmen. They were gentle people—small in stature and very humble.

Against her wishes, Justin bought her a beautiful sterling silver bracelet with inlaid stones of turquoise, coral, and alabaster. He insisted that she have something to remember this day, the day she began living life to the fullest.

Lunch was a quick stop at a buffet, where they had a surprisingly delicious meal of salads, baked chicken, rice, beans, and vegetables. Then it was back to the bus.

Upon arriving at the ruins, the tour participants were quickly given a brief introduction to Chichén Itzá and the layout of the surrounding area. The tour guide explained that he would take them around to most of the popular sites, then they were welcome to wander and explore as much as they wanted. Shuttles transported them to the site itself.

The Blakelys had found an elderly couple to spend their time with, making Morgan even more grateful that Justin had come along. She made a mental note to thank him.

A short walk through thickly forested trails delivered them to the first building, which was called the High Priest's Grave. The tour began, and the group of tourists was transported back in time as they learned about a people inhabiting the area during the ninth century. From her own knowledge of the Book of Mormon, Morgan couldn't help but wonder about the Nephites and Lamanites who could have lived in this area during an even earlier period in history. The buildings, the landscape, the entire area lent itself to the feel of the Book of Mormon. Morgan felt a sense of reverence surrounding the ruins and stood in awe as she learned about each structure.

Her amazement grew as she viewed each building and the remains of ninth-century construction and ways of life. Stones used in the construction of roads held fast in their original spots, and vibrant colors remained on the stone walls.

The group also visited the observatory, where it was believed that ancient priests studied the heavens, keeping an accurate account of time and seasons.

But above all, the main structure, the pyramid Kukulán, also known as El Castillo, captured her attention. Standing twenty-four meters high, its dominating presence was breathtaking.

"There it is," Justin said as the pyramid came into view. "What do you think?"

"I've seen it in pictures, but that's nothing like standing here in front of it."

Justin took both of her hands in his. "You have to climb to the top."

Morgan stepped back. "Justin, I can't. Heights terrify me."

"I'll be right beside you every step of the way, up and down. I'll help you. Look," he pointed at other people scaling the steep steps leading to the top, "it's not that hard. We'll take it slow and easy. If you get too nervous, we'll turn around and come down."

Morgan took in several quick breaths. "The cavern was enough for me in one day."

"Just try, Morgan. One step at a time."

She knew he'd respect her decision if she truly didn't want to climb the pyramid, but again, part of her really wanted to try. She wanted a picture from on top.

"All right. But if I change my mind halfway up, you have to help me back down."

"I promise."

Hugging the steps like a barnacle on a ship's hull, Morgan climbed slowly but surely up. The steps were so small and narrow they had to turn their feet to fit onto them. For Morgan, though, they seemed gigantic. She was so far out of her comfort zone she was in the almost-ready-to-freak-out zone.

Justin's calm assurance kept her going, steady and strong. And before she knew it, to her complete surprise, they were at the top. Justin let her cling to the walls of the two-room structure on top while she gathered enough nerve to actually open her eyes. She had a sudden flashback of when she was barely five years old and she'd followed her brothers up a tree in their backyard. Her mother had told her time and time again to stay out of the tree, but she hadn't listened. Her brothers had dared her to climb up with them, and sure enough, she'd fallen out of the tree and broken her arm. They'd all learned a very painful lesson that day about obedience. Her arm had healed, but her fear of heights had always remained.

"Hold onto me," Justin said, urging her away from the wall. "I promise I won't let you fall. You have to see this."

"Don't take me close to the ledge," she said. "I can't look down."

"I know. I won't."

She grabbed onto him as a slight gust of air hit her. "Why is the wind blowing?" she asked.

"Looks like some storm clouds are rolling in. We'll probably get some rain later on today. We're okay. Don't worry. I'm here, Morgan."

Digging her fingers into his arm, she held on tightly and opened her eyes. Her mouth dropped open with wonder. As far as she could see, thick, green jungle stretched out in front of her. Close up, the various structures of the Chichén Itzá ruins rose from the forest floor, stately and imposing, their presence a reminder of the past. The gray band of clouds moving into the area added a backdrop of drama to the view.

"Wow," was all she could say.

Justin kept a protective arm around her, and she kept her breathing slow and steady, feeling herself relax and marvel at the surroundings.

Just as he'd promised, the view was worth the climb.

They asked a young man if he would take a picture of them while they were up on top. Morgan knew that the only way her family would believe she'd actually done it was to show them a picture.

Grateful there weren't swarms of tourists with them, they made their way around to an entrance leading to the inner chamber, where they found a jade-studded sculpture of a jaguar still showing faint signs of red paint. It was magnificent.

The musty smell inside the chamber added to the ancient feel of the place.

A low-pitched rumble echoed inside, giving Morgan chills. "What was that?"

"Sounded like thunder," Justin replied.

They left the chamber and were greeted with a gust of wind swirling with leaves and dust.

"We've got to get down now!" Justin commanded.

Morgan's stomach clenched. The strong wind carried the scent of rain. Several wind-driven droplets stung her arms.

People scrambled down the steep steps, some scooting on their behinds, others brave enough to stand upright while they descended.

More frightened about staying on top of the pyramid during the storm than climbing down the stairs, Morgan followed Justin as he carefully made his way toward the bottom.

A streak of lightning split the sky, and seconds later, a loud crack of thunder rumbled the ground. Before Morgan and Justin could take one more step, the heavens opened and rain fell in buckets.

Morgan, blinking to keep the rain from blurring her vision, held onto a rope running down the center of the stairs and followed Justin, her eyes focused on each step. Each time she slipped, Justin reached out to steady her.

When they safely made it to the ground, they grabbed hands and ran for cover under a nearby tree. Morgan searched the crowd of tourists but couldn't find the Blakelys. Justin assured her they were fine, and even though neither of them knew for sure, his positive words eased her concerns.

"I've never seen anything like this," she said, digging into her bag.

"What are you looking for?" he asked, his voice raised so she could hear him over the noise of the pounding storm.

"Somewhere in here I've got . . . just a minute . . . there it is." She produced a small plastic packet. "A rain poncho," she announced. "We can share it."

His face registered surprise. "I'm impressed," he said as he helped her unfold it. They huddled underneath the clear poncho as drops of rain ran off in steady rivulets of water. "Sure glad you brought this along," he said. "Thanks for sharing it with me."

"You're welcome," she said. "It's plenty big for both of us."

The cloudburst continued with increasing intensity, drumming into the dry ground and creating puddles of water and mushy grassland. Even though it was loud and furious, the storm was also exhilarating.

Although they'd had the benefit of the poncho to protect them from most of the rain, they were still pretty wet. Morgan shivered, huddling close to Justin for warmth. He circled his arm about her shoulders and shifted the poncho so it would cover most of her legs too.

Then, as quickly as it had started, the rain stopped, the dark clouds broke apart, and warm rays of sunshine streaked to the earth.

"We still have time before the bus leaves. You want to see more?" Justin asked.

"Sure," Morgan said as steam rose from the ground. The extreme changes in weather had added an element of unpredictability to Justin's goal of helping Morgan explore outside her comfort zone. Even though her adventures so far would probably be considered mundane by most standards, to her they were a quantum leap into unknown territory. She loved it.

Justin took Morgan by the hand and led her to the structure known as the ball court. Here, it was said that games of skill were played using a hard rubber ball weighing about twelve pounds. The ball was hit through carved stone rings embedded in the walls seven meters above the ground. The athletes used only their elbows, wrists, and hips.

Morgan couldn't see how it was possible to get the ball through the rings at all, and when she found out that the losers lost their heads, she was completely perplexed with the entire game.

"Who would even be dumb enough to want to play the game?" she asked.

"It was considered an honor to participate, and an even greater honor to lose one's head."

"I can definitely see why I wasn't born back then," she informed him.

They moved on to the Temple of the Warriors, located next to the Group of a Thousand Columns. The stone columns were arranged in rows four columns deep and hundreds of columns long. It was believed to be the site of a great marketplace, but there was no firm explanation as to the use of so many intricately carved and painted columns.

A group of people from another tour approached, and Justin quickly asked one of them if they'd take a picture of him and Morgan with the carved stone columns in the background, then one more with El Castillo behind them.

Justin, in exchange, took pictures of the group of elderly tourists—three couples from Chicago—who were making an extensive trip to as many of the ruins in the area as they could. He laughed when the women told him to make sure the old relics were behind them, and they weren't talking about the ruins, they clarified. The three older gentlemen laughed good-naturedly and took their places behind their wives.

They thanked Justin for his assistance and went on their way, their laughter echoing through the grounds. Morgan admired the cute little couples and hoped that someday she would have a relationship like that; she wanted someone she could laugh with, someone she enjoyed being around . . . someone who was her friend as well as her husband.

It wasn't until they got back to the bus that they met up with the Blakelys again. Everyone was tired and hungry from their long afternoon and anxious to return to their hotels—everyone except Morgan. She'd enjoyed the day more than she'd expected she would, and it was largely due to Justin. He had a way of making her believe she could do things, and he'd been willing to stand by and help her every step of the way.

The bus wound its way along the same road it had come, through the thick, green jungles. An occasional souvenir stand popped up, dotting the highway. As they approached the flea market where they'd had lunch, Morgan paid closer attention to the small town where many of the Mayan people who worked at the flea market lived.

She shook her head slowly as she observed the extreme poverty. Their homes were nothing more than shacks made of the crudest of materials—cardboard, tin, or, if they were lucky, lumber of some type. Children, scarcely dressed and barefoot, wandered along the streets, some of them barely old enough to walk. Older members of the community sat in clusters near the food and souvenir stands, their hunched, weathered frames looking as old as some of the ruins in the area.

Morgan felt a rush of guilt at the bounty she daily took for granted. The money she'd spent that day on souvenirs alone would probably feed an entire family in this village for a month.

"What are you thinking about?" Justin's voice broke into her thoughts.

She kept her gaze fixed on the passing scene outside the bus window.

"I wonder how they survive. I wonder if they're happy."

They watched together in silence as the last few houses passed from their view.

"I think you'd be surprised at how happy they are."

"You think so?" she asked, wondering how he would know.

"Oh, don't get me wrong. Their lives are hard. Finding a way to get enough food each day is all they focus on. They deal with illness and death on a continual basis. Yet there's something serene about them, as if their poverty has spared them from becoming selfish, power hungry, and driven to do anything to acquire money and material things. Their focus is on survival and each other."

"How do you know so much?" she asked.

"I spent some time in Brazil. I saw entire sections of cities where people lived this way, begging for food if they had to, or even worse, sending their children to beg because it's harder to ignore a hungry child than hungry adults."

"Did you help any of them?" she asked.

"I try to donate money or volunteer whenever I can."

Morgan looked at Justin with a new perspective. She'd finally gotten past her first impressions of him enough to learn that the actions she'd misread as being self-absorbed were self-confidence and assurance. He was a very secure individual, and he had a very good heart, a tender heart. He was truly interested in other people. He'd taken an interest in her, for some reason, and he'd touched her life in just one short day.

"I think that's wonderful," she told him.

"Not really," he said. "I just have a lot of free time on my hands in the evenings and on weekends when I'm in Brazil. I'd just as soon be with people than by myself."

He definitely had a knack for helping people feel at ease. She'd known him such a short time, but already she felt comfortable with him, something that was unusual for her.

"So," he said, turning toward her, "you never did get to give your analysis of me."

"That's right," Morgan said, giving him a teasing smile. "Are you sure you want it?"

"It can't be that bad," he replied. "Can it?"

Morgan laughed. "That depends on how good of a guesser I am."

"I'm ready, then," he said with a nod.

"All right." She sat up straight and drew in a measured breath. "I think that growing up as an only child gave you a sense of confidence and an ability to communicate well with people, especially adults. You were obviously good at athletics, so you were probably well-known in the community. All the young boys probably wanted to be just like you, all the girls wanted you to like them, and all the adults were as proud of you as they would be of their own son."

Justin raised both eyebrows and gave a simple nod. She was obviously right on all counts.

"I'll bet in high school you were a practical joker. Not the cruel kind of jokes, just the good-natured kind."

"Like putting a 'For Sale' sign in front of the high school and toilet-papering houses?"

She laughed. "Yeah, stuff like that." Then she continued, "You're a bit of a contradiction, though, I have to say."

"Really? Me?"

"Yes. I would think that as an only child you would be self-centered and spoiled—you know, wanting your way, making everyone do what you want to do, stuff like that."

"How do you know I didn't do that?"

"I haven't known you for too long, but so far I haven't seen anything in your actions that even remotely resembles bratty behavior."

"And how do you know how brats behave?"

Even though Samantha was her best friend, Morgan had to admit that Samantha was also a spoiled princess. Yes, she knew bratty behavior, and Justin didn't exhibit it.

"I've just known a few." She continued, "An international job like you have tells me that you are adventurous and love challenges, but I see that you're also kind and thoughtful. And hardworking. I bet you're a very hard worker."

"Thank you. That's a nice thing to say. I'd like to think I'm a hard worker."

"There's one last thing, though," she said. "You're very loyal."

"What makes you say that?"

"The way you are with Trevor and your friends. You're still so close after all these years. Loyalty is important."

He nodded. "We've changed a lot since college. Things aren't exactly like they were, and we don't have as much in common as we used to. A couple of the guys act like they're still in college," he chuckled, "but they've always been there for me if I've ever needed them."

"And you've been there for them too."

"I've tried."

Morgan felt the sincerity of his words. This man in front of her, this person she'd misjudged earlier, was clearly a quality individual, a rare breed. She knew too well that men like Justin didn't come along every day.

Too bad they couldn't be anything more than just friends.

Chapter Five

After a long, hot bath, Morgan relaxed on her bed and waited for room service to bring her meal. It was too late to get dressed up and go to dinner, and besides, she didn't feel like going to one of the restaurants and eating alone.

Flipping through the channels on the television, she stopped to watch an advertisement promoting tourist areas around Cancún, Cozumel, and the Yucatán Peninsula as a whole. There were so many activities that a person would have to stay a month or more to do them all. It came as no surprise to Morgan that most of the activities involved the water: diving, snorkeling, swimming, and renting just about any motorized water vehicle. She watched as footage of the colorful coral reefs and abundant sea life were displayed on the television screen. There seemed to be a hidden paradise beneath the surface of the ocean, a world she'd never seen before.

The phone rang. She pressed the mute button on the TV remote and answered.

"So, how was your day?" Samantha's voice came over the line.

"Hi, Samantha," Morgan answered with enthusiasm. It was great to hear her friend again. They hadn't spoken since the wedding. "How are you doing?"

"Great," Samantha answered. "Everything's great."

Morgan detected something in her friend's voice that prevented her from believing Samantha's words, but before she could ask anything, Samantha continued, "But I want to hear about your day."

"Well, it was fun," Morgan said. Then she amended her response, "Actually, it was *really* fun."

"*Really* fun?"

Morgan knew Samantha would read much more into what she'd said than she meant. "I just mean it was more fun than I'd expected. The ruins were amazing, and we stopped at this cavern. It was quite a day."

"And how was Justin?"

Morgan shut her eyes and drew in a deep breath. She knew better than to give Samantha even the slightest hint that she thought Justin was a nice guy. If Samantha thought Morgan had any interest in Justin, she would never hear the end of it.

"He was fine," Morgan answered as blandly as she could.

"Fine? That's it? You spent the entire day with him, didn't you?"

"We were in the same tour group. It was hard not to," Morgan told her.

"But Mom said you two hung out together the whole time. She said you even went swimming with Justin."

Busted. "Yeah, well . . . we were the only ones our age on the bus. The rest were either senior citizens or families with young children. I guess it was only natural we would pal around together," she said, trying to downplay the situation.

"Pal around?" Samantha said, mocking Morgan's words.

"You know what I mean."

"So what do you think of him? I mean, isn't he the greatest guy?" Samantha persisted.

Morgan knew Samantha wasn't going to give up easily. "I'll say this—my first impression of him wasn't exactly on target. He's not quite as caught up in himself as I thought he was."

"I'm glad you've gotten to know him better. I've always thought you two would hit it off if you ever got a chance to meet."

Hoping to detour the conversation, Morgan asked, "So where's Trevor tonight? Are you guys going out on the town or anything?"

"Actually, he's out with his buddies."

"He left you all alone?" Morgan wasn't sure what kind of groom would leave his bride alone on their honeymoon and go hang out with his friends.

"Most of them are going home tomorrow, so he wanted to go have drinks with them to thank them for coming to the wedding."

It still didn't make sense to Morgan, but Samantha didn't seem too bothered by the fact that her husband was out for the evening while she was hanging out in her hotel room alone.

"I guess Justin went with them?"

"I don't know if he got back from the tour in time," Samantha told her. "Besides, he's not much of a drinker."

"He's not?" Morgan recalled seeing him at the bar with his friends.

"Oh, don't get me wrong. Justin loves to have a good time, but he's not a drinker. That's why I thought you two would hit if off."

"Because he doesn't drink?" Morgan remembered the virgin strawberry daiquiris they'd had at the pool.

"Not just that. He's also LDS."

Morgan nearly dropped the phone. Justin was LDS?

"Morgan?"

"Oh, sorry," Morgan pulled herself back to the flow of conversation. "But I got the impression he was a big partier in college."

"Yes, but he wasn't a Mormon the first couple of years they were in college. He joined the Church when he was about twenty. He blew out his knee in a football game and couldn't play anymore. One of the guys on the team was LDS, and they were good friends. He's the one who helped Justin join the Church. Justin even went on a mission somewhere in South America."

"Brazil?"

"Yeah, I think he went to Brazil."

Morgan was stunned at the news. She'd judged him wrongly. She felt as though she owed him an apology.

Then, something Samantha said hit Morgan. "Did you say Trevor was out with his friends because they're leaving tomorrow?"

"I think most of the guys are going. Why?"

"Is Justin leaving too?" Morgan asked.

Just as she feared, Samantha didn't let that comment go unnoticed. "Why do you want to know? You don't want him to stay longer, do you?"

"I was just wondering, that's all," Morgan replied.

"I'm not really sure what Justin's plans are. I can ask Trevor when he gets home tonight and call you."

"No, that's okay," Morgan answered quickly. If Justin was, in fact, leaving, she was surprised he hadn't said anything about it to her.

"Come on, Morgan. I know you better than that. You're interested in Justin, aren't you?"

"I don't even know him. Besides, we live on opposite sides of the country."

"So?"

"So I'm not interested in a long-distance relationship. I've been there and done that, remember?" Morgan's last serious boyfriend had lived in southern California. Even though they were in the same state, it felt like they were worlds apart. The distance had been a strain on their relationship and had proven too much of a challenge for him to stay true to her. She'd gone down one weekend to surprise him, but unfortunately she'd been the one who'd gotten a surprise. She'd waited at his apartment until he'd returned, and she was shocked to see him come in with a date. Trust in a relationship was a big deal to her, and long-distance relationships put that trust on the line. That had been a painful ending to a relationship she'd believed in. She didn't have it in her to deal with it again.

Maybe that's why she felt safe with Manny. At least he lived nearby and she didn't have to deal with the miles between them.

"Hey, if you want something badly enough, you can make it work. But I will warn you about Justin."

Morgan braced herself, knowing that there would inevitably be a major flaw.

"He's very involved in his career right now and has had some trouble in the past with commitment. Personally I think he's just waiting for the right girl, but I wouldn't want you to get hurt."

"What kind of problems?" Morgan wanted to know up front before she even considered getting involved with the guy.

"He's had a couple of very serious relationships. He was even engaged once to a gorgeous girl named Kelli. I really thought she was the one for him, but Justin decided he needed time and broke off their engagement. She started dating Justin's friend, Dave, the one who helped Justin get baptized, and they ended up getting married. I think Justin regretted letting her go, but it was too late."

"I'm not looking for a serious relationship right now anyway," Morgan told Samantha. "Besides, you know I'm dating Manny."

"But you still have to keep your options open. I mean, Manny's a nice guy and everything, but do you see yourself married to him? He's not very romantic or playful—especially with him being Latin and all."

Morgan was getting a headache from the conversation. "What's that supposed to mean?" She sighed. "Never mind. I don't care right now. I don't know what we are—we haven't dated long enough to even think about it." Wanting to change the subject, Morgan asked, "So what are you doing tonight?"

"I just painted my toenails and my fingernails, and now I'm going to bed. I'm sure Trevor won't get home until one or two in the morning, and I'm exhausted."

"Okay. I'll talk to you tomorrow?"

"Sounds good. Maybe the four of us can get together and have dinner."

"That would be nice," Morgan replied. "It might be kind of fun to go out as couples. That is, if Justin's interested."

"I'll have Trevor call him."

They said good-bye, and Morgan walked to the balcony to watch as the last few rays of the setting sun cast a fiery glow across the shimmering ocean. It was a beautiful evening, clear and warm. Morgan was glad she'd decided to stay longer to enjoy the exotic resort surrounded by the turquoise waters of the Caribbean. Voices and laughter from the outdoor café and bar drifted on the evening air along with the sound of the surf rolling onto the beach.

She relaxed a few more minutes before remembering she was supposed to call home and tell her parents her plans.

Her mother answered on the first ring. She sounded pleased to hear from Morgan and encouraged her to tell her about her trip. Morgan told her all about Samantha's wedding and about her day sightseeing, then mentioned she'd be staying a few days longer than she expected.

"I thought you were coming home today or tomorrow," her mother said with a disapproving tone in her voice.

"I thought so too. But I'm having such a nice time, I've decided to stay the rest of the week."

"But what about your job?"

"Mom, I'm using my vacation days."

"You still shouldn't leave your job for so long."

"They aren't expecting me back at work until next Monday."

"Well, I guess you know best."

"I'll be home late Sunday night. And I found some wonderful souvenirs for you."

"You don't need to spend your money on us."

"But I wanted to. I went to this little Mayan flea market today with—" Morgan stopped herself before bringing up Justin's name. Even though she was twenty-seven years old, her mother was still extremely protective of her. "With a tour group. I found some great stuff."

"All right, dear. Be careful, and don't drink the water."

"I won't, Mom," Morgan said, wondering wryly how her mother expected her to go for eight days without drinking water.

She hung up the phone and shook her head. Sometimes her mother took her to the edge of her patience. All her life she'd been told to be sensible, to use her head, to be a good girl and to not cause trouble. Well, she'd done that. She'd been a model child, and now as an adult she went about her day as if programmed by a computer, without much purpose or feeling. She fulfilled her callings, attended her church meetings, went to a movie occasionally with friends or, even more rarely, with a date. Most of her life was filled with doing the things she *had* to do, things that were expected of her, things that a responsible person did. Today was one of the first times she'd actually done something out of the ordinary. And it felt wonderful.

❦ ❦ ❦

Early the next morning, the phone rang, waking Morgan from a blissful sleep.

"Hello," she said, her voice groggy.

"Did I wake you?"

Her eyelids flew open. *Justin!*

"Hi," she said. "There's something about this air that makes me sleep better than I usually sleep."

"It's great, isn't it?" Justin said. "Hey, what are you doing today?"

"I don't have anything planned."

"Good. I want you to go somewhere with me."

"What about your friends?" she asked, wondering what they thought about him spending all his time with her.

"They're leaving today—that is, if they wake up in time to catch their plane. I think they were out all last night."

Morgan wondered if Trevor had been with them the entire time. "Where do you want me to go with you?" she asked.

"It's called Xel-ha," he told her. "You remember how you said you'd never been snorkeling?"

Her first reaction was to turn him down. She immediately fought back the urge and forced herself not to give in to her old, boring ways. He'd helped her realize that there were too many things in life to miss out on. She'd been a spectator long enough, and she wanted to participate in the fun.

"I can't even go under the water without holding my nose," she confessed.

"You don't need to worry about that." He went on to explain, "You wear a mask with a breathing tube. It's simple."

"I don't swim well."

"You don't even have to swim. They give you life vests so you can float on the current of the river."

"Gee, they've thought of everything, haven't they?"

"Yes, they have. So what do you say?"

She hesitated just a moment, then said, "Sure, why not? I think I can do that."

"Great. I already signed us up. The bus leaves at nine."

She glanced at the clock. It read seven forty-five.

"Can you meet me downstairs in the lobby at eight thirty? We can grab a bite to eat before we leave," he offered.

Morgan was nervous and excited—nervous to try something new, but excited to be with Justin again. Somehow she knew that with him there, she would be okay. She could do it.

"Sounds great. I'll see you at eight thirty."

After hanging up the phone, Morgan relaxed against her pillow, shutting her eyes for a moment as a current of excitement zipped through her veins. Her good sense warned her not to raise her hopes or expectations. Okay, so maybe he was LDS. That was one giant hurdle out of the way. In fact, she was still in a state of disbelief that he'd turned out to be the same religion as she was. But there was another fact she couldn't ignore. Being on opposite sides of the country didn't exactly pave the way for a future for them even if he did have any interest in her—which she assumed he did, since he had called her that morning.

The tingling inside her made its way to her fingers, toes, and scalp, and as much as she analyzed her feelings, she couldn't stop the reaction. He'd called all on his own.

She allowed herself to momentarily dwell on his good looks, magnetic smile, and charming personality. His fun-loving, live-life-to-its-fullest outlook and genuine optimism were contagious, and she'd caught his fever.

She was going snorkeling! That would definitely be a Kodak moment.

Making a mental note to take her camera, she glanced over at the clock and realized she didn't have much time.

Before rushing to get ready, she knelt down by the side of her bed and said a quick prayer. She'd learned long ago that this was the best way to start her day, and she wanted to express her gratitude for this new awakening she was experiencing.

Finishing her prayer, she jumped to her feet and ran to her closet. She couldn't remember the last time she'd looked forward to a day with as much anticipation as she felt today.

Chapter Six

Clutching her bag to her shoulder, Morgan rode the elevator to the lobby, her stomach dancing with excitement.

She tucked a stray lock of hair behind her ear and took a steadying breath. The bright orange of her T-shirt enhanced the blush of color on her skin. She wasn't much of a sun worshiper, but she liked the glow of bronze on her cheeks and arms. People back home would believe she'd actually taken a vacation.

The doors opened, and Morgan walked into the lobby, glancing quickly around to see if Justin had beat her there, but he hadn't arrived yet.

She sat on one of the tropical-print rattan chairs and watched as a steady stream of people checked in and out of the hotel. Other patrons sat at a small coffee shop in the lobby and watched television on the big-screen TV, the same one that had been used for karaoke.

Morgan checked her watch. It was exactly eight thirty.

The squawk of a parrot in a large cage near the hotel entrance caught her attention. She stood and walked over to the cage, admiring the colorful feathers of the three birds inside.

A movement nearby pulled her gaze away from the cage. A young man who was very tan, muscular, and tattooed smiled at her. He sat at one of the small café tables, drinking coffee alone.

Morgan gave him half a smile and turned her attention back to the birds. Out of the corner of her eye, she noticed the man at the table stand. Her stomach lurched. He was coming her way.

She jumped when a pair of hands grabbed her shoulders from behind. "Justin!" she exclaimed when she turned to see who it was. "I'm so glad to see you."

The tattooed man walked by, giving her a broad smile.

"Who was that?" Justin asked as he noticed the man.

"I don't want to know," she said.

"Was he hitting on you?" Justin asked.

"No, he didn't bother me. He didn't have a chance. You came along just in time."

Justin smiled. "I'm glad I did. Are you hungry?"

"A little."

Wordlessly, Justin took her hand and led her through the lobby and down a short hallway to the restaurant serving a delicious buffet breakfast.

"Do you like omelets?" he asked her.

"Mmmm, yes. With mushrooms, cheese, and green peppers."

"I'll be right back," he told her.

While he was getting their omelets, Morgan filled one plate with different breads and muffins and another one with fruit. She sat down at a nearby table and waited for Justin to arrive with the omelets. He soon approached with two plates and handed her one.

"Food tastes so much better when you don't have to prepare it," she told him after several bites.

"You're telling me?" he replied. "Even cereal tastes better when someone else pours it."

Morgan laughed. She'd forgotten he was a bachelor, stuck doing his own cooking.

She took a sip of her orange juice and caught his gaze over the rim of her cup. Their eyes locked for a moment. She felt the tang of the juice slide down her throat as she swallowed hard. He had incredible eyes.

"I can't blame that guy in the lobby for wanting to meet you," Justin said.

"Oh?"

"I wanted to meet you the first time I saw you on the beach," he told her.

Morgan was surprised he remembered.

"You did?" Morgan recalled how stupid she'd felt, all alone on a romantic, tropical beach.

"I saw you walking our way, so I missed the ball on purpose so it would roll out of bounds toward you."

A smile stretched across her face. "Really? Why?"

He shrugged, looking boyishly handsome. "I don't know. There was just something about you that made you stand out. Something different. I think it was the way you were dressed."

Her mind quickly scanned back to what she'd been wearing that day.

"I guess compared to all the other girls wearing string bikinis and skimpy clothes, I just thought that you must be a real classy lady."

Feeling her cheeks flush hot, Morgan looked down at her hands, then slowly back up to Justin.

"Thank you," she said.

"I knew there was something different about you. Something special. And . . . I was right."

Morgan didn't know what to say. This was all beginning to feel like a fairy tale, much too wonderful to be true.

"I tried to find you at the wedding dinner, but you disappeared so quickly. I was hoping we could dance. Anyway, I'm glad we've had a chance to get to know each other."

"Me too," she said. "I was a little hesitant at first to get to know you. I didn't know until last night that you're LDS, and I . . . well . . ."

"You weren't comfortable hanging out with a stranger who might have ulterior motives?"

She nodded. "I saw you with your friends and . . . I guess I figured you—"

"Partied and hit on girls like they do?"

"I'm sorry."

"Hey, why wouldn't you wonder? You saw me hanging around with them, so it makes sense that you'd think I was doing what they were doing." Morgan hoped the hurt on his face wasn't all her fault. He continued, "I love those guys, but I wouldn't want you to think I was like them. And I certainly wouldn't want any of them dating you. I know what's on their minds."

"I shouldn't have judged you."

"I'm just glad you gave me a chance to show you that I'm a decent guy."

"I'm glad I gave you a chance too." Morgan smiled, then asked, "When did you realize I was LDS?"

"I could tell at first glance," he answered.

"Really?"

"Yeah, your CTR ring gave it away."

She looked down at the small, diamond-studded CTR ring on her finger and laughed. "Oh, yeah. I forget I even have it on sometimes."

"I'm glad you were wearing it. I don't date outside the Church very often."

"Me either," she told him.

"Guess that explains why you didn't act too thrilled to get to know me."

"That makes me sound like a snob," she said.

"No, I completely agree with where you were coming from. You can't be too careful dating. Even if someone is a member, it's no guarantee, but I do think it improves your chances that they'll be someone more compatible with you."

They finished their breakfast, then made their way to the lobby to wait for their bus.

Morgan realized as they walked down the hallway that she didn't feel out of place at the resort anymore. Having Justin by her side, lavishing her with attention and compliments, and being surrounded by the tropical beauty of the resort and the ocean made her feel like a person she'd only dreamed of being, someone she never thought she could ever become. Someone living a fairy tale.

"Here," Justin said, pointing to an empty bench. "Why don't we sit down? I'll hold your bag for you."

It was refreshingly wonderful to have someone treat her this way, yet it still made Morgan a little nervous. Normally she was cautious with matters of the heart. At least she thought she was. But somehow, Justin was finding his way inside her heart. She was beginning to like him, and there was nothing she could do about it. Truth be known, she didn't *want* to do anything about it. For once, she wasn't letting her practical, analytical side decide her life. She was following her heart, and her heart was telling her to enjoy her vacation and this special time with Justin.

❧ ❧ ❧

"Okay, now suck air in through your nose, and the mask should seal tightly," Justin instructed as he helped get Morgan's snorkeling equipment fitted. They were at Xel-ha, a natural lagoon created by a reef barrier along the Caribbean Sea. It was an amazing place to snorkel, according to Justin.

She sucked in, and just as he'd said, the mask sealed itself to her face. She looked at him and crossed her eyes. He laughed along with her. She removed the mask and placed it with the rest of her gear.

Morgan was excited, but she still felt nervous about breathing through a tube underwater. She wasn't a big swimmer, therefore she was glad for the life jacket they'd provided. Given the chance, she would have gladly opted to sit on the shore and enjoy the sun, but she knew that with Justin that wasn't going to happen.

So, with snorkeling gear in one hand and Justin holding the other hand, off they went to catch a shuttle to the top of the river that would float them down to the lagoon.

Along the pathway, they saw an occasional iguana basking in the sun or poking its head out from underneath leafy ferns. At first, Morgan was skittish, thinking the reptiles would charge out and attack her, but she soon realized that the scaly lizards were so used to tourists that there wasn't much chance of that happening.

"Here we are," Justin said as they located the tram already loading for the next trip to the river head.

Morgan climbed aboard and clutched her gear tightly. What if she couldn't do it? What if she just couldn't get the hang of it? But then she took a deep breath and relaxed. Either way, she knew Justin would do his best to help her, which was a reassuring thought.

"You're going to love this," he said, giving her hand a squeeze. A breeze from the movement of the tram had tossed a strand of hair onto her face, and Justin reached up and tucked it behind her ear.

Morgan smiled, surprised at the comfort level between them. In a way, he was still a virtual stranger. They'd heard about each other through Trevor and Samantha, but that was it. How was it that they were so quickly at ease with each other? Especially since they were such opposites?

Morgan didn't waste much time trying to answer her own questions. It didn't really matter anyway. What mattered was the fact that they enjoyed each other's company and had fun being together. Still, she was amazed that a guy like Justin would be attracted to someone like her. While she knew she wasn't exactly homely, her personality was much more subdued than his, yet he seemed drawn to her. At least she assumed he was since he was always the one initiating their get-togethers. And she was fine with that, because being with Justin had turned her trip to Cancún into an unforgettable vacation.

Once off the tram, they walked the distance to the river and found a rock to sit on, where they put on their flippers, masks, and life jackets.

"Ready?" Justin asked.

Morgan nodded, feeling the muscles in her stomach clench. She was encouraged by the sight of a family with three young children who had just gotten into the water. The kids were facedown in the water, floating downstream.

If an eight year old can do it, I can do it, she told herself, following Justin's lead down the stone steps into the water.

The cool temperature of the water took away Morgan's breath as she entered, but she quickly warmed up as they left the shade of the trees. Justin gave her a last-minute lesson on relaxing and breathing through the tube. She managed to master the technique out of the water, but going under still had her worried. He assured her once again that she could do it, and together they put their heads into the water.

At first, Morgan held her breath. She liked the mask since she could look underneath the surface of the water, but she still didn't trust the tube.

Taking a breath with her mouth, she somehow gulped in water instead of air and went sputtering to the surface. Justin emerged a second later, and once again, in his calm, reassuring fashion, encouraged her to try again.

Slowly, this time face-to-face, they sank beneath the surface of the water, Morgan keeping her breathing strong and steady.

She hesitated for a moment as the water level reached her mouthpiece, tempted to hold her breath. Justin reminded her to focus on him and to keep breathing. Lower and lower they sank until they were staring at each other beneath the water, and to her amazement, she was actually breathing through the snorkel tube.

Justin gave her a thumbs-up and motioned for her to come along with him.

Kicking her fins, she felt herself glide through the water; the current made her movement effortless.

In front of them, a school of bright yellow-and-blue fish swam by. Morgan couldn't believe her eyes. Justin glanced back to make sure she'd seen it, and by the look on his face he was obviously delighted that not only had she seen it but was excited by the sight. Fish of every size and color swam around them. Occasionally Morgan felt a bubble of excitement fill her insides. She was doing it! She was actually snorkeling!

Together she and Justin floated along with the river current, exploring niches and caves, following groups of parrot fish, angel fish, and trigger fish. The river soon fed into the lagoon, where beautiful coral reefs and underwater plants created a magical background for the colorful marine life. They continued to explore and swim, delighting in their discoveries and sharing in the magic of the amazing underwater paradise.

Soon, however, they began to get cold and waterlogged and decided to climb out and lie in the sun on some of the lounge chairs provided by the park. As they slipped into the chairs and relaxed, Morgan felt as if she'd died and gone to heaven. The day couldn't get any more perfect than it already was.

"So, how did you like it?" Justin asked. He was lying on his stomach and propped himself up onto his elbows so he could see her better.

Morgan made enough effort to smile but kept her eyes shut. It was as if every muscle in her body was in complete and total relaxation. "Mmmm," she sighed. "I feel like an iguana."

Justin laughed. "How's that?"

"Like I've lived my life under a rock. This place is incredible. I didn't know places like this even existed."

"It is amazing, isn't it?"

She rolled onto her side, propping her head on her hand. "Thank you," she said.

"What did I do?" he asked.

"You helped me open my eyes. I've seen more and done more in these last few days than I have most of my adult life. I'm so glad I met—"

He tilted his chin, waiting for her to finish.

She knew she'd said too much to stop there, and even though she was hesitant to continue, she did anyway. "I'm so glad I met you."

His dazzling smile assured her he was pleased by her words, which caused Morgan to grow warm inside.

"Me too," he said.

After they warmed up and dried off, they decided to visit some of the other attractions at the park. Across the Path of the Wind, a wooden bridge floating on the water's surface, was an underwater cave they wanted to see. They grabbed their snorkeling gear and followed the path that meandered through the park, which was busy with tourists. Several food courts bulged with hungry swimmers, and souvenir shops were also packed with browsing travelers. Loudspeakers played festive Caribbean music, and Morgan felt as though she'd been transported to another place and time. Compared to her boring, sheltered life at home, this was the adventure of a life-time. She was seeing exotic places and having fascinating experiences with a man who was handsome, fun, and kind.

"There it is," Justin said, pointing at the bridge. "Here, let me carry your gear for you while we cross."

The swaying, rippling bridge was crowded with park visitors. Morgan took one step and felt her balance leave her. Justin caught her by the elbow, steadying her as she got her footing.

Ocean water sloshed onto the boards with each crashing wave. The bridge was placed at a break in the reef where the lagoon met the ocean, and there was enough wind that day to make the crossing a bit treacherous.

Taking careful steps and keeping hold of Justin's hand for balance, Morgan made her way across, grateful when they finally reached solid ground again.

"Okay, so now I know how it feels to be seasick," she said, still swaying a bit.

Justin laughed. "I was getting a little green around the gills myself," he said.

They followed the arrows along the path that led to the cave, and for a split second Morgan felt her stomach churn. She wondered how dark and narrow it was going to be inside the cave, but her fears quickly vanished as she recalled her earlier adventures. She knew she could do it. And not only that, she wanted to do it.

After slipping into their fins and snorkel masks, Justin and Morgan slid into the water, which was warm and inviting. They were excited to have the cave to themselves and hurried ahead to get there before other visitors joined them.

The cave entrance was rocky, and the sides were covered in moss and vines. It looked like something out of a Tarzan movie. The tunnel-like entrance echoed their voices and splashing fins.

Once they were inside, an emerald pool spread out before them. One round hole at the top of the cave let in a small column of sunlight.

"This is so cool!" Morgan exclaimed. She looked down at the water, which was so clear that the fish swimming around were visible.

Justin smiled and swam close to her. He took her hands in his and pulled her to the spot where the water reflected the sunlight. It was shallow enough that they could sit on the rocks under the surface. Together they sat in the serene silence of the cave, marveling at the natural beauty surrounding them.

She liked it when he slipped his arm around her—it was just enough to send her heart soaring. She didn't know what was going on or where all of this was leading, but she wasn't about to get all cerebral and analytical about it now. All she wanted to do was enjoy the moment.

"I don't want to go home," she said. "I haven't gotten enough adventure in."

"I know what you mean," he agreed. "Life shouldn't be so dull that a vacation is like a completely different world."

"That's how I've been feeling," she replied, surprised he had put her thoughts into words for her. "I feel like I've been transported to another place and time. It's like a dream." She lifted one of her fins out of the water and let it fall gently back in. "Of course, your life isn't much different from this, is it?"

He looked out across the pool of water. "I guess traveling with my job seems exciting and adventurous," he said. "But it's no fun when you can't share it with someone, you know?" He turned and looked at her, his eyes searching deep into hers.

Morgan kept her eyes fixed on his. "I do. I know exactly how you feel." Slowly they drew closer together, their eyes locked. The water had become like glass and the cave was perfectly silent. Morgan awaited his kiss with a pounding heart. Her eyelids began to close.

Just then, the silence was broken by a dozen or more teenagers splashing into the water, charging toward the cave with hurricane force.

The spell was broken, the magic gone, but the feeling remained in her heart, and she saw it in Justin's eyes. There was something happening between them, something wonderful and amazing.

Chapter Seven

❦

"What do you think?" Justin gestured to the fawn-colored leather hat on top of his head. A brightly colored band encircled it. Morgan thought he looked like an explorer or archaeologist—rugged, handsome, and outdoorsy, but classy.

"That's the best one," she told him. He'd tried on several other hats, but none fit him like this one did. "I really like it."

"I've always wanted a hat like this. I don't know why, though. I'd never wear it anywhere." He took it off and placed it back on the rack.

"You should get it. It would be a nice souvenir."

He shrugged. "I'll think about it."

They moseyed down the path, browsing in other shops and boutiques. They'd had a bite of lunch and were working their way back to the dressing rooms. It was almost time to leave.

A rack of swimsuit cover-ups and sarongs caught Morgan's eye. She searched through the rack and found a sarong in shades of aqua, purple, and green. The bottom of the garment was edged with beaded fringe.

"That looks like you," Justin said.

"It's pretty, isn't it?" Morgan checked the price tag and quickly put it back on the rack. Forty dollars was too much to spend on something she'd only wear until the end of the week.

"You should get it," he encouraged.

"I'll think about it," she said, mimicking his earlier answer.

They clasped hands and wandered to the next store, which had an ice cream stand in front. The scorching heat of the day made the ice cream irresistible.

Sharing tastes of each other's ice cream, they sat in the shade enjoying the cold, creamy treat. As she watched snorkelers swim around the enormous lagoon, Morgan wished they could go out again, but their bus left soon and there wasn't enough time.

After finishing their ice cream, they went to the dressing rooms to change. On the way to her dressing room, Morgan saw the boutique where Justin had found the hat he'd liked so much. Without a second thought, she bought it for him. He'd looked so fabulous in it, and she wanted to get him something to thank him for all he'd done for her.

Her purchase wasn't easy to conceal, but she managed to use her beach towel to hide it. She waited outside the men's dressing room for Justin, and when he walked out a few minutes later, Morgan was thrilled to see how his face lit up when he saw her waiting for him.

Hand in hand, they followed the path leading to the park exit. Along the way they passed a smaller lagoon, where dolphins zipped through the water and then rocketed into the air, arching into perfect dives back into the water. It was a beautiful sight, and Morgan prayed the day would never end.

All too soon they arrived at the bus, found their seat, and stowed their belongings in the overhead storage compartments. She discreetly covered Justin's hat with her beach towel, hoping she could keep it a secret.

The bus was quiet on the ride back to Cancún. Most of the people were tired from the day in the sun. Morgan was relaxed, but she couldn't sleep. She was anxious to make each moment with Justin count. Their time together would end in three days, and who knew when or even if they'd see each other again?

As they talked, they realized that they had a lot in common. They both loved Beatles music, Chinese food, tennis, and vintage movies. His mother had always watched the classics, especially those starring Cary Grant, Doris Day, John Wayne, Fred Astaire, and Ginger Rogers. Justin confessed that though it wasn't something he would ever admit to his friends, he actually enjoyed musicals and, to her delight, knew all the songs from most of her favorites.

"Tell me about how you joined the Church," she said, liking how he held her hand and gently ran his thumb back and forth over her knuckles.

"Growing up, my best friend was LDS. I'm surprised my parents let me play with him because they weren't fans of the Church at all. In fact, my father thought the members were a bunch of crazy religious fanatics—much too straightlaced for him. My mother tolerated them better than my father, but she thought the women needed liberating. She thought they were too tied to their children and husbands and needed lives of their own."

"Is that why you're an only child?"

He nodded. "My mother's an attorney, and my father's a doctor. I was a disappointment to them because I didn't go to an Ivy League college and follow one of their paths."

"What happened with your friend?"

"Straight out of high school, Dave went on a mission, which my parents thought was outrageously stupid. He played football with me and received several scholarship offers, which he turned down. They couldn't understand it."

"Were your parents proud you got a scholarship?"

"They were. They hated that it was clear across the country, but they were supportive and came to as many of my games as they could. That's one thing I can say about them—they are very supportive. In high school, they didn't miss one of my games. Not one."

"That's really great," she said, wishing her parents had been a little more supportive of her, a little more encouraging of her pursuits.

"And even though they were critical of Dave's beliefs and home life, they appreciated him being my friend when we were back in high school."

"What do you mean?"

"Dave didn't party or do anything too wild, so they knew when I was with him I was doing good things. Dave was still a blast to be with, though. Anyway, my parents thought the world of him and even got to know his parents and family a little bit."

"So was Dave the one who brought you into the Church?"

"He's the one I give the credit to because his example and friendship all through high school made a huge impact on me. He wrote me while he was on his mission and bore his testimony, and in one letter he even challenged me to meet with the missionaries to find out more."

"Did you?"

"I thought about it, but I never got around to calling them. But a weird thing happened. Barely one week later, the missionaries knocked on the door at my apartment."

"That's amazing."

"That's what I thought," he said. "I took it as a sign that I was supposed to talk to them."

"What did your friends say?"

"They thought I was a nut, like I'd taken too hard a hit during a game or something. They couldn't understand what I'd want with a religion that wouldn't let a person have any fun. But I wasn't into partying all that much anyway, especially during the season. I didn't want to risk messing up my performance."

"What did your parents say when you told them you wanted to get baptized?"

"They took the news better than I thought they would. I know it was hard for them, but they supported me all the way. They were at my baptism, and I know they felt something that night. They haven't shown an interest in joining yet, but who knows? Maybe someday down the road they will."

"And your mission?"

"Again, they were cool about that. It was hard for them to understand why they couldn't come and visit and I couldn't ever come home or call that often. My grandmother died while I was in Brazil, and they were upset I couldn't come home for the funeral. But for the most part, they've been supportive. I think they also notice how much the gospel is a part of my life and that it makes me a better person. They've got friends whose children really struggle with drug abuse, divorce, unwanted pregnancies, all sorts of problems, and they're grateful I've turned out the way I have. In fact, I wouldn't have the job I have if it weren't for my mission."

"What do you mean?"

"One of the families I baptized had a tile business. They were very poor, but they made beautiful tile, and I thought that if they could somehow get their product to the United States, they could increase their business. And I was right. My father knew a man in the import business, and he showed an interest in the tile. That family now has a million-dollar business going, and they employ half the members of the Church in Santa Maria. My parents think it was luck that all of this turned out like it did, but I know that Dave's influence and the gospel have shaped me into the person I am today. I'm not sure what I'd be like without it."

"I've had that same thought many times. I'm not sure I would have figured things out by myself." Morgan had never taken for granted the fact that she had the gospel to help her through life's challenges, always knowing what a blessing and a strength it was to her. "What about your friends? Has it changed things with them?"

"The guys are cool with everything now. We still have a great time together, and they respect me when I don't go along with them and do things they want to do. I keep hoping that someday my example will touch them, like Dave's did me. They're great guys, but let's face it, we're not getting any younger. None of them seems to be the least bit interested in settling down and having a wife and family. Trevor took a lot of ribbing when he decided to get married, but I'm proud of him for doing what he wanted to do—not what they wanted him to do. Someday they'll realize that friends and fun aren't enough. They'll want to get married, but by the time it happens, it won't be that easy to find someone."

Morgan wondered if he was saying that friends and fun weren't enough for him anymore but didn't want to ask. Instead she said, "Have they said anything to you about spending time with me?"

"Are you kidding? Those guys were all jealous because I met you first. They all had their eyes on you. But as much as I love those guys, I wouldn't want any of them to date you, whether or not we were dating."

She smiled, flattered at his protectiveness.

"I mean, if you consider the times we've spent together to be dates." There was uncertainty in his voice.

"Do you?" she asked with a slight hesitation.

"Well, yeah. I mean, I think they are."

She smiled, causing the uncertainty in his expression to fade. "I think so too."

He reached for her hand and laced his fingers through hers.

Morgan was taken aback by everything happening so fast. Given her track record, she would have expected all sorts of red flags and warning signs to be in the way, but they weren't. In her heart, she felt peaceful, and even though she didn't know what was down the road, for some reason she wasn't worried about it.

❦ ❦ ❦

Early the next morning, a knock came at her door. Morgan was awake but still lying in bed, thinking about the day before—the day that she would never forget. To her it had signified a pivotal moment in her life, a time in which she had decided she would never go back to being the same person she was before. There was too much in the world to see and experience. No matter what happened between her and Justin, she knew she would never be the same. For that, she would always be grateful to him.

Pulling on her robe, she checked the peephole in the door and saw no one. She opened the door and looked down to see a gift box and a note.

Immediately she thought of Justin, then chastised herself for assuming the gift was from him. Yet Justin didn't play games or make her guess about his feelings. She knew he liked her. And it boggled her mind.

They were truly opposites, yet for some reason, they had so much in common, and he pulled out a side of her that she'd never given herself permission to express. Her family was very conservative, traditional, and, for lack of a better word, predictable. Until now, she had been just the same. Justin had helped her discover that within herself was a person who wanted to experience life.

She picked up the package and note and took them inside her room and closed the door. Opening the curtains wide, she exposed a gorgeous tropical morning with a clear, blue sky and a startling turquoise sea. A small boat with a rainbow sail gently cut through the smooth water. It was picturesque.

Turning back to the gift, she pulled the card from the envelope and read the message.

> *Morgan,*
> *I couldn't resist buying this for you. I want you to have something to remind you of this time we've had together. I'd give anything to not have it end.*

Yours always, Justin
   P.S. Meet me in the lobby at nine for breakfast and
beach combing, if you can.

Morgan hugged the card to her chest. He felt the same way she did. It was just too perfect. The weather, the atmosphere, the sites, the beauty, and, of course, being together.

She opened the lid of the gift box to find another smaller box sitting on top of something wrapped in tissue paper. Curious as to what was in the box, she lifted the lid and gasped. It was a sterling silver charm bracelet with three charms—a tiny pair of snorkeling fins, a palm tree, and a miniature pyramid like El Castillo.

Immediately she put it on her wrist and admired the charms that would serve as reminders of their time together in Cancún. She then separated the pieces of tissue paper to expose the beautiful, aqua-colored sarong she'd admired at Xel-ha. He'd had the same idea she'd had. She thought of the hat she'd purchased for him and decided to take it to him when she met him for breakfast.

Wrapping the sarong around her, she twirled in front of the mirror with joy, the charms on her wrist tinkling with the movement.

Rummaging through her suitcase, she found the lilac-purple swimming suit she'd purchased before she'd come on this trip. It had been purely an impulse buy, but Morgan couldn't have been happier now that she had it. It matched the purple flowers in the fabric of the sarong perfectly.

Slipping into a pair of flip-flops, she stood in front of the bath-room mirror and studied her reflection. She couldn't remember the last time she'd spent so much time in the sun and was surprised at the pretty golden brown her skin had turned since she'd been there. Her blonde hair had even reacted to the sun, showing honey-colored highlights.

Forgoing her normal ponytail, she twisted her hair on top of her head and fastened an opalescent clip to it, then let the ends of her hair cascade down to her neck in a flirty fountain of curls. After applying a light coat of sunscreen to her face and shoulders, she used a little makeup to darken her lashes and gloss her lips. With a satisfied smile, she checked her reflection one last time. Something caught in her throat, and she swallowed and blinked a few times to clear the film of moisture in her eyes.

She felt beautiful inside, a feeling that was reflected in her outward appearance. She still looked like herself, but in her eyes she noticed a look of self-assurance that wasn't usually there.

After grabbing her bag and Justin's hat, she dashed from her room and headed for the gift shop to buy a gift bag. She had just enough time before they were to meet.

Several young men rode the elevator down with her to the lobby. They struck up a casual conversation with her, asking how long she'd been there and where she was from.

"How long are you staying?" she asked them.

"We're leaving this morning," one of the them replied.

"It's too bad, too," the other one said. "Where have you been this whole time? I think I would have noticed you around the resort."

Morgan smiled. "I haven't stayed around the hotel much. I went to the ruins one day, and snorkeling at Xel-ha—"

"See! I told you we should get in on some of the tours instead of hanging around here the whole time," the second guy said to the first, smacking his friend on the arm.

"Sorry," his friend said as the elevator bell announced their arrival.

"Well," Morgan cut in, taking a brisk step into the hallway, "have a nice trip home."

At the gift shop, she found what she needed right off and was about to make her purchase when something else caught her eye—a picture frame covered with seashells. It gave her an idea.

"Is there a place to get film developed at the hotel?" she asked the clerk.

"Yes, ma'am, right here. I can have it done for you in an hour."

That was perfect. She would wait to give Justin the picture and frame a little later.

With that taken care of, she hurried to the lobby.

Her breath caught in her throat when she saw him. He looked handsome with his twinkling blue eyes, dark curly hair, and bronzed skin, but it was his smile that got to her.

"You look great," he said, giving her a hug.

"I love the sarong, but you didn't need to buy it for me."

"I couldn't resist," he said.

"And the bracelet," she said. "Justin, really, it's too much."

"I wanted to give you something to remember all the fun we've had together."

"Thank you."

Their gazes met, and she felt her heartbeat increase. She'd never fallen so quickly for a guy, and she knew her parents would be surprised and skeptical. She wasn't doing anything wrong—she knew that—but after hearing that she'd spent all her time with a man while she was in Mexico, they wouldn't exactly be elated. Yet she knew in her heart that the time she and Justin had spent together had been wonderful and had felt right.

"I have something for you too," she said, lifting the gift bag so he could see. She handed him the bag so he could open it.

"You didn't have to get me anything," he said, but his smile showed his pleasure.

Peeking down inside, he pulled out several sheets of tissue paper, then saw the contents of the bag. His face lit up. "All right!" he exclaimed. "This is so cool. I've been kicking myself for not getting this hat. Thank you so much." He pulled her into a crushing hug and held her for a moment, then tried on the hat.

"That hat was made for you," she told him. "I couldn't resist buying it."

"You didn't need to," he said, "but I'm so glad you did. It's awesome."

They spent a lingering moment captured in each other's gaze. Morgan couldn't help but wonder what would happen when she flew home to the West Coast and he flew to the East Coast. Would that be it for them? Would they ever see each other again?

Forcing the thought from her mind, she refused to let anything ruin their time together. She had enough faith to know that if it was right, it would work out. And in the back of her mind, she prayed it would.

Chapter Eight

❦

"Hungry?" Justin asked, pulling her out of her thoughts.

"Starving," she replied.

Hand in hand, they walked to the breakfast buffet, where they were soon enjoying a delicious meal over small talk. Of course, Morgan realized she could have eaten packing peanuts and cardboard and it still would have been a great meal. Being with Justin made everything enjoyable.

After breakfast, she and Justin strolled to the beach. The day was already warm and sunny, without a cloud in the sky or a whitecap on the sea—just a gentle breeze and a white, sandy beach practically all to themselves. This was the ultimate stress-free life—no phone, no job, no obligations. Just doing what they wanted, when they wanted, without responsibility. Morgan knew it was the complete antithesis of reality, but she didn't care. She was going to enjoy every waking moment.

And to think she'd wanted to go home the day after the wedding!

"So tell me, Morgan," Justin said as a low wave rolled onto the beach, splashing warm water over their bare feet, "how has an intelligent, beautiful woman like yourself managed to stay single all these years? I'm assuming you don't have a boyfriend back home."

Morgan smiled, giving him an honest answer. "I date a little, but I don't have a boyfriend. I haven't really had a lot of luck with men."

"I find that hard to believe."

She was glad he didn't know the Morgan back home. The boring, predictable, still-at-home Morgan was now just a memory because the Morgan who returned to California would never be the same. And if anything came out of meeting Justin, it would be eternal gratitude for her changed view on life and herself.

She had no trouble sharing her thoughts and personal feelings with Justin—he was someone she could trust with her emotions. She felt as comfortable talking with him as she did with Samantha, and now that Samantha was married, Morgan's relationship with her would inevitably change. It was likely the perfect time for Morgan to change because she would need to. And, she realized, perhaps all of this was part of a plan, something more spiritual and eternal.

"I'm a member of the date-and-dump club," she continued. "I meet guys who seem to be really nice, but after I get to know them, I start seeing a side of them I'm not sure about. Just as I'm realizing that, though, I usually get dumped. What can I say?"

"Well, it's their loss," Justin said, looking her straight in the eye. They continued to wander down the beach until an employee from the resort approached them about participating in one of the water activities.

"You feel like snorkeling some more?" Justin asked her.

"Are you kidding? I'd love to." Morgan wasn't about to turn down an opportunity like that. She wanted to pack as much fun in as she could before it all ended.

After storing their belongings in a locker, they got fitted for flippers and masks. Morgan remembered how scared to snorkel she'd been the day before. Now she couldn't wait to get into the water.

Geared up and ready to go, they waded into the ocean. Then, lowering their faces into the water, they entered the undersea paradise together.

❦ ❦ ❦

After an exhilarating morning of snorkeling, Justin got them a table for lunch while Morgan ran to the gift shop to pick up the pictures and frame. She was all smiles as she glanced through the photographs of the cavern, the ruins, and Xel-ha. For her frame, she chose a picture of her and Justin at Xel-ha, standing with arms around each other next to a shady palm tree with a view of the ocean behind them. After sliding it into place, she hurried back to the restaurant to meet Justin.

As she approached, Justin signaled her over to their table, then stood and helped her into her chair. They'd chosen to eat outside next to the ocean, where they could still enjoy the view and partake of the Caribbean atmosphere.

"I hope you don't mind, but I ordered us some fruit to start off our meal," Justin said.

"Fruit sounds great," she said, touched by his thoughtfulness. "By the way, I have something else for you."

"Something else! Morgan, the hat was plenty."

"I know, but I couldn't resist. Here," she said, handing him another gift bag.

Shaking his head, he pulled out the tissue-wrapped gift and peeled away the paper. "Oh, wow!" He gave her an excited smile.

"I'm glad you like it."

He took her hand and pulled her toward him. He then gave her a kiss on the cheek and said, "This is the best gift you could've given me." He studied the picture again. "We don't look too bad, do we?"

"Not bad at all," she replied, also looking at the photograph. In her opinion, they did look good together. There was something about his dark, handsome features and her fairer complexion that seemed to fit together just right.

They spent the remainder of the meal reminiscing about the past two days together. It seemed as though they'd packed months of excitement into those two short days, and Morgan wanted to savor every last moment before they said good-bye.

Later that afternoon, with their lounge chairs side by side, they relaxed in the sun and talked about their childhoods and family vacations. Morgan didn't have much to tell. Her family vacations were few and far between. Money had been tight in their family, and her parents never felt like a family vacation was important enough to miss work for. As she heard Justin talk about going to Disneyland, Hawaii, and Europe with his parents, it was evident why they had turned out so differently. But she also realized it didn't matter. There was still a lifetime ahead of her to experience adventures.

Justin had given her a taste of life, and she would never be satisfied with anything less again.

ॐ ॐ ॐ

In her room that evening, Morgan tried on several outfits in front of the mirror, finally deciding on a floral-print rayon skirt and a soft, lightweight pink sweater. It was feminine and fun, and she was glad she had taken the time to go shopping before the trip. She had Samantha to thank for that. Her mother had thought she was wasting her money buying clothes she'd probably only wear while on vacation, but Samantha had said that she wouldn't regret having some fun new outfits for Cancún. She had been right.

After slipping into a pair of sandals, Morgan spritzed on some perfume and glanced at the clock. She was meeting Justin at seven thirty for dinner by the ocean. It had become their favorite place to eat together.

Just then, the phone rang, sending her heartbeat racing. Hoping it was Justin, she quickly answered it.

"Morgan?"

"Sammy, hi," Morgan said with surprise. "What's going on?"

"I've been trying to reach you since last night," Samantha said. "Where have you been? I thought maybe you went home without telling me."

"Sorry. Justin and I went snorkeling yesterday and just messed around at the beach and at the pool today. Why? Is something wrong?" She detected a slight tremor in Samantha's voice.

"I don't know, Morgan," her friend replied. "I mean, I knew when I married Trevor that I shouldn't expect him to change for me. But he . . . well . . . he . . ."

Morgan listened, her heart pounding in her chest.

"The night he went out with his friends, he didn't come home until six in the morning."

"Oh, Sammy," Morgan sympathized, not knowing what to say.

"I understand that he doesn't get to see these guys all together that much anymore, but still, it's our honeymoon. Am I wrong to be upset?"

"I don't think so," Morgan said. "But maybe they didn't mean to stay out that long—they just lost track of time or something."

"That's what he said," Samantha replied. "But he stays out all night and the whole next day all he wants to do is stay in bed and sleep. So I end up sitting around our room waiting for him to wake up. This hasn't been . . ." Samantha was quiet for a moment.

Morgan listened, knowing what her friend's next words would be.

"This just hasn't been what I thought it would be," she said.

"Where's Trevor right now?"

"In the shower. We thought we'd get something to eat."

"Why don't you join Justin and me for dinner? Unless you two want to be alone."

"That would be fun," Samantha said. "I'd love to get together. Maybe that would diffuse some of the tension between Trevor and me. By the way, what's going on between you and Justin?"

Morgan laughed. "I don't really know," she answered. "We've had so much fun together—it's like we've known each other for years instead of days."

"Do you see a future?"

"Slow down, Sammy," Morgan told her with a laugh. "We aren't even close to discussing any future plans. I would love to see him when I get home, but I'm not sure how we'll ever be able to get together. Please don't say anything tonight. I don't want to put any kind of pressure on our time together."

"I won't, but I'm just so thrilled you two have hit it off! What a surprise, eh?"

"Yes, total surprise. But a wonderful surprise."

They made arrangements to meet for dinner and said good-bye. Morgan felt for her friend, but she also knew that Samantha had been aware of what she was getting into when she married Trevor.

How grateful she was for the common ground the gospel laid between two people! Even with Justin, a person she'd barely met, she knew there were certain fundamental beliefs and ideas they shared, certain lifestyle choices that would be the same for both of them, even life goals they would have in common. These things presented a foundation upon which a solid relationship could be built. Samantha and Trevor didn't necessarily have those things, and it was for that reason she was truly worried about her friend.

❦ ❦ ❦

"They aren't in their room," Justin said as he returned to the table. "Maybe they changed their minds."

Morgan shrugged, hoping that everything with Samantha and Trevor was okay. They had had a stormy relationship even before they were married, sometimes saying things they didn't really mean. While they'd always been able to patch things up, Morgan knew that those exchanges left scars.

During their delicious Italian dinner, a lovely half-moon graced the sky, sprinkling the ocean with silver kisses. A live band near the pool played romantic music, and once again Morgan found herself unable to believe she was actually experiencing something she had never even had the nerve to dream would happen to her.

She sighed with contentment and found Justin staring at her. "You look so beautiful tonight."

Glad it was dark so he couldn't see her blush, Morgan smiled. "Thank you. You look very handsome yourself, especially in that shirt. The color matches your eyes perfectly." He was stunning in a light blue cotton shirt and white linen pants.

"Thank you for a perfect day," he said. He took her hand in his and raised her knuckles to his lips. "In fact, for three perfect days."

"I've had a wonderful time," she replied.

"But the day's not over yet. The night's still young." He pulled her to her feet. "Would you like to dance?"

She opened her mouth to protest but knew it wouldn't do any good. He wouldn't take no for an answer, and she'd made a pact with herself to enjoy new experiences. She just hoped she didn't make a fool out of herself in the process.

"I haven't danced much," she said. "Actually," she amended, "I haven't danced at all since high school."

"Nothing to it," he said. "Just shut your eyes and let the music move you."

He led her to the terrace where other couples were dancing. The beat of the music wasn't hard to follow, and soon Morgan floated in Justin's arms.

"The Caribbean suits you," Justin said.

"You think?" she said, surprised.

"Since the wedding, I've watched you blossom like a rose."

"I guess that's only appropriate since Rose is my last name," she said.

"That's right!" he exclaimed. "I didn't even make the connection." They continued to sway with the music. "You seemed a little uncomfortable that first day we met, but now you're more relaxed and content. I hope this means you've been enjoying yourself."

She looked into his eyes. "I've never had this much fun in my life, Justin. This isn't like me. I'm usually quiet and reserved—more of a spectator than a participant."

"I think you mean you *used* to be a spectator."

"You're right. You've introduced me to a whole world I didn't know existed. I'll never be the same."

"Neither will I," he said, pulling her close to him.

She rested her head on his shoulder, and together they swayed back and forth to the rhythm of the band and the sound of lapping waves upon the shore. The only light came from the moon above and the lanterns hanging from the trees.

"Hey," he said, after a moment, "you're not falling asleep on me, are you?"

She smiled dreamily. "I'm just trying to memorize every detail of this moment. I want it to last in my memory forever."

"Maybe this will help," he said. Bending toward her, he kissed her gently on the lips. It wasn't a long kiss, but enough to make her feel weak at the knees. She was glad he had a firm hold on her.

After the kiss they smiled, their gazes locked. Morgan prayed the magic would never end but knew it was almost over. Then it was back to everyday life and reality.

Chapter Nine

"You in the mood to shop?" Justin asked. He'd called first thing the next morning.

"I'm always in the mood to shop," Morgan said, stretching one arm overhead. "Why?"

"I haven't gotten one souvenir. I need to take something home for my parents. My mom has this . . ." he paused, searching for the right word, "shrine is all I can think of to call it. Everything I've ever brought her back from my trips is displayed in the corner of the living room. There are rows of shelves and two small tables, all of them loaded with stuff."

"She sounds very sentimental. I like that."

Justin chuckled. "She even keeps the boxes they were packed in and the bags I got from the stores."

"You're her only child, so of course she treasures everything. She probably kept every drawing you ever made and every worksheet from school."

"Yeah. The storage room is full of boxes with my junk in it."

"I think it's probably hard for a mom to let her child grow up and pull away from her." Morgan's parents were the same way. "She must not be too bad. You turned out fairly normal," she teased.

"Gee, thanks," he snorted. Then he added, a bit more seriously, "I guess I should be flattered I'm so important to her."

"Yes, you should. And you should take her something wonderful home. I'd love to help you pick something out."

"Thanks for the offer. I never know what to get her. She's got everything."

"I'm sure we'll find something."

ॐ ॐ ॐ

The flea market was busy with swarms of tourists when they arrived. Some of the stores were indoors, and the rest were outside in the heat, shaded only by thin canvas coverings.

They had barely made it through the front door before they were bombarded with salespeople pushing their wares. Justin waved them away and kept walking, even though some of the merchants followed after them. Morgan stayed close to Justin's side.

"I feel like live bait in a shark pool," she told him.

"You just have to ignore them," Justin told her. "I've been around these people enough to know how to deal with them. Most of them are pretty nice, but they are desperate to make a living."

Morgan suggested they look at some leather goods, since she'd heard that leather was a good buy in Cancún and she thought Justin's mom might like a new bag. In fact, she wouldn't mind a new purse herself.

The leather shop was packed full of goods ranging from wallets and belts to bags and jackets. It didn't take long for Morgan to find a beautifully crafted bag made from sleek, black, top-grain leather. She showed it to Justin, who seemed pleased and grateful she'd found something that would suit his mother so well.

After haggling with the shopkeeper over the price of the purse, Justin concluded they could get a better price elsewhere. "Let's keep looking," he told Morgan as he shielded her from more salespeople ready to pounce on them as they walked by.

They spied another leather shop outside and looked over the assortment, eventually finding a bag similar to the other one, but not nearly as stylish.

"How do you know Spanish so well?" Morgan asked, referring to his earlier conversation with the storekeeper.

"Even though I do most of my business in Portuguese, I work with a lot of Spanish-speaking people from other countries in South America. I took an evening course in Spanish, then picked up the rest on the job."

They decided to keep looking but in the meantime found some beautiful, crystal-beaded bracelets to go along with his mother's purse.

Of course, Morgan couldn't resist purchasing some for herself, her mom, and her two sisters-in-law.

Just as they were about to concede that they weren't going to find anything as nice as the bag they had found earlier, Morgan and Justin stopped at a small kiosk with just a few various items for sale—sunglasses, colorfully woven blankets, T-shirts, and . . . purses.

"Look at that!" Morgan said, in amazement. "There's the same bag. And there's another one."

Justin approached the small, elderly shopkeeper and asked him about the purses. In the meantime Morgan looked at T-shirts for her father and brothers.

The two men spoke rapidly for several minutes before Justin finally reached into his back pocket and pulled out his wallet. After handing the man some bills, Justin took both purses from him and handed them to Morgan.

"How much?" she asked under her breath.

"Both for fifty dollars."

Her eyes opened wide as she held in her excitement. She almost felt guilty that the man had given them such a good deal, but they just couldn't turn down such an amazing price.

"I want to get these T-shirts for my father and brothers," she said.

Justin got her another good deal and even bought a T-shirt for himself. As they walked away, Morgan remarked, "That poor old man probably didn't make much off these purses."

"Don't feel too badly. I bet he can get them made for ten or fifteen dollars."

Carrying their purchases under their arms, they strolled back through the market past the first leather shop they had stopped in. The owner saw them and hurried toward them anxiously, assuring them he was willing to come down a few more pesos. When Justin told him how much they paid another vendor for the same bag, the man got agitated. Justin just shook his head and hid a smile. It was the man's own fault he'd lost a sale. He'd just been too greedy.

After leaving the angry shopkeeper, they wandered through a shopping district, taking pictures of each other and asking friendly tourists to take pictures of them together.

They soon found a small restaurant and ordered lunch, then took their food outside and sat in the shade.

"So," Justin said, "what time does your plane leave tomorrow?"

"I leave for the airport at nine. The plane leaves at eleven. How about you?"

"Mine's not till one."

They both suddenly became quiet, and Morgan noticed her appetite had diminished. She'd known this day would come, but she still wasn't ready for all of it to end. If someone had asked her to describe the perfect vacation, including the place, the atmosphere, and the company, she would describe exactly what she'd been experiencing the last four days. And now it was almost over.

"Have you talked with Samantha yet?" Justin asked.

"I did for just a second last night. She called to apologize. She said they decided to call room service and stay in. I think they needed to talk about the night Trevor stayed out with his friends until morning."

"I hope I'm wrong, but I'm afraid this won't be the last time Trevor will do this. Before the wedding, he was bragging about how cool Samantha was and that she would let him hang out with his buddies anytime he wanted to. I had a feeling that Samantha might say otherwise if we asked her."

"She understands that Trevor's friends are important to him, and I think she's a lot more understanding than most women would be. But now that they're married, I don't think she'll be quite as understanding."

"Then I'm afraid they're going to have a tough marriage. I wish I believed Trevor would change—and who knows, maybe he will—but it's going to take something pretty powerful to make it happen."

As Morgan thought about her friend, she and Justin browsed through more shops, took full advantage of the relaxed atmosphere, and, most of all, enjoyed each other's company. They talked and laughed with the ease of old friends, and Morgan couldn't deny that they'd been able to connect in a way that she'd never experienced before. In previous relationships she'd had, she'd felt like it had always been about pleasing the guys—their needs, their goals, their agendas. Her feelings and dreams didn't seem to matter much to them. Even

Manny, as sweet and good as he was, was focused on his future and what he needed to do to make things happen according to *his* plan. Morgan appreciated the qualities of being hardworking and goal oriented, but Manny seemed to take those qualities to extreme levels.

Dating had never seemed easy, natural, or comfortable to her until she met Justin. But Samantha's words haunted her in the back of her mind. Did he live only for the moment? Was his resistance to commitment something that would rob them of seeing each other again and of possibly continuing their relationship? That reminded her of another obstacle in their way, one they couldn't ignore. Soon they would be on opposite ends of the continent.

She couldn't help but wonder what the point of it all had been. If they seemed so compatible, so right for each other, such a comfortable fit, why couldn't they be together?

"Hey, there," Justin said, lifting her chin with his finger. "Are you okay?"

Morgan mustered a smile. "I'm fine." The brightness in her voice was forced. She cleared her throat and tried to sound more natural. "Why?"

"You look a little sad."

Morgan knew there was no fooling him, but there was also no point in telling him what was on her mind. Nothing could change where they lived.

He took her hand in his and they walked in silence until they found their bus stop. Sitting on a bench in the shade, Justin put his arm around Morgan's shoulders. She turned her head and rested it against him, fighting off the tears that threatened. She wanted to talk to him about what things would be like after they both returned home, but she couldn't force herself to bring it up.

How could she ever tell him good-bye?

ॐ ॐ ॐ

They enjoyed the rest of the day at the resort swimming in the pool, playing volleyball at the beach, snorkeling in the lagoon, and drinking virgin strawberry daiquiris at the bar. Staying active kept her mind off the inevitable, but Morgan still found herself having moments of sadness. Now that Justin was in her life, and especially in her heart, how did she just walk away?

That night, after dining outside by the ocean, they held hands and watched the waves, avoiding the subject of their farewell. Morgan knew this was it. She'd have to be up early in the morning to pack and get ready to leave.

"You're awfully quiet," Justin said. "What are you thinking about?"

She bit her lip and tried to steady her emotions. How could she begin to thank him for helping her spread her wings and see how wonderful the world really was? More than anything, though, she wanted him to tell her that it wasn't the end, that somehow, some way, they would still see each other.

Pulling in a steadying breath, she gave his hand a squeeze and said, "I'm thinking about how wonderful this place is and how wonderful you've been. You spent a lot of your vacation time keeping me entertained."

"It was my pleasure, Morgan. I didn't do anything I didn't want to do. In fact, I would've left a few days ago had I not met you. I wasn't all that excited about hanging out with the guys the entire time. Their hours are completely opposite of mine. Just as I'm getting up for the day, they're coming in from a night on the town. When they're ready to start partying again, I'm ready for bed. You saved me."

"I'm glad I could."

"Me too," he said, gazing at her for a moment. "So what happens now?"

Here it comes, she thought. "What do you mean?"

"Well, I don't want our good-bye to be final, you know? I'd like to see you again, Morgan."

Her heart soared. Tears stung her eyes.

"I'd like to see you again too," she whispered.

"Well," he began. "I'll be traveling back and forth to South America for the next six months or longer. It just depends on how things go down there. I have extended stays a few times, maybe a month or so, but I'll also have some free weeks in between trips. I rack up enough frequent flyer miles to make as many trips to California as I want."

"You'll come and see me?" she asked, her voice still a whisper.

"Morgan," Justin said, "you'd have to get a restraining order to keep me away. I've never enjoyed being with someone as much as I've enjoyed being with you. I feel like you give me balance."

Morgan smiled. "And I feel like you've given me freedom."

The mood grew somber as the reality of their imminent good-bye sank in.

Justin looked at her, his expression completely serious. "Morgan, I *will* come and see you. And I know there's always a chance that we might each meet someone else, but I'd like to think there's something special between us. If it's as right as it feels, then things will work out."

She nodded. It would take faith, but she believed with all of her heart that if they were right for each other, the Lord would help them get together.

"Do you feel like taking a walk on the beach?"

"That would be nice."

Hand in hand, they walked away from the busy restaurant and the lights of the resort onto the cool, moonlit sand along the shore. Gentle waves lapped at their feet, and the spray of salt filled the air.

Justin put his arm around Morgan's waist, and she leaned her head on his shoulder as they strolled in comfortable silence. Not only did she like Justin, but she liked how she was with Justin. She was herself, but a part of her was opening up. She felt more alive and more passionate about life than she ever had before. Their feelings and hopes were the same, and she prayed that if it was the Lord's will, they would find a future together.

Chapter Ten

Fighting back tears, Morgan stood on her balcony, watching the sun come up over the Caribbean Sea as the water turned from a deep blue into a vivid turquoise.

It was over. She was going home, and as she realized what awaited her upon arrival, she was filled with dread. How could she go back to her normal, boring life when she knew what else the world had to offer?

She couldn't. In those few, short days, she'd grown. No matter what happened between her and Justin, she'd made some big decisions for herself. When she got home, things were going to be different—very different.

Moving out on her own would be the first step. It was time for her to get out and gain some independence. She'd also decided she was going back to college to get her art degree and a teaching certificate.

The ringing of her telephone broke into her thoughts.

"Hello?" Justin said when she picked the receiver up.

"Hi!" she answered, her spirits lifting.

"Are you ready?"

"No."

"Don't you have to meet your shuttle in a few minutes?"

"Yes."

"Do you need some help getting packed?"

"I'm packed, I'm just not ready to leave."

Justin paused. "I know what you mean."

"Maybe we could get jobs here at the hotel and they'd let us keep our rooms," she joked.

"Hey, that's a good idea. You could be a maid and I could wait tables."

"It'd be worth it," she replied, trying to chuckle even as her voice cracked.

"Morgan, are you okay?"

Squeezing her eyes shut, she swallowed the knot in her throat and took a deep breath. "I don't want it to end."

"I know. Me neither. But this isn't good-bye for us. I promise."

Morgan remained silent.

"I'm going to come to your room and help you take your bags down to the lobby."

"Okay," she said, sniffing. "Thanks."

She was heading for the bathroom to get a tissue when the phone rang again. Morgan picked it up, trying to maintain her composure, but when she heard Samantha's voice, she knew her friend would pick up on her mood.

"Gee, don't sound so excited to talk to me," Samantha began in a gently teasing tone.

"I'm sorry. I'm just sad to be going home."

"Are you sad to go home or sad to say good-bye to Justin?"

"Both," she said.

"You'll see Justin again. I mean, they have airplanes that fly from California to New York, you know. It's not like you can't get together. And think how exciting it will be to look forward to those trips when he comes to see you or you go to see him. Besides, having me and Trevor in Sacramento will give him another reason to come and visit. It'll be fine. You'll see."

Morgan smiled, grateful for her friend's encouragement. Glancing at her watch, she realized that Justin would be at her room any minute. "I need to go, Sammy. I've got to catch the shuttle at nine. Call me when you guys get home so we can talk."

"I will. Have a nice flight home. And Morgan, I know everything will work out for the best."

After she hung up, Morgan barely had time to stack her suitcases by the door and double-check the room when she heard a knock. She opened the door to see Justin wearing his hat and a silly grin. "Hi."

Morgan stepped aside and let him into the room. He pulled her into a hug, then gave her a welcome kiss. They walked out onto the balcony, and Morgan rested her head on his shoulder. "I hate good-byes."

"Me too," he said, holding her close for a moment longer.

"I just wish I knew when I'll see you again."

"I leave for Brazil in a month." Then, with a sudden movement, he pulled back. "Hey, I have an idea."

"What?" she said, waiting for him to explain.

"On the fifteenth of August, six months from the exact day we met, we're going to have lunch in San Francisco at one o'clock. There's a restaurant called Gauchos. It has great Brazilian food, and I eat there every time I go to San Francisco. No matter what has happened between us, whether we've gotten involved with someone else or not, we will meet there to celebrate the anniversary of when we met, okay?"

"Unless one of us gets hit by a car," she said, unable to hide the teasing in her voice.

"Huh?"

"You know, in *An Affair to Remember*? Deborah Kerr gets hit by a car on her way to meet Cary Grant at the Empire State Building. He takes that as a sign that she doesn't love him anymore."

Justin smiled and placed his hand on her cheek. "Neither of us will get hit by a car, I promise."

"All right, then. Lunch at Gauchos in six months. It's a date."

"Now, that doesn't mean we can't eat there before that—when I come to visit."

She nodded, hopeful that those visits would be often.

"Morgan, I know I can't promise you exactly when I'll come and see you, but I will come. In fact, I'll probably see you so much you're going to get sick and tired of me."

Morgan gave him a smile. "I can't imagine ever getting tired of you," she said. "But I'd love a chance to try."

"That's my girl," he said, giving her a kiss on the forehead.

"I do have one last little present for you," she said, taking a small, tissue-wrapped item from her pocket.

"Another one?"

"It's nothing big or expensive," she told him as he opened the gift, a leather key chain with "Morgan and Justin, Cancún, Mexico," and the date inscribed underneath.

"This is great," he exclaimed. "I love it."

"I wanted you to have it because you found the key to my heart," she said, only half joking.

He clasped the key chain tightly in his hand. "I'll keep it with me always," he said, a serious look in his eye despite his humorous tone.

"Think we'd better get downstairs?" she said.

They stole one last kiss on the balcony, then took a final look at the amazing view before walking away.

♥ ♥ ♥

"Don't you have to go to work today?" Morgan's mother, Laura Rose, asked.

Morgan buttered a piece of toast and smeared raspberry jelly on it. "Yes. Why?"

"Is that what you're wearing?"

Morgan took a bite of toast and nodded. Instead of wearing her usual dark skirt and drab-colored sweater, she had on a khaki skirt and a small cotton T-shirt with a deep orange, button-front shirt over the top. It was comfortable and casual, and Morgan loved what the color did for her tan.

Leaving her toast half finished, Morgan gulped down her orange juice and grabbed her purse. "Gotta go, Mom. See you tonight."

Just then the phone rang. Laura Rose looked at the caller ID before she picked it up. "It's Manny."

"I don't have time to talk," Morgan said. "Tell him I'll call him later."

"But—"

"Mom, I don't want to be late for work." Morgan grabbed her purse and dashed to her car.

It was only her third day back home, and she was somewhat chagrined by the lack of excitement with which her family was responding to her changed self. The new Morgan was met with resistance. She'd gotten her vacation pictures developed the day before, and her mother had expressed great concern at the amount of time she and Justin had spent together. She had given Morgan the classic mom lecture about not trusting strangers, and how men preyed upon naive young women like her. She had also voiced disapproval at the idea of her daughter spending time with someone she knew so little about. "How does that look to others?" her mother had asked.

"It probably looked like we were having fun," Morgan had answered.

To Morgan's surprise, her father had been the one to stay cool and not jump to conclusions. In fact, he had said he thought Justin was a "right handsome fellow" and was fascinated by Justin's job taking him to South America. He had also expressed an interest in seeing the ruins sometime, much to the dissatisfaction of her mother, who had told her husband not to encourage their daughter.

The reaction from Morgan's co-workers had been just what Morgan had hoped it would be. Everyone noticed her tan right off, and they wanted to know about the places she had visited and things she had seen. For once Morgan was actually able to tell them something. She described the cavern, the ruins, the snorkeling, the beaches, and the resort. Many of the women got a faraway look of longing in their eyes, as if wishing they could go on a romantic adventure like Morgan had. And some of the single men looked at Morgan as if they were seeing her for the first time.

All through the day, Morgan hummed as she worked and chatted cheerfully with the other employees.

"Okay, Morgan." Rhonda Witherspoon cornered her when it was near closing time. Rhonda was her closest friend at the library. Even though she was seven years older than Morgan, she was as spunky and energetic as a teenager. "What else happened while you were on your trip?"

"What do you mean?" Morgan asked her.

"I mean, you have been transformed into another person. You were always sweet, hardworking, and pleasant, but you are simply glowing. If just going to Cancún did this to you, then I'm booking a flight as soon as I get home."

Morgan hugged the book she was holding to her chest. "I met the most wonderful guy down there."

"You met someone?"

"He was one of the groomsmen at my friend's wedding," Morgan told her.

"And . . ."

"And we spent almost every day together. He's incredible. In fact . . ." Morgan reached under her desk and pulled a picture of Justin out of her purse, " . . . this is him."

Rhonda raised her eyebrows. "You say he was *one* of the groomsmen? Are there others?" Rhonda had been divorced for a few years and had also gone on her share of bad dates.

"Believe me," Morgan said, "Justin was the best of the groomsmen. While the others were partying and staying out all night, Justin was with me. It was so amazing."

"So where is this Prince Charming?"

"In New York for a few weeks, then he's on to Brazil."

"What's down there?"

"You mean besides a country full of beautiful women?"

Rhonda nodded.

"His job. He works for a marketing firm in New York. Their main office is based in São Paulo, but he's in charge of the southern region. Because he served a mission in Brazil for the LDS Church, he knows the people and the language very well."

"How cool is that?" Rhonda exclaimed. "Just think—if you marry him, you'd get to travel and see the world."

"Rhonda! I've only known the man six days."

"Doesn't matter. If the chemistry and the timing are right, you can't stop love from happening."

Morgan had to admit that he was an incredible guy—so incredible that her heart ached for him. Still, a week wasn't enough time to decide who she'd spend eternity with. But it was long enough for her to know that they'd made a special connection. She wanted them to have the chance to get to know each other better. There was always the possibility that they'd find out they weren't right for each other, but there was also the possibility that they could have a future together. Either way, she felt compelled—and courageous enough—to try.

"So," Rhonda said, "when do you see him next?"

"When he gets back from Brazil, which could be in a month. It could also be longer."

"Well, girl, you just keep busy and have faith that things are going to work out and he'll be here before you know it. In fact, come hang out with me. We can go to a movie or to the city and see a play, or hit the flea market in San Jose sometime."

"I'd love that!" Morgan felt a flicker of excitement grow inside of her. She was ready to grow more, to discover who she was inside and what she wanted out of life.

"How about this weekend?" Rhonda suggested. "We'd have to get there early in the morning."

"That would be great."

"And if you want, since we live kind of by each other, you could come to the gym with me. We've got the best yoga instructor. Have you ever done yoga?"

"Me? No, never. I'm not very flexible."

"Oh, you have to come with me. Before you know it, we'll be able to tie you up like a pretzel."

"I don't think so. I can hardly sit on the floor cross-legged," Morgan said.

"Lucretia can do wonders with the most inflexible body. You'll see. Just wear comfortable clothes. It'll be fun."

Morgan had always enjoyed working with Rhonda, and she was suddenly amazed that it had never occurred to her that she ought to get to know her friend better.

"You're on," Morgan suddenly answered, feeling a rush of excitement.

ॐ ॐ ॐ

Morgan's old Honda Accord was about to fall apart. It seemed that rust was the only thing holding the body together. With well over 200,000 miles on it, it was time to think about a new car, so with her father's help Morgan found a used Acura. It was shiny red and had a sporty spoiler on the back as well as sleek, tinted windows. She loved it at first sight.

"Now this is a great car," her father exclaimed as they drove home after making the purchase.

"What do you think Mom's going to say?" Morgan asked, changing lanes and enjoying the tight handling of the car.

"Before or after she passes out?" her dad replied.

Morgan chuckled, grateful to have at least one parent's support. Not that her mother wasn't supportive in other areas of her life, but when it came to taking any kind of a risk, her mother just couldn't seem to handle it. If there were ever a person addicted to security and predictability, it was her mother. Though Morgan understood that her mother's overprotectiveness came from the death of her sister, Morgan still had to live her life—now that she'd found it.

"Either," Morgan answered.

"Well, she'll think we've completely lost our minds, bought way out of our price range, and done something totally unnecessary. Then she'll accept it, get over it, and that will be that."

"Dad, was Mom this bad when we were little?" Morgan asked, suddenly.

"Well, first you have to remember that she came from a home that was near the poverty level. I think I've told you that her father walked out on the family when she was ten, and after that her mother worked as a maid in a hotel, haven't I?"

Morgan nodded.

"Well, your mom once told me that the gifts she and her siblings got for Christmas and birthdays were things her mother found in hotel rooms that people left behind and never claimed. So her fears about you spending money are based on the fact that she never wants you to have to go without like that—she wants you to always feel financially secure."

Morgan's heart constricted in her chest. For the first time, her mother's chastisements suddenly meant something more to her. Her mother had reminded their family of her growing-up circumstances every time they hadn't eaten every scrap of food on their plates, or when they'd complained about something like their shoes getting a little too tight. But Morgan was beginning to realize that her mom was motivated by love—however misdirected her actions were.

"Security is very important to her," her father continued. "And after Erin died, she wanted to prevent something like that from ever happening again. I think that's why she clings to each of you kids so much. She wants to protect you from anything that might hurt you, physically or mentally."

Morgan understood, but she also knew she had to have the chance to spread her wings and fly. She had to be her own person, to be strong and independent, to stand on her own convictions and testimony. And she felt confident she could do it, but she was afraid her mother wouldn't let go of her long enough to let her find out for sure.

Cancún had given her a taste of freedom, a freedom she longed to pursue. She'd thought long and hard about her life and the changes she wanted to make. Her decisions would probably cause her mother some heartache, but Morgan knew that it would have to happen.

Chapter Eleven

The doorbell rang several times before Morgan answered it. She was surprised to find Manny on the porch.

"Morgan, I finally caught you home!" Handsome was the only way to describe him. He had jet-black hair and dark eyes that complemented his creamy-brown skin. He was a little taller than average and broad shouldered. His quick smile and easy manner were magnetic, drawing people to him wherever he went.

Morgan gave him a surprised smile, not knowing what to say. He evidently wanted to be invited in, but Morgan was on her way out.

"Hi, Manny. I'm sorry I've been so hard to get ahold of. It's been crazy ever since I got home from Mexico."

"You said you'd show me your pictures sometime."

It was obvious by his tone that he was hoping that "sometime" would be tonight.

Giving him an apologetic smile, she said, "I was just going to meet Rhonda at the gym. But maybe we can get together later?"

While he didn't try to hide his disappointment, he was still very gracious and understanding. "Sure, why don't you call me when you get home?"

He paused for a moment, and Morgan expected him to say something else, but then he turned and went back to his car.

"Who was that?" her mother asked as she came into the room from the kitchen.

"That was Manny."

"Why didn't you invite him in?"

It was no secret that Laura Rose thought the world of Manny. For that matter, so did Greg Rose. Morgan didn't blame her parents for liking him. He really was a great guy. She found it interesting, however, that while Manny had seemed interested only in casually dating her before the trip, ever since she'd gotten home he seemed to call a dozen times a day.

"I was just on my way out," she told her mother.

"But what about dinner?" her mother asked. Delicious smells from the kitchen filled the entire house. Laura Rose was known for her culinary skills.

"I'll eat when I get back."

"Where are you going, anyway?"

"To the gym with Rhonda. I'm going to try a yoga class."

"Don't you have something better to do with your time? Besides, who is this Rhonda person?"

Morgan didn't want her mother's questions to turn into a lengthy lecture, so she just replied, "I work with her at the library. You've met Rhonda."

"Do you two really have anything in common? I mean, isn't she the one who's divorced and quite a bit older than you? Is she even a member?"

"She's not that much older, Mom, and no, she's not a member, but she's a good person. Can we talk about this later? I'm going to be late."

"All right," her mother said with a frustrated huff.

"And if anybody calls . . ."

"I know, I'll have them call your cell phone. Of course, you can't answer the phone if you're in the middle of a yoga class, now, can you?"

Even though it had only been five days since she'd seen Justin, it felt like an eternity and she'd begun to wonder why he hadn't called. With each passing day, she worried more and more that his feelings for her had changed. Had they just been caught up in the moment? Was their attraction just a result of the enchanted atmosphere and intoxicating romance of the Caribbean?

"I'll turn off the ringer," she answered, coming back to the moment. "I'll see you later." She burst out the front door and ran for the car, hoping she would make it in time.

ह ह ह

"I can't move," Morgan said to Rhonda the next morning at the library.

"You just need to move around and the stiffness will go away," Rhonda told her. "But you still liked it, didn't you?"

"I loved it, but I still can't imagine ever being as flexible as you are. And Lucretia? She's more flexible than Gumby."

"Keep at it and you'll be amazed at how quickly your body adapts. I was just like you when I started."

"I don't believe it," Morgan said, groaning as she got up from her chair. "I feel like a ninety-year-old woman."

"You'll feel like a new woman if you keep coming. I promise."

"I need to get some decent clothes, though. Everyone in class had all these cute little outfits on, and I felt stupid in just a T-shirt and sweats."

"Hey, you looked great, and I loved having you there. It's fun to work out with a friend."

"Yeah, it was fun," Morgan agreed. The teacher had made her feel welcome, and the other women in the class had been warm and friendly. She'd enjoyed herself and liked how her muscles felt after the class—that is, until she'd woken up and felt like she'd been run over by a tractor.

"Why don't we go to lunch together and then shopping? There's a great store in the mall that has some nice workout clothes, and the prices are reasonable."

"That would be—" Morgan paused, listening. She heard a faint ringing sound. "My phone!" She lunged for her purse with a fair amount of pain tearing though her muscles. She located the phone and, glancing down at the name and phone number, saw that it was her mother. A twinge of disappointment stung her.

"Hi, Mom," she answered breathlessly.

"Why are you breathing so hard?"

Morgan moved the phone away from her mouth and took a deep breath. "No reason. I wasn't close to my purse, so I had to hurry so I wouldn't miss your call."

Her mother didn't comment.

"So what's up, Mom?" Morgan asked as Rhonda waved at her and mouthed, "We'll talk at lunch."

"You know I hate to bother you at work, but I thought you should know that boy called."

"That boy? You mean Justin called?"

"Yes, and he left his phone number. I didn't know if you wanted him to call you at work or not."

Morgan didn't say anything. She knew her mother didn't approve of the "stranger from Cancún" and wasn't going to help more than she absolutely had to. Morgan just bit her lip. "What's his number?" she asked, striving to keep any anxiety from her voice.

After her mother had given it to her, Morgan clutched the phone to her chest, tingling with excitement.

Telling one of her co-workers that she would be back in a few minutes, she stepped outside and found a quiet bench in the shade. Her fingers trembled so badly she could barely dial the number. "Come on," she prayed. "Answer!"

"Hello?"

Morgan opened her mouth and managed a "hi" that sounded like she had a bad case of laryngitis.

"Morgan?" Justin asked, sounding happy.

"It's me. How are you?" Morgan found her voice.

"I miss you. How are you?"

"I miss you too. I'm good, though. Trying to stay busy."

Morgan proceeded to tell him about work, her new car, and her yoga class.

"What have you been doing?" she asked.

"Nothing too exciting. I'm helping my dad fix his roof this weekend. That's about it."

They were silent for a moment.

"I want to see you," Justin suddenly said.

"Me too."

"Maybe I can take a couple of days off before I leave for Brazil and fly out to see you. I can leave for South America from San Francisco just as easily as I can from here."

"Do you think you can?" Morgan couldn't believe she might actually see him soon.

"I'll try. It may be tricky since I just took a vacation, but it doesn't hurt to ask."

"I hope it works out."

"I hope so too. Say a prayer."

"I will."

"I'll call you when I talk to my boss. Keep your phone on."

"I'll keep my fingers crossed."

They said good-bye, and Morgan hung up the phone. For a moment she sat and sorted through all the emotions inside of her. Soon a smile grew on her face. Not only did he miss her, but he was going to try to see her!

🍅 🍅 🍅

Morgan walked through the door from work at the same moment the phone rang.

"You're home," Manny said after she answered it.

"Just barely," Morgan replied, dropping her purse onto the counter and snitching a piece of a freshly baked roll. She was starving.

"You want to go grab a bite to eat?"

Since she and Manny hadn't been able to get together after her yoga class earlier that week, she didn't have the heart to tell him no, even though she just wanted to have dinner and then relax in a long, hot bath with a good book.

"Sure," she answered, forcing perkiness into her words. "That'd be fun."

Just as she hung up the phone, her mother walked into the kitchen. "Who was that?"

"Manny called to invite me to go out to dinner."

"That's nice. Your father's working late, so I was just going to open a can of soup to go with these rolls. You go have fun."

Morgan went to her room to change and freshen up. She pulled on a new pair of black capris she'd just purchased and a raspberry-colored blouse to go with them. Before her trip, she'd shopped for more conservative clothing, but she and Rhonda had recently gone into some of the more fashionable stores at the mall. Morgan had blown nearly her whole paycheck on new clothes, even though she knew she was going to have to start being more careful with money. Rhonda had just found out that there was a single-bedroom apartment for rent in her complex, and Morgan felt this was the time to make the next step in her quest for growth and independence.

"Morgan," her mother called up the stairs a few minutes later. "Manny's here."

After putting on some lip gloss, she spritzed herself with perfume and headed downstairs.

"Hi, Manny," she greeted as he turned to see her coming down the stairs.

"Wow, Morgan, look at you."

Morgan smiled. There was nothing extreme about her outfit, but apparently he had noticed the change from her usual librarian attire.

They arrived at the restaurant before the dinner crowd and were seated almost immediately. It wasn't a fancy place, but it was cozy and fun, and the food was delicious.

After placing their order, they talked about what they'd both been doing the last several weeks. Manny worked for his uncle in his tire shop, and even though it wasn't a job he particularly enjoyed, the money was good. He was just biding his time until he headed to Burley, Idaho, at the end of the summer to teach seminary.

"How about you?" Manny asked. "You seem kind of preoccupied."

Morgan knew the time had come for her to tell him her next big news. "I've decided to get my own apartment."

Manny raised his eyebrows. "Why?"

"What do you mean?" she asked.

"You've got the perfect setup at home. You don't have to pay rent, and it's just you and your parents. Think of all the money you'll spend having your own place."

"I have thought about it. You're right, staying at home has been nice in terms of money, and I've been able to save a lot, but I need to do this for myself. I've never been on my own." The confused look on his face told her he didn't get it, so she continued. "You served a mission, so you were out in the world seeing things, growing, gaining your independence, and finding out who you were. I haven't had any of that, and I need it. It's important to me."

His eyes narrowed. "Something happened while you were in Mexico."

"What do you mean?"

"You seem different."

She didn't know how to reply. Meeting Justin wasn't the whole reason she had changed, but it had given her courage to go after her dreams and the prospects that lay before her. She had realized that she didn't want to look back on her life and have regrets because she hadn't had the courage to try. "I had the chance to really think about my life and where it was going, and I realized I wasn't living up to my potential. There are things I want to do with my life, and I've decided I'm going to do them."

"Like what?"

"Well, like getting out on my own. The other thing is going back to college."

Manny blinked, looking startled. "Why? You have a wonderful job."

"I enjoy my job, but it's just not totally fulfilling. I've felt this way for a while, but I just didn't understand why."

"And?"

"And I realize that the reason I'm not fulfilled is because I sold out in college. I went for the easiest route to graduation instead of the one I wanted to pursue."

"What was that?"

"Art." Her mind flashed back to the days when she'd immersed herself in art projects, staying after school to work on them until janitors kicked her out of the building. Creating and seeing her work take shape and come to life had been one of the most rewarding times of her life. "Mr. Tobler, my art teacher, told me that he'd never seen such natural talent in a student. I knew then that I wanted to study art and maybe even teach someday. But I let people talk me into taking other paths, and before I knew it, I was going down one I didn't really want to take. Ever since then, I've regretted it, and I don't think I'll ever find real fulfillment and satisfaction until I pursue my degree in art and get my teaching certificate."

"What do your parents have to say about all of this?"

"They don't know yet. I didn't want to say anything until I found out for sure about the apartment." She looked at him, unable to read his expression. "What do you think about all of this? I mean, it's like selling tires. It's a good job, but you wouldn't want to do it the rest of your life, would you? Don't you feel your calling in life is to teach seminary and to work with the youth?"

Manny thought for a moment, then nodded.

"That's what I feel. And I need to at least try. Even if I fail and never make it, I need to at least know that I tried."

❦ ❦ ❦

The next night at dinner, Morgan looked at her parents sitting across from her at the table and braced herself for their reaction when she told them her news. "I need to talk to you."

"Oh?" her father said, cutting a piece of chicken and popping it into his mouth. "What about?" he asked as he chewed.

Her mother's expression was skeptical and Morgan found her resolve weakening. But she knew this was right. She'd prayed about her decision, and she had no doubts—at least, not until this moment.

"Well . . . " She pushed her plate away. "I've decided it's time for me to get out on my own."

"What do you mean?" her mother questioned.

"I mean, well . . . I mean move out of the house. I've found an apartment not far from here."

Her mother's eyebrows rose. "Your own apartment. By yourself?"

Morgan nodded. "I thought I'd ask around at church to see if anyone knows of someone else who needs a place, so I could maybe get a roommate, but for now I can handle it on my own."

"Why do you want to move out?" her mother probed. "You've got everything you could ever want here at home. Plus you get to live here for free."

"I've appreciated being able to stay here as long as I have. But I feel I need to do this."

"But—" her mother started.

"Laura," her father cut in, "I think Morgan is right. If she feels it's time to get out on her own, then we need to support her."

Morgan smiled at her father appreciatively. She had recently discovered a new side of him and felt happy she could count on his support. She supposed she'd never needed it before since she'd never tried anything risky. "That's not all," she continued.

"There's more?" It wasn't hard to tell that Laura Rose was struggling with her daughter's announcement.

Morgan nodded. "I've decided to go back to school."

"Whatever for?" her mother exclaimed.

"I realize that I'm not going to be happy until I finish my art degree and get a teaching certificate. I know I should have just done it the first time, but I really thought I'd enjoy working in a library."

"We didn't know you were unhappy there," her father said.

"I'm not unhappy, Dad, but I know that it's not what I want to do with my life. I miss painting and sculpting and creating. It's in my blood, and I've decided the only thing to do is go back and finish what I've started."

While her mother shook her head, her father nodded and smiled. "Honey, if that's what you want to do, I think that's great. We know how talented you are, and I think you'd make a great teacher."

"Thanks, Dad." Morgan looked at her mother. "Mom, please say something."

"I don't know what to say," Laura replied. "I want you to be happy and do what you need to do, but I don't see why you have to move out."

"I know," Morgan said, "but I do. Eventually I'm going to have to move out. I think I need to do it now. You two have taught me everything I need to know, so I guess I just feel like it's time for me to leave the nest."

Her mother nodded and remained silent. Morgan hoped she'd achieve a level of understanding that would eventually lead to acceptance.

♥ ♥ ♥

Restless was the only way to describe how Morgan felt. When she was home she couldn't relax, and between boxing up her things to move into her new apartment and waiting for Justin to call, she was in a constant state of excitement and anxiety.

Fortunately, Rhonda, her yoga classes, and an occasional outing to a movie or dinner kept her mind off Justin and helped her keep her sanity amid all the changes she was making in her life.

One Saturday morning as Rhonda and Morgan drove to San Jose to the flea market, Morgan's phone rang. She quickly answered when she noticed it was Justin, excited to find out when he was coming.

"I'm sorry, Morgan," he began, and her hopes faded as he continued. "I need to leave earlier than planned, so there's just no way I can squeeze in a visit before I go. But I promise I'll come straight to see you when I come home."

Surprised at the intensity of her own emotions, Morgan felt her eyes sting with tears.

"I feel terrible. I did everything I could."

"I know," she answered, forcing her voice to stay steady. "That's all you could do."

"We're building a new tile plant in southern Brazil, in a city near Santa Maria. It's a big project, and they're sending me to oversee things. I have to be there as soon as possible. I'll be in touch when I get there and get settled. Good luck with your move. I'm proud of you."

"Thanks," she said, appreciating his vote of confidence more than anything.

He said good-bye, and Morgan couldn't help but wonder how long it would be until she saw him again.

❦ ❦ ❦

At church the next day, Morgan's friend Stephanie Jepson ran up to her, grabbed her by the arm, and pulled her outside.

"You're never going to believe who's speaking in church today."

"The prophet?" Morgan said, looking over Stephanie's shoulder. Judging by her friend's level of excitement, it had to be someone pretty special.

"No, silly," Stephanie said in exasperation. Stephanie and Morgan had been friends throughout their high school years, and though they hadn't really hung out at school much, they had always had fun at church activities. Morgan had always admired Stephanie, and even though Stephanie was now married, with children, she was still fun and crazy.

"Okay, who?"

"Manny Lopez."

"Steph, I've seen Manny since he moved back to town. I guess I didn't tell you we've been dating a little."

"You have?" Stephanie looked surprised.

"Yeah. I guess I haven't talked to you much since you had the baby."

They walked into the chapel together, and Morgan wondered why Manny was speaking in their ward and why he hadn't told her about it.

"I'll talk to you later," Stephanie said, as she headed toward her family's pew. "I want to hear about everything."

Morgan nodded and made her way to the row where her parents sat. As she took her seat, she looked up and saw Manny smiling at her. She gave him a slight wave and returned his smile. He did look good sitting up there on the stand in his dark suit and white shirt.

Her mind was at once flooded with memories. Manny had been a member of their ward when she had been in high school, and Morgan had had a crush on him for several years while they were growing up. He'd been the star of the basketball and baseball teams and had won academic awards along with being offered full-ride scholarships to a dozen universities on both coasts and in Utah.

Before Manny's family had moved to Salt Lake, soon after high school graduation, he and Morgan had dated a little bit before his mission. It was all due to Stephanie, who had played matchmaker for them. Morgan remembered her first date with Manny. Before that he'd always seemed untouchable, out of her league. But Stephanie had talked him into going out with her, and to Morgan's surprise, they'd hit it off.

At the time, it was obvious that Manny was full of himself. He'd known he was good-looking and popular, but Morgan had managed to overlook his conceit in light of the fact that he was taking an interest in her, something she'd never thought possible in high school.

After his mission to Fiji, Manny hadn't returned to his Sacramento ward. He'd stayed in Salt Lake City, near where his family had moved, and, she'd thought, had gone on with his life, just as she had.

Then he'd unexpectedly returned to California a few months ago to work at his uncle's tire business until he started teaching seminary in Idaho. Morgan had been swept away when he first came back into her life, convinced that they were meant for each other. But Manny had changed over the years. He was still handsome and confident, but the magic just wasn't there like she had hoped.

It didn't help that her parents were crazy for Manny. She got pressured more concerning him than any other guy she had ever dated. Morgan always felt they'd been a little surprised that she'd managed to date a guy like Manny. Their disappointment that nothing had come of their relationship after he had returned from his mission was expressed more often than she cared to hear. And then, when he came back into her life, they had a hard time not pushing her straight into his arms. She wondered if her parents wouldn't push so hard if she were more excited about her relationship with Manny.

The meeting soon started, and Morgan felt self-conscious, knowing that he was looking at her. "Doesn't Manny look handsome?" her mother whispered during the rest hymn. "I wonder if he has plans for dinner," she continued. "Why don't we invite him over?"

"Mother, he probably has somewhere else to go."

"He has to eat," her mother insisted. "I'm going to ask him. I've got a lovely roast in the oven. He loves my pot roast."

Morgan remained silent, knowing that one way or another, her mother was going to get her way.

Chapter Twelve

When it was Manny's turn to talk, the bishop introduced him and made a point of explaining what a wonderful young man he'd been in his youth.

"We're pleased to have Brother Lopez with us today, and we're grateful that he agreed to share a few words with us. He left from this ward to serve a mission but his family moved to Utah and he never got a chance to report on that mission when he returned. We felt it would be appropriate to take this opportunity to have him share some remarks and his testimony now."

Manny took his place at the pulpit. "It's wonderful to be back with my brothers and sisters of this ward."

Morgan's mother elbowed her, and Morgan scooted away discreetly.

He began to talk about experiences on his mission, focusing his stories and comments on the power of prayer. Morgan felt faint stirrings of sentimentality as her memory recalled emotions from her past. Manny had been her first love, and she couldn't deny that he was the type of guy all parents prayed their daughter would marry.

After Manny closed his talk, the meeting ended, and the mass exodus from the chapel began. The aisles were crowded, and Morgan waited patiently to leave the room. She turned to speak with Sister Sparks, the Primary president, who sat behind her.

As they chatted, Sister Sparks's gaze traveled beyond Morgan's face, and Morgan sensed someone standing behind her. Sister Sparks quietly excused herself, and slowly Morgan turned and saw Manny. She couldn't deny she felt attracted to him.

"Hi," he greeted her.

"Hi," she replied. "Why didn't you tell me you were speaking in my ward today?"

"I didn't know until last night when the bishop called. I guess their original speaker got sick, and he'd been wanting me to come later in the month anyway."

Morgan knew everyone was watching them. Many of the ward members had been there during Morgan and Manny's courtship before his mission, and Morgan was sure they remembered all the talk and speculation of what would happen after. It had embarrassed Morgan then, and it still embarrassed her now.

They exchanged small talk for a few moments, and finally Manny said, "You know we haven't been out much this week. Do you think you could squeeze me in sometime?"

She nodded and smiled. "Yeah, I think I could do that."

Just then, Morgan's mother approached them. "Manny, dear, is there any way we could talk you into joining us for dinner after church?"

Manny didn't hesitate. "Sure, Sister Rose, I'd love to. I can't turn down your delicious cooking."

Laura Rose glowed. "We'll see you after church, then."

As Manny and Morgan left the chapel for Sunday School, several members stopped to greet Manny and express their delight in seeing him again. None of them left without giving Morgan an encouraging wink. Suddenly Manny turned to her in the foyer, which was quickly growing empty. "You know, Morgan, I haven't told you this, but I've thought about you every day since I returned from my mission," he said.

Morgan was surprised and unsure how to reply, so she said nothing.

"You've grown into a beautiful woman."

"Thank you," she finally said.

"There's something else I haven't told you."

"Oh?" She swallowed.

"I didn't come here just to work in my uncle's tire shop. I came here hoping to find that you weren't attached, engaged, or married."

"Not me," she said, feeling her stomach tense. Where was this conversation going? "I was surprised when you came back to town. I couldn't believe you were still single."

"I came close to getting married, but it didn't work out."

"I'm sorry."

"It's okay. It wasn't right."

She nodded, feeling uncomfortable. "Oh!" she said, stalling as she looked at her watch. "I guess I'd better get to Primary. I'm supposed to be leading the music."

"Can I come with you?"

His request caught her off guard. "Um, yeah, I guess. If you want to."

They walked together to the Primary room and took seats toward the back until it was time for Morgan to do the music. She fanned herself with a folded piece of paper as she walked to the front of the room. How was she going to get through music time with him watching her?

ত ত ত

"So tell us how you went from getting a business degree at BYU to wanting to teach seminary in Burley." Morgan's father asked Manny as he passed a bowl of mixed vegetables to him.

"Well, sir, while I was on my mission I realized that nothing gave me greater joy than helping others understand the principles of the gospel. We taught many investigators in Fiji, but we also helped strengthen the youth of the Church there. Being involved with those kids and seeing them gain their own testimonies helped me decide what I ultimately wanted to do with my life. I know that teaching seminary isn't going to bring in a lot of money, but teaching is something I love, and it's something I feel I'm supposed to do. With my business degree, I'll hopefully be able to find ways to supplement my income."

Greg Rose nodded thoughtfully, clearly impressed by the young man sitting in front of him.

After the meal, Morgan gathered some plates and carried them into the kitchen while her parents continued the conversation with Manny.

"So how's Samantha doing?" Manny asked Morgan as she came back for more dishes. "How does she like married life?"

Morgan shrugged. "We haven't talked much since she got home from Mexico. Her wedding was very different from a temple wedding," she continued. "But Samantha thought the beach would be romantic."

"And was it?" he asked.

"It was romantic, but I could tell there was something missing from the ceremony. It just didn't seem complete." Manny nodded with understanding as she gathered more dishes and headed back to the kitchen.

As Morgan loaded the dishwasher, her thoughts drifted to the resort, the turquoise water, and to Justin. Her heart constricted inside her chest as she thought of where the experience in Cancún might lead her.

Suddenly she heard her mother in the next room and realized it was her cue to come out. "Well, if no one's going to have more pie, I guess I'll straighten up the kitchen. Honey," Laura Rose addressed her husband, "do you mind giving me a hand?"

As her parents took their place in the kitchen, Morgan and Manny went into the living room to relax and talk. Manny asked her about her apartment plans and offered to help her move in. She appreciated his offer, and even though she knew he didn't fully understand why she wanted to move out, she appreciated his show of support.

As they talked, Morgan noticed subtle differences in the way Manny was now, as opposed to before his mission. He'd been such a charmer, flirtatious and funny. Now, though he was still charming, he seemed a bit more serious and focused on his future. Morgan admired the man he'd become and knew he would be successful at anything he pursued. But something was missing for her now, though she wasn't sure what it was.

"I know you probably have a lot going on," Manny said, "but I've been wanting to go to San Francisco. I was wondering if you'd like to go with me sometime this week? We could have some dinner, walk around the wharf, and I wouldn't mind going to Alcatraz if we could fit it in. Have you ever been there?"

Morgan shook her head.

"What do you think? I'd enjoy it more if you'd come with me."

She opened her mouth to speak, but nothing came out. Thoughts of Justin flooded her mind. She felt she would be somehow untrue to him by going out with Manny, but she knew she hadn't committed to Justin or agreed not to date others.

"Morgan, is there something you want to tell me? Ever since you came home from your trip, you've seemed different. Have you . . ." He looked her straight in the eye, which made her uncomfortable. "Have you met someone?"

Morgan tried to swallow. Manny waited for an answer.

"Well, kind of, but . . . I . . ." She stopped, then started again. "Yeah," she finally managed to say, "I did meet someone while I was in Cancún. He was a friend of Trevor's."

Manny nodded, as if relieved to hear she hadn't hooked up with a complete stranger.

"But he lives in New York, and he's on his way to Brazil soon. So . . . I'm not even sure why I told you all that, because—yes—I'd like to go to San Francisco with you."

"You're sure?"

"Yes. In fact, I get off at three on Wednesday. Would that work?"

"I'll be there a few minutes before to pick you up."

❦ ❦ ❦

True to his word, Manny picked Morgan up a few minutes before she got off work on Wednesday. He looked particularly handsome in a red polo shirt and loose-fitting jeans, and Morgan chuckled to herself as she waved to her gawking friends at the library.

She'd like to see their faces when they met Justin!

❦ ❦ ❦

As they drove to San Francisco, Morgan had a couple of hours to realize just what a strong, grounded person Manny was. He told her about his daily routine, which consisted of morning prayer and scripture study, followed by a forty-five-minute jog. He then showered and left for work, and in the evenings he did some sort of gospel reading or visited the temple.

She shook her head just thinking about it all, knowing that she was nowhere near his spiritual level, but nonetheless truly impressed by the depth of his commitment.

They drove straight to the wharf and found a wonderful chowder house. Throughout the meal, they grew more and more comfortable with each other as old feelings and memories seemed to be reawakening. Morgan had never forgotten just how deeply she had cared for Manny at one time, and she pondered for a moment the possibility that there was a reason they were together again now. Everything felt so strange. She felt as if her feelings for Manny had suddenly rekindled, and yet she was more hesitant than ever to want to commit to him. Why would the Lord put Manny and Justin into her life at the same time? And was either of them the right one for her?

She and Manny held hands as they walked to the dock to await the ferry that would carry them across the bay to Alcatraz. The evening was beautiful and clear, with a soft breeze blowing. They stood side by side, looking out over the harbor, with the San Francisco Bridge stretched out before them. Morgan had always loved this city. It was beautiful, exciting, and fun. She'd attended Broadway plays, spent hours shopping and sightseeing, and ridden trolley cars up and down the streets. On several of those occasions she'd been with Manny.

They boarded the ferry and found seats on the upper deck so they could have a view of the bay. Morgan admired the city from a distance and drew in a breath of ocean air. It felt good to have a break from her regular routine. She was glad she'd agreed to come.

Just then, she turned, catching Manny looking at her with a strange expression on his face.

"What?" she asked.

"I'm sorry if I keep staring, but sometimes I just can't believe I'm really with you again."

She laughed. "I've had the same thought."

"I can't get over how much you've changed since I've been gone. You're wonderful with people, especially children. When I saw you yesterday in Primary, well, I . . . was truly impressed. You are an incredible woman, and I really feel like I was led back here for a reason."

Morgan felt her panic level rise up a notch. "You do?" she managed to say.

"Yes."

Just then, an announcement came over the loudspeaker giving instructions about getting off the ferry and how to get to the entrance of the prison.

Morgan glanced away, relieved that their discussion had been interrupted. She wasn't ready for this. Not now, when her heart was with Justin. But Manny was practically handing his heart to her on a silver platter. She couldn't help wondering where it was all going to lead.

Chapter Thirteen

"Mom, I'll be back in a couple of hours." Morgan headed for the door with her gym bag slung over her shoulder. In the beginning her workouts had been to improve her physical condition, but now she needed them just as much for her mental condition.

"What about dinner?"

"I'm not hungry," she replied and sped out the door before her mother could delay her any longer. She didn't tell her mother that she was fasting. If she did, her mother would make a big deal out of it, and right now Morgan didn't need that.

She needed to clear her head. What had once been a boring life had now become so complicated she couldn't concentrate anymore. She needed peace, guidance, and inspiration, and for her, fasting was the surest way to make her prayers more effective and to fine-tune her reception of the Spirit.

As she drove to the gym, her mind was awhirl with questions. She'd spent a lot of time with Manny recently. They'd been to movies, out to dinner, and even shopping. Each time she'd come home, she'd sworn she was going to slow things down with him, knowing she needed distance and space to look at the situation clearly. But every time he had called to ask her out, she had said yes.

After a relaxing workout, she came home feeling somewhat calmer. Even nicer was the fact that she came home to a quiet, empty house. Her parents had gone out.

She dumped her things in her room, then went to the study and turned on the computer. She opened her e-mail account and noticed she had several messages waiting for her. To her delight and surprise, two were from Justin.

Her fingers actually trembled as she clicked to bring up the first message.

> Guten Morgan. I just found out that the word morgen in German means "morning." There are a lot of Germans here in the southern part of Brazil, and one of the gentlemen I work with told me how to say "good morning" in German. Your name fits you. Morning. I'm a morning person, and I love to watch the sun come up, all warm and radiant and beautiful, just like you.
>
> Anyway, how are you? Believe it or not, it's freezing cold down here! The seasons are reversed, as you probably know. Spring there is fall here, and it's been raining ever since I arrived. I didn't even bring a coat, so I guess I'll have to go shopping.
>
> I'm sorry I didn't get a chance to come and see you before I left. If you only knew how badly I wanted to see you . . . I miss you so much that my heart aches. Does that sound weird?
>
> My body is here in Brazil but I left my heart in Sacramento with you. That's kind of like the song, isn't it? Next time we're together I'll sing it for you. Something to look forward to.
>
> Ever since we parted in Cancún, I've felt empty inside. Does that sound even weirder? In my mind I try to re-create our time together. It was magical for me, as I hope it was for you too. I would give anything to be with you again, if only for a moment.
>
> Write back when you can. I'm sure your life is much more exciting than mine.
>
> Com muito amor, Justin.

Morgan reread the e-mail and sighed.

She clicked on the next e-mail from him.

Hi, me again. Did I tell you how much I miss you?
Justin
P.S. Watch your mail. I sent you something.
P.P.S. Your passport's still valid, right?

Her passport? Why did he want to know that?

She clicked on the "reply" button and wrote back to him. Yes, she missed him. Yes, her heart ached. Yes, her passport was still valid—

Morgan stopped typing. Was that why he was asking? Was he thinking of having her come to Brazil?

That was crazy. There was no way her mother would approve of her going to Brazil to see him. But she knew she would if he asked. It would be scary but exciting—another adventure, another exotic land.

A quiver of excitement rippled through her. She quickly finished her message and clicked on the "send" button.

It was time to break her fast.

After saying a heartfelt prayer, she went to the kitchen to see what her mother had made for dinner. She found some sort of meatloaf and a baked potato in the fridge and decided that wasn't going to cut it.

"Italian food," she said, guessing she wanted it because she was thinking of what she and Justin had shared on vacation.

She called a local Italian café, thrilled to find out that they did offer take-out service. She ordered, then dashed up the stairs to change her clothes, figuring she could shower later. Right now, all she wanted was something to eat.

After dressing, she grabbed her purse and flew to the front door. She yanked it open and jumped when she saw a man standing there. Then she realized it was Manny.

"Sorry," he said. "I didn't mean to startle you."

"I . . ." she took a breath to slow her racing heart, "I didn't expect anyone," she finally managed.

"Where's the fire?" he asked.

She smiled. "I was just running to get some food I ordered. I'm starving. Have you eaten? I ordered more food than I can eat."

"I could use a little something," he said. "Where are you heading? I'll give you a ride."

She jumped into his car, and within minutes they had grabbed the order and were back at her house. Manny blessed the food once they settled in at the kitchen table, and then Morgan launched into the containers.

While they ate, Manny brought up the subject of her trip to Cancún. He asked her if she had any pictures. Looking at his near-casual expression, she wondered if he was bothered by the fact that she had met someone. He hadn't really said much about it when she'd first told him, but she could tell he wanted more information.

For a moment she worried about him seeing all the pictures of her and Justin, but then she realized it was stupid to care. She wasn't going to hide the fact that she'd spent time with Justin, nor the fact that they had something special going on between them.

After grabbing her photo album, she returned to the kitchen, and as they ate, they looked at pictures. Manny was surprisingly less inquisitive about her and Justin than she'd thought he'd be. He appeared to be very impressed with the pictures of the ruins and just as impressed with all the underwater pictures she'd taken while snorkeling.

"Looks like you had a great time," he said.

"I did," she answered. "It really was awesome."

"Tell me more about this Justin," he said suddenly. "How serious is it?"

Morgan hadn't really expected him to ask her outright about Justin, but she didn't intend to hide anything from him. "It's hard to explain," she answered. "We really hit it off and enjoyed spending time together. It was like being with someone I'd known for a long time instead of just a few days. But now he's in Brazil, for I don't know how long, and I'm here."

Manny looked as though he were about to ask another question when the back door opened and Morgan's parents walked in. Morgan's father was quick to greet Manny, but Morgan's mother didn't follow suit.

"Morgan," she said when she saw the take-out meal, "I made plenty for dinner tonight. You didn't need to go buy food."

"I know, Mom," Morgan answered, "But I was in the mood for Italian. So was Manny, right?" She directed her comment to Manny, hoping that his involvement would help her mother chill just a little.

"The shrimp is really good. You should try it," Manny commented.

Greg Rose grabbed a fork, spearing one of the Alfredo-covered shrimp. "Mmmm," he said with his mouth full. "That really is good. Honey, you should try this."

Laura Rose declined, but her husband persisted. She finally tasted the shrimp and the pasta dish and couldn't deny how good it was. Morgan was happy to see her mother relax a bit and join them, wishing she did that more often. She would fuss and labor over a nice meal, then barely take time to sit down and eat it. Morgan admired her mother's hard work and discipline, but wished she wouldn't put it above enjoying moments with her family.

Manny didn't stay much longer after they finished eating. He asked her if she wanted to go on a double date with Stephanie and her husband, Leo. The thought of going with Stephanie and Leo made the date hard to resist, so she accepted.

ভ ভ ভ

Morgan waited until after dinner the next evening to present her mother with her gift—a day at the spa that included a massage, facial, pedicure, manicure, and a deep-oil treatment for her hair. It was pricey, but Morgan had decided that as much as she loved having money saved in the bank, she was going to allow herself a few splurges now and then. And she wanted to do this for herself and her mother.

"Mom, have you got plans on Saturday afternoon after I move?" she said as casually as she could.

Her mother was busy folding a load of laundry. "Just yard work, dear. The flower beds are loaded with weeds."

"Well, how about after we get my stuff moved into my apartment, you and I spend the rest of the day together. I'll help you weed another time. And there's no hurry to put my stuff away."

Her father looked at Morgan with raised eyebrows and took his newspaper to the living room.

Morgan waited for her mother's response.

"Doing what?" her mother asked.

Morgan handed her the envelope, feeling herself bubble over with excitement. She looked forward to having a mother-daughter day they could spend growing closer.

"What in the world is this?" her mother asked as she opened the envelope.

"It's a certificate for the day spa at my gym. They have a wonderful facility, and Rhonda tells me—"

"Did Rhonda give you this idea?" her mother interrupted her, shaking her head as if amused.

"No, Mom. It was my idea. I thought it would be fun for us—"

"It's a nice idea, sweetheart," her mother continued as she picked up the laundry basket and headed for the doorway. "However, I don't have time to go and soak my hands in dish soap—I can do that at home while I wash the dishes. And I couldn't possibly let you spend that kind of money on me when you have so many important things to spend your money on right now."

Morgan was stunned—how could her mother not see what that time would have meant to her. Before she could say anything else however, her mother was already out of the room. There was no one to express her disappointment to. She didn't doubt that her mother loved her, but why couldn't she show it in a way that Morgan appreciated? Why couldn't her mother support her and try to understand her feelings for once? As she made her way to her bedroom, she realized she'd give anything to have a mother who was also a best friend, someone in whom she could confide, someone she could share her hopes and dreams with. She knew her father did the best he could, but he still couldn't fill that void in her life. There was only one person—other than Samantha—whom she'd felt that comfortable with, and that had been Justin. And he wasn't there.

After lying down on the bed, she rolled onto her back and hugged her pillow close to her. She couldn't call him, but she could call Samantha. They'd only chatted briefly a few times since the wedding, and right now she needed a friend. Hopefully she could catch her at a good time.

Trevor answered the phone. "Samantha's out right now. She ran to the grocery store. I can have her call when she gets back."

"Thanks, Trevor."

"So, what do you hear from Justin?" he asked.

"He seems to be doing fine."

"When does he come back?"

"He thinks it might be six weeks or so," she said. "He said he'd come and visit when he gets back to the States."

"Cool. Let me know when he's coming so we can hang out."

"I will. Thanks, Trevor."

They hung up, and Morgan still felt empty inside. Feeling lost and alone, she sighed and turned on the lamp beside her bed. She opened her scriptures to the nineteenth section of the Doctrine and Covenants, which she'd read a lot lately in search of answers since her life had become so complicated. Her eyes fell on the thirty-eighth verse.

> *Pray always, and I will pour out my Spirit upon you, and great shall be your blessing . . .*

The simple words of direction were a healing balm to her aching heart. Even though she felt she didn't have anyone close she could turn to, she knew she could always depend upon the Lord to be there for her. In His gentle way, He communicated with her and gave her the peace she needed, just as He always had. She'd learned to find meaning in the small, simple answers she received, knowing that they were the key to which direction her life should go—even if she couldn't always see the path ahead. Her prayer helped her now in her moment of despair. Peace enveloped her heart. All would be well. With patience and faith, things would work out the way they were supposed to.

ভ ভ ভ

"I've heard about this place," Morgan said as the four of them pulled into the parking lot. "It's supposed to be a lot of fun."

"We came about a month ago with another couple," Stephanie said. "We've been dying to come back. The food is great. They have the best barbecued brisket in the world. And the atmosphere is a blast."

Morgan was in the mood for some fun. Her week had been hard both emotionally and physically. She had taken that day off to box up the rest of her stuff and get her neighbor's truck and trailer loaded. He was letting her borrow it for her big move.

Now that she was, for the most part, done loading, she just wanted to relax with her friends and enjoy the evening. When they walked in, they noticed that the place was packed. Over the dull roar of voices and laughter, music blasted.

The hostess led them away from the bar and around to the back of the building. Morgan laughed as two of the employees, a waitress and a waiter, began dancing to the Beatles' "Twist and Shout." This brought some of the customers to their feet, and soon the floor was full of people twisting and shouting. The fun was contagious, and Morgan and Stephanie looped arms and added a little twist to their step as they found their seats.

Morgan felt a rush of excitement grow inside of her. This was exactly what she needed. Stephanie and Leo were such a fun couple to be with. Stephanie was still as enthusiastic as she'd been in high school, and Leo complemented her personality well. They were the "coolest" little family Morgan had ever known, and she vowed she would enjoy marriage and having a family as much as those two did. It was obvious that they were as much in love now as they were when they had gotten married. To Morgan, that was the most romantic thing in the world.

"Look!" Morgan exclaimed. "They have karaoke."

"Are you going to get up tonight?" Leo asked.

Morgan opened her mouth to say no, but Stephanie cut in with, "You bet she is. We're getting up together, aren't we?"

Morgan immediately suppressed the urge to decline the invitation and instead said, "It does sound kind of fun."

Manny's eyes narrowed slightly when he heard Morgan's answer. She couldn't tell if he gave her a look of disapproval or just surprise that she would be open to the idea. Regardless, she didn't let it discourage her. She wouldn't be up on the stage alone, and it wasn't like she couldn't sing. Still, it took all the willpower she had to ignore her feelings of fear and shyness.

Their waiter, a Jamaican with dreadlocks and a heavy accent, took their order. He told them that tonight's karaoke theme was Motown. Morgan and Stephanie both happened to be huge Supremes fans.

"You're not really going to sing tonight." Manny looked somewhat skeptical.

"Of course we are!" Stephanie exclaimed. "And we expect you to get up there too. C'mon, Manny. You used to be the one leading all the fun."

"We're not in high school anymore," he replied.

"So?" Stephanie quipped. "Does that mean we can't have fun anymore?"

"Well, no," he said. "But doesn't it embarrass you to do stuff like this?"

"It might if I couldn't sing. But you just wait, boy. We're going to bring down the house, aren't we, Morgan?"

Morgan looked silently at Stephanie as worry began to choke out her confidence. What if they *did* embarrass themselves?

When their food arrived, all attention turned to the delicious, steaming plates of barbecued ribs and brisket and the plentiful helpings of potatoes, vegetables, and freshly baked garlic-cheese bread.

As they ate, Leo entertained them with stories of his latest escapades on the ski slopes. He had a group of companions from his mission that he'd been particularly close to, and their families had recently gathered in Tahoe for a mission reunion. He related a few humorous incidents that had occurred, and everyone seemed to appreciate his gift for storytelling.

Morgan noticed that Manny finally relaxed a little bit and was able to enjoy the meal and laugh along with them. While she appreciated his discipline and focus, she also saw no reason that he couldn't laugh and have fun too.

"Can I get you some dessert tonight?" the waiter asked when he saw they were finishing up.

Stephanie and Morgan decided to split a piece of hot-fudge cake. Leo had his own, and Manny declined to have any.

"What time does karaoke start?" Stephanie asked the waiter.

"Nine o'clock. Are you ladies going to sing for us tonight?"

Stephanie nodded for both of them and winked at Morgan.

"Then you need to go over to Randy and choose a song. He'll put you down on the list. How about you?" he asked Leo.

"I'm thinkin' about it," Leo answered.

The waiter turned to Manny.

"Not me," Manny said, holding up both hands in a gesture of defense.

The waiter left to get the dessert, and Stephanie grabbed Morgan's hand. "Let's go choose a song." She turned to her husband. "Honey, do you want me to put you down?"

Leo asked Manny if he wanted to join him, an offer Manny quickly declined. "I guess I'll pass tonight." Leo said. "After I eat that fudge cake, I know I won't be able to breathe, let alone sing."

The women went to the stage, where an employee was handing out lists of song choices.

"What's with Manny?" Stephanie asked Morgan. "He's not as fun as he used to be."

"He's gotten a lot more serious, but he's still a great guy," Morgan said in his defense.

"I guess I just thought he'd be his old self. He used to be the life of the party."

Morgan shrugged, realizing that just as Manny had been different in high school, so had she. And she was grateful for the opportunity to change.

After they read through the songs, they realized they were going to have a hard time deciding what to sing. While Stephanie narrowed down their options, Morgan found herself thinking of Justin. She knew he'd be proud of her tonight, and she'd give anything to have him there with her. She decided that when he came to visit, she'd bring him here along with Stephanie and Leo and Trevor and Samantha. They'd have so much fun.

After selecting "Stop! In the Name of Love" by the Supremes, Stephanie and Morgan went back to their seats. Morgan's stomach churned. It was taking every ounce of courage she possessed to go through with this, yet she was determined not to let her fears stop her from enjoying life.

Chapter Fourteen

From their seats, the two couples had a great view of the stage. They ate their dessert as the show started, cringing with the first performance as one young girl got up and tried to sing "Heat Wave." She did okay on the verses, but the chorus was almost painful to listen to, and Morgan felt herself sliding down in her seat with dread. What if she sounded like that?

As it got closer to their turn, Morgan's confidence weakened. She just couldn't do it, and she was about to tell Stephanie when Manny took her hand. "You look nervous," he said.

"It sounded fun at first, but now I'm not so sure."

Stephanie turned to her. "Hey, girlfriend, are you ready?"

"I can't believe I let you talk me into this."

"It's going to be fun," Stephanie assured her. "We'd better go up there. We're after the next guy."

Manny gave her a thumbs-up and Leo gave Stephanie a kiss for luck.

"I don't remember the words," Morgan said as they walked to the stage. "I can't do this."

"Will you calm down?" Stephanie said. "You're going to be fine. Hey, look at it this way. We *can't* be as bad as some of the people who've already gone tonight."

Morgan had to agree with her there, but she was just glad that she didn't know any of these people. She would never have to see them again.

Stephanie showed her a couple of little steps they could do together, and Morgan suddenly began to panic. She'd be lucky to sing, let alone do choreography! She swallowed and tried to joke. "I think you missed your calling in life. Why didn't you become a performer?"

"Actually, I'm trying out for the temple pageant this year. So are Leo and the kids. We're going to do it as a family."

Onstage, a guy was desperately trying to get through "I Heard It Through the Grapevine," but he was so nervous he could barely get the words in. Morgan felt embarrassed for him, then scared when she realized what was coming.

"We're next," Stephanie said, grabbing her hand.

"I can't do it," Morgan said, panicking.

"Of course you can," Stephanie told her, watching for the guy on the stage to finish. "You're going to be . . ." Stephanie turned and looked at her. "Sick? Morgan, you look like you're going to throw up."

Morgan felt like she was going to do that or pass out.

"Here," Stephanie said, pulling up a chair. "Sit down. Breathe," she instructed.

Morgan pulled in several deep breaths but still felt her nerves slipping.

"You two ready?" Randy, the stage coordinator, asked them.

Stephanie looked at her. "Can you go on?"

Clutching her stomach, Morgan shook her head. "Sorry."

"Lady, you going on or what?" Randy pressed.

Stephanie gave Morgan one last imploring look, but Morgan knew her legs wouldn't hold her if she stood. She shook her head again.

"All right, yes," Stephanie said. "I'm doing it."

The guy handed Stephanie a microphone and announced her name and the song. Morgan watched with relief and disappointment. She was too frightened to go onstage, but she was mad at herself for being frightened.

Once Stephanie found her voice, she began to relax and find her groove. She got through the first verse, then belted out the chorus as if she were Diana Ross herself. The crowd cheered, and Stephanie beamed. She was in her element, a natural performer. And when the song ended, the crowd erupted in applause.

"Hey, that wasn't bad," Randy said to Stephanie when she came off the stage. "Not bad at all."

"Thanks," Stephanie said breathlessly.

"You can sing on my stage any time you want," Randy told her.

By now Morgan was feeling better, but she was still upset with herself for not having had the courage to go onstage. She'd come a long way but still had so far to go.

Morgan gave Stephanie a hug and said, "You were great up there. Sorry I backed out."

"Don't worry about it. I had a blast. Maybe next time, huh?"

"Yeah," Morgan said, appreciating her friend's understanding. "I'd like to."

Several people told Stephanie what a good job she'd done, and others high-fived her as she and Morgan made their way back to their seats.

Morgan was still berating herself for being such a chicken but promised herself that one day she'd do it. She'd get up on a stage in front of a crowd and sing, if it was with her dying breath.

Leo and Manny were on their feet when the women returned.

"You were great, sweetie," Leo said to his wife. "I didn't know you had so much 'soul' in you."

Stephanie laughed and took her seat.

Manny agreed. "Very impressive. I knew you had a nice voice, but you really blew the audience away."

Stephanie took a quick drink of water. "Thanks. And next time, Morgan's going to be there with me, right?"

Morgan gave her half a smile. "Right."

"Hey, it takes a lot to get up on that stage," Leo said.

"More than I have," Manny said. "I couldn't do it."

"You did in high school," Stephanie reminded him. "You were always in front of a crowd."

"I know. Guess I've changed," he said.

Morgan pondered the fact that as he was changing one way, she was changing another. Their differences would either complement one another or drive them apart.

❧ ❧ ❧

The move to her new apartment was actually easier than she'd thought it would be, partly because she didn't have a lot of possessions. Except for the used couch from her parents' basement, the old color television, and her bedroom furniture, her apartment was bare.

After her things were moved in, Morgan's mom stayed a few hours longer and helped her make her bed and put her clothes away. Most of the cupboards and drawers in the bathroom and kitchen were empty, but Morgan didn't care. It was her own place, and she was excited about the prospect of gaining her independence.

Since she had only a gallon of milk, a loaf of bread, and a box of cereal to her name, Morgan took Rhonda's offer to go to dinner that evening after her mom left.

"So, why do you keep going out with him?" Rhonda asked once they'd sat down to dinner.

"Manny?" Morgan replied, breaking off a piece of sourdough bread and popping it into her mouth.

"Of course, Manny. That's who we've been talking about all this time, isn't it?"

Morgan had asked herself this question a dozen times these last few days. She felt like a cloud had settled in on her and was fogging her heart and her brain. She couldn't think clearly, and she wasn't sure about her feelings for Manny. Her feelings for Justin were as strong as ever, but having him gone and being limited in their correspondence had allowed doubt to creep in.

"I don't know," she replied. "I mean, I enjoy being with him. He's very attentive to me, and he's such a good person."

"Does he have all the qualities you'd want in a husband?"

Morgan shrugged, then nodded. "Yeah. I mean, any girl would be lucky to get him. He's focused on what he wants, and he's a pillar of strength in all areas of his life."

"Then I don't see what the problem is," Rhonda said.

"I know," Morgan replied. "He's almost perfect."

"Almost?"

Morgan let her fork drop into her salad bowl and sighed. "His only flaw is that he's not Justin."

Rhonda gave her a sympathetic smile.

"I don't know if I'm going out with Manny just because he's the one who's here, or if I'm developing true feelings for him. And the other problem is that I don't know if there's even a future for Justin and me. Every time I hear from him, the time he has to stay in Brazil gets stretched a little longer. If I'm ever going to see him again, I'm afraid I'm going have to learn Portuguese and go down there!"

"*Have* you ever considered going to Brazil to see him?"

Shaking her head, Morgan answered, "My mother would definitely have a stroke, and I wouldn't do anything like that until I knew *for sure* there was something serious between us with a guaranteed future."

Rhonda paused for a moment before answering, "Morgan, I know you've been hurt a few times in the past."

"A few?" Morgan replied. "Ha! Try every relationship I've ever had."

"Okay, okay. I know you've had some bad luck with guys, but you have a wonderful man right here in front of your face who adores you and is not going anywhere. He's not going to hurt you like the others. He's clearly in love with you. I'd think long and hard before doing anything to mess that up."

Shutting her eyes for a moment, Morgan couldn't believe she was hearing from Rhonda the same speech she'd heard from her mother.

"He's not asking for a commitment, is he?"

Morgan shook her head.

"He isn't pressuring you to be with him or to spend time with him when you don't want to, is he?"

Morgan shook her head again.

Rhonda threw up her hands and fell back against her chair, "Then enjoy the ride, girl! Don't make this harder than it needs to be. Let your heart lead the way, and follow the natural course where it takes you. Manny sounds wonderful. Justin does too, but you know what your friend Samantha said about him. The fact that he's not the type to commit to a relationship and that he was born into wealth are red flags in my opinion. Plus he's never been around small children, and I know a family is very important to you. Doesn't that concern you a little?"

Morgan hadn't really thought about it. She couldn't imagine that Justin would be anything but marvelous with kids.

"I believe it's possible to love more than one person, but ultimately, circumstances and life in general are going to determine which one you end up with. You could probably be happy with either one, really. It will just depend on which relationship develops and leads to marriage."

Morgan thought about Rhonda's comment, then asked, "So, you don't believe there's one perfect person out there for each of us?"

"Do you?"

"I guess I always thought there was one who was 'best' suited for me, although I don't believe in a 'one and only.' I mean, it would be kind of scary to think that out of all the people on the earth, *one* of them was the person I was supposed to marry. What if I never found him? What if I didn't recognize him when I did meet him?"

"Exactly!" Rhonda said. "I'm not saying just any two people can fall in love and get married. It has to be right, and there has to be chemistry, friendship, and common goals. I believe you could fall in love with Justin, and if that works out, you could probably be very happy with him. But if you end up falling in love with Manny, I think you could be very happy with him. How lucky are you to have a choice?"

Morgan didn't consider herself lucky. She considered herself confused and full of conflict. She'd been toying with the idea of telling Manny that she didn't think they should spend so much time together. Since his feelings for her were obvious, she knew he wanted to take their relationship to a more serious level. But she just wasn't ready to do it.

"Maybe this will help," Rhonda said. "You've kind of told me all the things about Manny that you admire. What are the things about him that you don't like?"

"That's a good question," Morgan replied. "Okay, well, sometimes he's too perfect."

Rhonda raised her eyebrows.

"I know, I know, but you have to understand that there are times he's almost like a robot."

"Morgan—"

"No, listen to me. He's punctual, always in control of himself and his emotions, dresses just right, says the right thing, and treats me like a queen. I know this is hard to see, but it gets annoying sometimes."

Rhonda looked confused.

"Let me give you an example. The other day, we planned a date to go out to dinner and then to a movie that we both wanted to see. Dinner was fine, but when we got to the theater, the movie was sold out."

"So?"

"So, even though we ended up going to a different movie, one I really enjoyed, Manny couldn't seem to get over it. He couldn't handle the fact that the night didn't turn out like he'd planned, you know?"

"Maybe he just really had his heart set on seeing the first movie," Rhonda ventured.

"Yeah, I guess, but we can go see it another time. It's not the end of the world. He just likes his life in control so much that it's a little overwhelming at times. And for someone like me to say that is big, because I used to be a real day-planner addict."

"I remember. What did you do with your day planner?"

"I still have it. I just don't carry it around with me now. That was the old me. I like having my day structured, but now I'm not a slave to my planner like I used to be. Being the new me is much more enjoyable."

"I liked the old you," Rhonda began, "but you're right—the new you seems to be much happier, and you're much more fun to be around." Then her face lit up. "I almost forgot—I have something to ask you. You know Mike, that guy I've dated a few times?"

Morgan nodded. "Of course. How's that going? Is he back in town?"

"He got back last night, and we talked for a couple of hours on the phone. He asked me if I'd be interested in getting certified in scuba diving. He's a dive master and is starting a class next week. He said he'd give me a great deal on the course and that I could bring a friend if I wanted to."

Scuba diving. The old Morgan's first reaction would have been, "Absolutely not!" But it wasn't. It was exactly the opposite. Sure, the thought of diving deep under the water with only a tank of oxygen on her back was somewhat terrifying, but she knew it was only because she didn't know that much about diving. Besides, what was the harm in trying? She'd loved snorkeling, and if scuba diving were anything like that, it would really be fun.

"Sure, why not?" Morgan answered.

"Are you serious? You want to do it?" Rhonda couldn't hide her amazement at Morgan's immediate interest.

"I'd love to give it a try. Justin told me how much he loved diving. I think it would be fun to know how."

"I can't wait to call Mike and tell him to sign us up. I thought I was going to have to do all kinds of convincing to get you to even go to the first meeting." Rhonda gave her a smile. "You really have changed. I like it."

"I have Justin to thank for that."

"What exactly did he do?"

"He taught me how to enjoy life instead of just exist. He helped me see that I could believe in myself and my abilities." She lifted her wrist and showed Rhonda the silver bracelet with the turquoise, coral, and alabaster inlay. "That's why he gave me this bracelet—to commemorate the day I left my comfort zone, never to return."

"What's that other bracelet for—you know, the charm bracelet?" Rhonda asked.

"That's so I don't forget him," she replied.

Rhonda's smile softened to one of warmth and tenderness. She reached over and patted Morgan's hand. "Things will work out the way they're supposed to. Try not to worry. Trust your heart and trust in your God, and everything will work out."

❦ ❦ ❦

Morgan went to her regular home ward for church, then over to her parents' house afterward. Her mother was unusually quiet, which made Morgan hesitant to share her news about getting scuba certified.

"You're what?!" Morgan's mother exclaimed when Morgan broke the news. "But that's so dangerous! People die doing that."

"Mom, it's very safe. Millions of people go diving every year and don't die."

"Still, there's that chance. Plus, what about sharks and other dangerous creatures?"

"I wouldn't dive somewhere dangerous, Mom."

"I just don't understand what's gotten into you," Laura Rose said to her daughter. "You used to be so—"

"Predictable?" Morgan finished for her.

"Well, yes. Predictable, dependable, focused . . . levelheaded."

"Mom," Morgan said, striving to be patient, "I'm not trying to do something irresponsible or dangerous. I just want to discover what the world has to offer. I want to learn and grow."

Laura didn't reply, but instead she put her napkin on her plate and excused herself to the kitchen.

Morgan and her father sat at the table in silence. Finally her father said, "I was certified when I was young."

"Greg, don't encourage her," her mother called from the kitchen.

Morgan's father smiled and shook his head. "Actually, I wouldn't mind taking a refresher course."

"Dad, are you serious? You could take it with me and Rhonda."

He nodded, as if thinking through the possibility. "Yes, I'd like to do it. I did some diving off the coast of Florida when I was young. It's certainly an amazing experience."

"We meet next Wednesday for the orientation and the first lecture."

"Wednesday is good. That's when your mother volunteers at the care center, so I'm home alone anyway."

Morgan grinned. Having her father there would take a lot of the fear out of the experience.

"I'll talk with your mother," he said in a low tone. "Don't worry. She'll settle down."

Morgan knew scuba diving was definitely going to take her to a whole new level of self-discovery. And the more she learned about herself, the more she liked the person she was becoming.

Chapter Fifteen

⸱

Morgan reread his message.

A bad storm came through the area and flooded many of the homes. Along with the full-time missionaries, we organized a group of men to work on fixing the damage. These people are amazing. They have so much faith. Instead of blaming God for the bad things that happen in their life, they thank Him for the good things, no matter how tiny those things are. For example, the storm caused a lot of damage to many of the poorly constructed homes, yet the people were grateful for the water it provided.

Have you received the package I sent? It's nothing fancy, but I wanted you to know I was thinking of you. I'm sorry I've been gone so long. But while I'm here, I have to take care of everything that needs to be done. The government is very slow sometimes. We need licenses to open this new manufacturing plant, and they don't seem to want to cooperate, even though it means creating needed jobs for so many people.

I miss you. Every night I look at pictures of us in Cancún and remember how wonderful it was. I think of your laugh and it makes me smile. I don't know when I'll be home, but it can't be much longer. Hopefully by the end of May. Please don't forget about me.

Justin

She loved his perspective and how much he respected the people in Brazil. He was a good man.

❦ ❦ ❦

"My uncle just gave me tickets to that new play," Manny said over the phone. "Is there any chance you could get away tonight and go with me?"

Morgan had always loved getting dressed up and going to the theater in the city. She'd been lucky enough to see several of the classics when they'd come to town, and she was excited at the chance to see another production.

"Sure, I'd love to go," she said, realizing that this was the most spontaneous thing Manny had done since they'd started dating again. She'd planned on going to her yoga class but she knew Rhonda would understand.

"If I pick you up in a half an hour, we'd have time to go to dinner. Can you be ready that soon?"

"I'll be ready," she told him.

Dashing to her room, she raced to her closet, where she pulled out a new black dress she'd found on sale. It was a slim-fitting dress and fell just above her ankles. It was simple and very elegant and looked wonderful with the tan she'd maintained since her trip to Cancún. *Dinner and the theater—what a perfect evening,* she thought as she touched up her makeup.

Glad that Manny was taller than she was, she put on a pair of strappy stiletto sandals, then stood to check her reflection again. Since she'd been working out, her muscles had become more toned, her arms and calves revealing the hours on the stairmaster and in the yoga studio.

After piling her curls on top of her head, she pinned several rhinestone-studded clips into the mass to add some elegance and glitter to her hair.

She glanced at her watch and realized Manny would be there in a few minutes. She quickly spritzed some perfume on and grabbed her dressy handbag and a black silk shawl, something she'd found at a flea market with Rhonda. Then she went to the computer desk in the front room to check her e-mail. She had just sat down when the doorbell rang.

Opening the door, she was pleasantly surprised to see Manny there with a bouquet of spring flowers for her in his hand.

"Manny, you didn't need to bring me flowers. Thank you."

He smiled and followed her inside to the kitchen, where she filled the only vase she had with water and put in the flowers. "Aren't they colorful! They sure brighten up my apartment."

"I'm glad you like them."

"And look at you," she said, stepping back. He wore a black, double-breasted suit, a starched white shirt, and a tie; with his tall frame, he looked very handsome.

His reaction toward her indicated he was every bit as pleased. "You look pretty incredible yourself." Morgan blushed and smiled.

"Thank you for coming with me tonight," he said.

"Thank you for asking," she replied, looking up into his eyes.

Their gazes held for a brief moment before the telephone rang.

"Excuse me," Morgan said, reaching for the receiver. It was her mother inviting her to dinner.

"Sorry, Mom. It sounds wonderful, but I'm going out to dinner."

"Are you sure? I made your favorite—barbecued ribs." Her mother's disappointment was evident in her voice.

"Manny's taking me to dinner, and then we're going to a play in the city."

"Oh. Well, tell him hi for us," her mother's voice immediately brightened. "We'll have you over another time."

"Everything okay?" Manny asked when Morgan hung up the phone.

"Yeah, it was my mom. She's been having a hard time since I moved out. But she sounded fine once she heard I was going out with you."

Manny smiled, obviously pleased by the information.

ಠ ಠ ಠ

"Thank you for tonight," Morgan said as Manny pulled into the parking lot in front of her apartment. She covered a yawn and wondered how she was going to stay awake at work the next day.

The evening had been interesting and fun. She'd learned over the course of their past dates that Manny was very frugal, and except for the flowers, tonight had been no exception. Their dinner had been at a fish house that wasn't exactly elegant, but the food was good. They'd used two free coupons that Manny's uncle had won over the radio. She understood Manny's need to be money conscious, though. He was trying to pay off his student loans and make his car payment, plus he wanted to build up his savings before he moved to Burley at the end of summer. "I had a great time. I'm glad you could come," he told her.

Another yawn overtook Morgan, and she couldn't stop it. It was nearly two in the morning.

"I'd better get you inside," he said. After helping her from the car, he slipped an arm around her waist, and guided her up the walk to the front door.

She was about to open her purse to get out her key when Manny stopped her, pulling her into a gentle embrace. "I really like being with you, Morgan," he said, holding her close.

"Thanks. I like being with you too," she replied, not sure where he was going with the conversation.

"I'll be leaving toward the end of August, and these next three months are going to fly by. I hope we can spend a lot more time together before I go."

"Uh . . ." She paused. "Sure. That would be great."

The next thing she knew, Manny had kissed her.

The kiss didn't send her heart rate soaring and her head spinning, but it did leave her a little breathless and pleasantly surprised.

"I'll call you at work," he said, giving her a smile.

"Good night," she said.

Manny waited a moment before leaving, then with a wave, he was gone.

❦ ❦ ❦

"I don't know what to think, Rhonda," Morgan said during their break the next day. They'd walked outside to get some fresh air and found a bench in the shade. "I like Manny—I really do—and my family loves him, but I still have such strong feelings for Justin."

"Do you ever worry that the feelings you have for Justin are just part of being caught up in the romance of your trip to Cancún? I mean, do you know what he's like day to day, week to week? You spent five days with him on a tropical vacation in paradise, but what's he like in the real world?"

Morgan didn't admit that the same thoughts had crossed her mind. Was she just infatuated, or were her feelings more meaningful? Justin was every bit as admirable and stalwart as Manny. Justin truly cared about others, and he had a kind and giving heart. His testimony was unwavering, and he was dedicated to giving service and sharing the gospel. At least, all that seemed to be the case. But the passage of time and the separation of so many miles was causing her to second-guess herself.

"You know what you're getting with Manny. He's real, and he's right here, right now. Justin is based on a fantasy," Rhonda continued.

"But it *was* real," Morgan countered. "The feelings Justin and I shared were real—I know they were." Then she added sadly, "But it's all beginning to blur. And you're right—I'm beginning to wonder if we were both under the influence of the Caribbean atmosphere, or if it was genuine. I just know that I loved the way I felt when I was with him. I can't explain it."

"Maybe what you need to do is decide what qualities you want in a man so you'll know if either of these guys is what you're looking for."

With a nod, Morgan agreed. She'd always thought she wanted someone like her father, and she still did, but she had yet to compile a list of specific qualities. "That's a good suggestion," she told her friend after a thoughtful pause.

"Luckily you don't have to make a decision anytime soon. I would just let your heart lead the way, and things will work out. Don't fight what's happening between you and Manny, but . . . maybe you should pray that Justin gets home before it's too late," she added with a playful jab at Morgan's ribs.

Morgan closed her eyes and sighed. How she wished she had a crystal ball to get a peek into her future! She believed that things would work out for the best, but she wondered what she was going to have to go through before that happened.

❧ ❧ ❧

"Your package from that *boy* is on the counter," Morgan's mother told her as Morgan hurried through the door.

Dropping her purse on the counter, Morgan rushed to the table and found a package addressed to her from Brazil. She grabbed a pair of scissors out of a drawer. Tingles of excitement raced through her veins. The box looked like it had been used for soccer practice, with its chewed corners and worn edges, but it was still intact. She could barely slit the tape, her hands were trembling with so much anticipation.

The first thing she found was a note inside.

> *Dear Morgan,*
> *I found a few things I thought you'd enjoy, and there's something for your parents, too. I couldn't resist. I hope you like what I've sent. Tell your parents that I look forward to meeting them someday. Don't forget about me.*
> *Justin*

Inside the box she found a beautiful white linen shirt with intricate embroidery on the edges of the sleeve and around the neckline. It was loose and airy and would look great with jeans or a skirt. Morgan loved it immediately. Even her mother commented on the lovely hand stitching.

Next was a small box. Inside Morgan found charms for her bracelet—a small figure of a man and a woman dressed like the native gauchos from the area Justin was in, Rio Grande do Sul. He'd told her a little about the culture and the amazing sights in the area, and she had been fascinated by it all.

"Oh, look, Mom," she said, lifting a black leather handbag out of the box. It was similar to the one they'd picked out for his mother. "This is for you."

"For me?" Laura exclaimed. "He didn't need to get me anything. Here," she handed the bag back to her daughter. "You keep it."

"Mom, it's for you."

Her mother accepted the gift, but it was apparent she felt awkward accepting it from someone she'd never met.

Morgan reached inside the box for the last item. "And this is for Dad." It was a sleek, black leather wallet. Morgan recalled that her father had just been saying he needed a new wallet, and she admired Justin's thoughtfulness.

"That boy doesn't need to spend his money on us," Laura said.

"That's the kind of guy *Justin* is—thoughtful and generous," Morgan replied, emphasizing his name. Her mother knew his name, so why couldn't she just call him by it?

"Well, it *is* a beautiful bag, but I don't want him sending us anything else."

"Okay, I'll tell him," Morgan said, striving to keep the annoyance out of her voice and wondering why it was such a big deal to her mother.

ꕥ ꕥ ꕥ

When she checked her e-mail, Morgan was pleased to find a reply from Justin. She'd written to tell him that the package had arrived and to thank him for his sweet gifts. She told him that her father had loved the wallet and that her mother had cleaned out her old purse and moved all her things into her new one, unable to deny that it was much nicer than what she had been using.

Morgan had also sent him another e-mail, telling him about her diving classes and how her father was going to recertify with her. It was going to take six weeks to get through the course since they could only meet once a week, but it would hopefully help the time go faster until Justin got back from Brazil.

She asked him when he thought he was coming back to the States. He had already been there much longer than he'd originally planned, and it seemed as if every time she heard from him there was another reason he needed to stay even longer. After she sent the e-mail, she sighed and found herself wishing she could fly as quickly as her message did on the Internet and arrive in mere moments where Justin was.

ꕥ ꕥ ꕥ

Each day Morgan watched her e-mail, waiting for the message that told her Justin was coming back to the States. She was grateful for anything that helped time pass quickly. Even though her dive class was challenging for her, she looked forward to the weekly lectures with her father that were necessary to complete the written portion of their certification. They also began Saturday sessions in the pool, learning skills and mastering the techniques of diving.

Morgan was glad she had someone as patient as her father to dive with. She'd never been a big water fan. Holding her nose was the only way she knew to go underwater. So when Mike, the dive master, told her she needed to go under the water, fill up her mask with water, then clear the water out of it, she panicked. Up to that point she'd managed to work through every other skill required, but this wasn't something she wanted to try. It didn't help that Rhonda took to diving like the proverbial fish to water.

Rhonda didn't seem to struggle with the skills at all. Maybe it was due to the fact that Mike was her dive partner.

"I can't do it," she told Mike.

"Yes, you can," he said. "It's very easy." Above the water he took her slowly, step by step, through the process, then left her to practice with her dive buddy.

"Dad, I can't do this," Morgan said. "The last time I tried, I breathed in through my nose instead of my mouth and I got a lungful of water. If I did that under the ocean, I would probably drown."

"Morgan, you're going to be fine. I'll help you."

She shut her eyes, wishing she could just quit. She didn't need to dive this badly.

"Just try," her dad urged. "If you have any trouble, we'll come right back up to the surface."

Her breath came in panicked and short choppy gulps.

"Morgan, look me in the eye. You can do this. You've come so far. Don't let this be the skill that makes you stop."

He was right. It was dumb to give up everything because of this one challenge.

Focusing on her father's face, Morgan steadied her breathing and felt herself calm down. She could do it. Everyone else in the class had, even the twelve-year-old kids.

"Okay," she said, bracing herself to go under. She rehearsed the steps one more time, knowing that the biggest trick would be to breathe through her mouth while her mask was full of water.

As she sank below the surface of the water, Morgan's father motioned for her to keep her gaze focused on him. In her mind she repeated the phrase *I can do this*, over and over.

Shutting her eyes, she focused on breathing through her mouth, then lifted the bottom edge of her mask, allowing it to fill up with water. A rush of panic rippled through her stomach, but she didn't give in to it. Instead, she remained focused, drew in a deep breath, pushed on the top edge of her mask, and blew hard through her nose.

Continuing to breathe as she'd been taught, she opened her eyes and saw the delighted look in her father's eyes. Her mask wasn't completely clear, but she'd done it! She'd actually done it! Clearing the mask one last time, she got rid of the rest of the water and felt herself completely relax under the water.

The dive master, who'd been underwater as well and watching from a short distance, swam over and gave her a thumbs-up, his signal that she'd performed well. She nodded, and he gave her a wink. She'd passed.

Morgan ascended from the water and burst through the surface with an amazing sense of accomplishment. She'd faced an enormous fear, and she'd conquered it.

Her father hugged her. "I knew you could do it, sweetie. I am so proud of you."

"Yeah, Morgan. You got the worst one out of the way," Rhonda said. "The rest will be easy."

Then her dive master gave her a pat on the back. "Nice job," he said.

That night, Manny called to see how her class had gone. Even though he tried to be happy for her accomplishment, she knew he still didn't quite understand what it meant to her to pass off that skill.

After she had hung up with him, she tried to call Justin. He would understand and he would be proud of her for her accomplishment. But he didn't answer his phone, which either meant his phone wasn't receiving service or he wasn't able to get to the phone. Her heart filled with sadness. Things just weren't going the direction she wanted them to, no matter how hard she tried to make them. And it hurt. Her heart kept wanting to go one direction but her life kept taking her another. And the weeks were passing slowly but surely. Justin been gone over three months. How much longer would they be apart?

Chapter Sixteen

Justin's e-mail didn't seem right.

She read it again and tried to figure out what it was, but she couldn't put her finger on it. He had written less frequently, but the e-mails still came.

This one was full of news and was interesting, but it was as if his heart wasn't in it. He told her that he'd been working in the evenings with the full-time missionaries to teach someone he'd met while on his mission. The girl had accepted the invitation to baptism, and Justin had been able to baptize her. It had been a wonderful, spiritual experience, and he knew that it was one of the reasons he'd stayed longer in Brazil than planned.

The e-mail was short, but he still told her he thought about her and planned to return home as soon as he could. He even reminded her of their agreement to meet six months from the fifteenth of February, the day they officially met. But it almost sounded as if he were trying to hide his guilt by mentioning their promise. Would she see him before the middle of August?

She didn't know if he was changing or if she was changing, but something was different and the doubts that had filled her heart now troubled her mind. She ached to talk to him, but contacting him by phone had proved a futile effort.

Maybe he didn't want to talk to her.

She didn't know what to think. He said he still cared about her and thought about her, but the reality of their situation was getting harder and harder to ignore.

It was time to face facts. She knew better than anyone what it felt like to be brushed off. She didn't need a house to fall on her to tell her what was going on. And that was what she believed was happening. His feelings for her had faded away. She sensed it, even from halfway across the world. She didn't even reply to his e-mail. She didn't know what to say, nor could she see through her tears to type a message.

Not ready to accept that their relationship was ending, Morgan decided to get out of the apartment and clear her mind. She grabbed her purse and headed out the door. The phone rang just as she opened the door. A hope that it was Justin soared in her heart, but her mind quickly snuffed it out.

Once again, her mind was right—Manny's number was on her caller I.D.

She almost pushed the button to talk, then changed her mind. She needed some distance, some space to think and hopefully to receive guidance and answers.

Without another thought, she hurried out the door as the phone continued ringing until the answering machine finally clicked on. She pulled the door shut just as Manny's voice sounded.

❦ ❦ ❦

She usually called before she went to Samantha's, but this time she just found herself in the driveway, not really sure how she got there. She'd been driving, trying to make sense of her life, her emotions, her future, but there didn't appear to be any chance of it happening, and the next thing she knew, she was at Samantha's house.

Trevor's truck was gone, but Samantha's car was in the driveway. Morgan was glad Trevor was out. She didn't feel up to seeing him; right now she just needed the shoulder of a friend.

"Morgan!" Samantha exclaimed when she opened the front door. "What in the world are you doing here?"

"Are you busy?"

"Hardly. Trevor went to his city-league baseball game and I'm folding laundry. I'd love some company."

Morgan stepped inside and immediately detected the smell of cigarette smoke. Trevor had smoked occasionally in the past, but Samantha had said it was a disgusting habit she wouldn't allow him to continue. He'd quit for a while, but obviously it hadn't lasted long.

"Have a seat," Samantha said, clearing an armload of clean laundry from the couch. "What's going on? You don't look so good. Hey, can I get you something to drink?"

"No, thanks," Morgan told her. "I just needed to talk."

"This is about Justin, isn't it? Did he finally tell you what's going on?"

Morgan swallowed hard. "What do you mean, what's going on?"

Samantha mouthed, "Uh-oh," but Morgan still made out what she said.

"Samantha? What do you mean?"

"Nothing," Samantha said quickly. "Really. I mean, like how his job is going and stuff."

"Samantha," Morgan said firmly. "You know something."

"I don't," Samantha countered. "I mean, not really." She placed a folded towel on a stack and grabbed another.

"I have been going crazy over Justin," Morgan told her. "Something's different, I can tell. You're my best friend, Sam. If you know something, you need to tell me."

Samantha blew out a defeated breath. She let the towel drop to her lap. "Morgan, I . . ."

Morgan's gaze became fixed on Samantha's face. "Yes?"

"I . . ." Samantha shut her eyes. "I don't know how to say this."

A familiar pain clenched Morgan's heart—a pain she'd felt too many times in her life, one she still hadn't gotten used to, one she'd hoped she'd never feel again. How many times, she wondered, could a heart be broken and mended? How many?

"Go on," she managed to say.

"Did he tell you about the girl he baptized?"

"Yes," Morgan answered.

"She's . . . he's . . . they . . ." Samantha couldn't get the words out, but Morgan managed to fill in the gaps between the pronouns.

"They're dating?" she finally asked for clarification.

Samantha nodded and expelled a relieved breath of air. "Her name's Marika. I guess she's beautiful, some kind of model or something. He taught her on his mission, and they met up again awhile back. I guess she works in Rio de Janeiro but went back to visit her family for a while, and that's where they ran into each other again."

Morgan chewed her bottom lip as Samantha continued the explanation that was becoming excruciating to digest.

"I guess he started talking to her about the Church again, and they've been spending a lot of time together. I think at first it was to teach her the discussions with the missionaries, you know? But after he baptized her—"

Feeling as though a charging bull had rammed her in the stomach, Morgan collapsed back into the cushions of the couch. Why hadn't he told her this? If he cared even a little for her, wouldn't he at least be honest with her about a new relationship? But then, she'd never said anything to him about Manny. Still, there was nothing to tell. She wasn't serious with Manny, was she?

"Hey," Samantha said brightly. "Maybe there's not really anything to it. It's possible he's just helping her since she's a new convert."

Morgan shook her head. "Things are different. I feel it. It all makes sense now."

"I'm sorry," Samantha said. "But this doesn't really surprise me. I mean, Justin's thoughtful and considerate, but he's got this spoiled, rich-kid side to him that shows up sometimes, you know? He just doesn't appreciate what he's got, so he lets good things go. I told you how he is with commitment."

Morgan expelled a weary sigh. "I know, and I don't have a right to be upset, because we didn't have any arrangement or agreement not to date others. I mean, I'm dating Manny, right?"

"Right," Samantha agreed.

"I just don't understand how I fall into the same trap, over and over and over again. You'd think I'd learn. You'd think I'd see it coming—" Her voice broke. "I'm so stupid."

Samantha scooted next to her friend and pulled her into a hug. "No, you're not. He's not perfect," she said. "I don't think any man's perfect," she added. "But Justin's a wonderful person and you two shared something very special, very magical. I wouldn't give up hope."

Morgan wiped her eyes and sat back, taking in a deep breath. "I really did think it was going to be different this time, but I should have known magic doesn't last. You can't build a future on a few romantic walks on the beach and kisses in the moonlight."

"Maybe," Samantha said, "but I wouldn't write him off. Maybe you should just confront him about it. Ask him what's going on."

With a nod, Morgan agreed. "You're right." She didn't give it another thought, knowing that was the next step she needed to take. "I'll do that." She gave her friend a hug. "Thanks for being here for me."

"Anytime. And if I find out anything else, I'll let you know."

An hour later, Morgan left Samantha's house with a heavy heart, angry at herself for not being smarter. She should have known that the time she spent with Justin was too wonderful to last, too wonderful to be real. She should have listened to her head, not her heart.

෴ ෴ ෴

Morgan's heart had been broken before, and it had devastated her each time. But she was older and stronger now, and she knew—as badly as the thought of never seeing Justin again hurt—she would survive. She had to be strong. And she had to find out what was going on. Taking charge of her life and her own happiness was a big step for her, and this was just one more thing she needed to do in moving toward her goal of self-realization.

She'd start with an e-mail.

> Dear Justin,
>
> I can't believe it's been almost four months since we were in Cancún. Sometimes it doesn't seem real, like it never really happened. I guess that's because we haven't seen each other since.
>
> I've been thinking about you, about us. I wonder where our relationship is going when there's no opportunity in sight for us to see each other again.
>
> The memories I have of us together are something I think of often and treasure deeply, but I don't know how much longer I can keep those memories alive.
>
> How are you feeling about us?
>
> Love,
> Morgan

She read it again and again before sending it. She didn't want to sound desperate and whiny, but she did want to make a point. The memories just weren't enough anymore, not without some kind of possibility of meeting again to find out if what they shared in Mexico worked in the United States too!

No, she needed to know where he stood and what he thought. She wanted to do everything she could to find out what they had together, but he wasn't making it very easy. And one thing she had learned from all her bad relationships: she didn't have time to waste on a guy who had no intentions of taking their relationship to a more serious level.

Many times throughout the evening and the next day, she checked her incoming e-mails. The good news was that she'd heard from two of the universities she'd contacted about their art programs. The first one, UC Davis, was the college where she'd received her history degree. She'd heard great things about their art program. The other school, San Francisco State University, was the college her high school art teacher had recommended. That was where he'd gone to school, and he'd encouraged her to go there and immerse herself in its excellent art program.

The bad news was that nothing had come through from Justin.

Burying her emotions under a whirl of activity, Morgan stayed as busy as possible the following days. The less free time she had, the less time she spent thinking of Justin.

Between workouts with Rhonda, her scuba classes, and dates with Manny, Morgan didn't stay idle for long. It helped, but it still didn't erase her fears concerning Justin.

Then, early one Saturday morning in June, Manny called. He caught Morgan just as she was going to the grocery store.

"Do you have plans today?" he asked.

"Just some shopping," she told him. "Why?"

"It's such a beautiful day, I wondered if you'd like to go on a picnic, maybe go bike riding or something."

Morgan had to hand it to him, Manny was very creative when it came to inexpensive dates. She didn't mind at all—in fact, she admired his frugality—except that sometimes she wished they could see a movie at the regular theater instead of waiting for it to come to the dollar theaters. And she'd given up any chance of them getting popcorn at the movie. They usually made a stop at the grocery store on the way and stashed treats in her purse.

"Sure," she said, knowing that her plans for the day consisted of painting her toenails and preparing for the Primary's singing time the next day. "I'll need a couple of hours, though."

"That's fine. I'll see you soon, then."

Morgan hung up the phone and stared at the receiver. Manny had been constant, caring, and open with his feelings. She didn't have to guess how he felt or wonder if he'd call. He didn't play games. He was up-front and honest, and it was something she appreciated. And she had grown to care for him too. It wasn't quite the tingly, butterflies-in-the-stomach, breathless anticipation that she sometimes wished for, but there was a sense of security and comfortableness that came with having spent so much time together. He was kind and considerate, thoughtful, and attentive. Those characteristics were important to her.

She knew it was selfish of her, but why did she wish there was more?

❦ ❦ ❦

Running her errands and stopping at the grocery store kept her busy most of the morning, and she arrived back at her apartment just as the mailman was leaving. Taking the mail inside, she poured herself a tall glass of apple juice and relaxed on a bar stool at the counter. Absentmindedly she leafed through the rest of the stack of letters, sorting bills and junk mail. Suddenly, she stopped.

There, in front of her, was a letter from Brazil. Justin had written to her.

Her heart jumped into her throat. She swallowed, wondering what the contents held—afraid to look but dying of curiosity.

Bracing herself for whatever it said, she slid her finger under the flap of the envelope and pulled out the letter. A picture tumbled out.

Tears filled her eyes. There was Justin, standing among a crowd of Brazilians, knee-deep in mud with shovel in hand. In the background were the remains of several homes with their roofs collapsed and walls crumbling to the ground. She read the enclosed letter.

Dear Morgan,

The picture probably says everything. We had another bad rainstorm, this one worse than the first. I've never seen anything like it. The flooding caused incredible damage and the wind destroyed many of the homes. Many were left with nothing. Some even lost their lives. I've wanted to contact you, but we haven't had phone or Internet service. I actually thought I was going to get to come back to the States, but then this happened. I can't leave these people this way, so I will be here awhile longer. They're my friends. Many I've grown to love as family. I try not to get too attached, but it's hard not to. These people are so humble and loving. They need my help, so I'll be staying to help them get back on their feet—these people can't count on the government for help. The Church has sent volunteers and food. Perhaps this is the Lord's way of furthering His work in this area. Many are listening to the discussions as they try to make sense of their trials.

I hope all is well with you. I miss you and have your picture on the nightstand next to my bed. You're the first thing I see in the morning and the last thing I see at night.

Sorry this isn't long. I don't have much time, but I wanted to let you know I was still alive and well. I don't know when I'll be back.

Love,

Justin

P.S. Please don't forget me.

Tears poured down Morgan's cheeks. The thought of him helping all those people in their time of disaster touched her heart. He was such a good man. His capacity to love and serve his fellowman was inspiring.

Holding her head in her hands, she continued to cry. She admired him and the difference he made in people's lives. Even though they'd only been together a few days, he'd made a huge difference in her life.

That was the type of man he was. Why wasn't she getting a fair chance with him?

And if she was, how did it all fit together? What did the future hold? And what about this girl, Marika? How serious was Justin about her? Morgan had fished for answers in her e-mails, even asking directly about her, but he never gave her a solid answer as to the seriousness of their relationship.

The sound of the doorbell nearly caused her to jump out of her chair.

"Manny!"

She'd completely forgotten about him coming.

When she opened the door, the smile he greeted her with quickly faded when he saw she wasn't ready.

"Sorry," she said, inviting him inside. "My errands took longer than I expected. Make yourself at home and I'll hurry as fast as I can. There's juice in the fridge and some of my mom's brownies on the counter. Help yourself."

Manny assured her there was no hurry, but she knew how he was about keeping on schedule.

Racing to her room, she jumped into the shower. Manny had dressed casually, so she pulled on a pair of comfortable walking shorts and a soft, lime-colored T-shirt. Keeping her look casual too, she donned a white visor and let her wet hair hang loose down her back. A quick swipe of lip gloss and a few strokes of mascara completed her makeup. She was ready to go.

Hurrying from her room, she found Manny at the kitchen table, looking at the picture of Justin in Brazil.

"Is this your friend?" he asked.

Her heart did a triple beat, but she didn't get flustered. "Yeah. That's him in Brazil. He's down there on business. He served a mission there so he's close to a lot of the people."

Manny nodded. "Looks like quite a project."

"It's very poor where he's at. They've had some really bad weather this winter. This storm didn't help them."

He took one last look, then got up from his chair. "Ready?"

"I sure am. Is there anything you want me to bring?"

"I got it all."

Morgan appreciated him being so thoughtful and going to so much work. She'd dated guys who seemed to lack the ability to come up with a creative date—even if their lives depended upon it. Manny was different. He put a lot of effort into their dates. Maybe the fact that he was trying to save money forced him to be more creative, but Morgan appreciated his efforts.

The day was clear and beautiful. They drove to the park, where they spread a blanket out on the lawn under some trees and brought out the picnic basket Manny had prepared.

"This looks wonderful," Morgan said when she saw the fried chicken and potato salad. She'd been expecting peanut butter and jelly—he was a guy, after all.

"I wanted this meal to be special," he said with a peculiar tone to his voice.

She looked at him as he pulled paper plates and napkins out of the picnic basket.

"Why's that?" she asked, popping open the lids of two Sprite cans.

He shrugged, then flashed her a mysterious smile. "You'll find out later."

Morgan noticed that he seemed a bit fidgety and unfocused, as if his thoughts were somewhere else. She wondered if it had anything to do with the picture of Justin. Or maybe . . . the letter? She held her breath for a moment. Was that it? Had he read Justin's letter? Not that Justin's letter was anything romantic, but it did allude to the fact that they had some sort of relationship. What that was exactly, even she couldn't say.

They shared small talk as they ate, and slowly the awkwardness disappeared—that is, until he brought up the topic of the picture.

"So, tell me more about Justin."

Morgan swallowed a piece of chicken and asked, "What do you want to know?"

"How much do you like him?"

Feeling the chicken suddenly stick halfway down her throat, Morgan took a swallow of her drink.

"Uh—well," she stammered. If they were to have an honest, open relationship, then she needed to be exactly that—open and honest. "Justin and I really had a great time together in Cancún. I guess it's hard for me to answer your question because we were only together five days. We haven't spent any time together since then."

"But you still know how you feel about him."

She nodded and took a deep breath. "You're right. Okay. I like him a lot. He's a wonderful person. We hit it off like we were old friends from the moment we met."

Manny listened, his expression revealing nothing of what he thought.

Morgan continued. "But it wasn't just spending time together that I enjoyed. Justin helped me discover a person inside I never knew existed."

Manny's forehead wrinkled.

She knew she needed to explain what she meant. "It was like he allowed me to explore my personal potential and dreams. Like he gave me permission to step outside my comfort zone and see if there was more to me than I thought."

"And was there?"

"Yes." She looked him directly in the eye. "Much, much more. That discovery is what gave me the courage to finally move out on my own and to make the decision to go back to college. I've just received two acceptance letters. My dream is finally going to come true!"

"Then if you care so much for each other, why is he still in Brazil? When is he coming home?"

Morgan licked her lips and took another long breath before answering. "I don't know. I guess that's the biggest problem. We haven't been able to spend any more time together to determine if there's really something between us. I don't know when he'll be back. I don't think he knows for sure either."

"So where do I fit in? Am I just someone to kill time with until he returns, or—"

"Of course not!" she interrupted, hurt to realize he actually thought she was merely using him. "That's not it at all." She cleared her throat, trying to gather her thoughts. "I've enjoyed our dates. I haven't had a plan or an agenda. I guess I was just letting things take their natural course, to see where it all led. I'm sorry if you thought I wasn't interested in you, because it's not that way at all." She looked into his eyes, searching to see how he was taking all of this—it mattered to Morgan that he believed her.

A corner of his mouth lifted. The glimpse of pain she saw in his eyes turned to one of understanding and relief. "I'm glad to hear that," he said. "Because I've enjoyed our dates too." He leaned toward her. "I think you're the most incredible woman I've ever met."

Their gazes lingered for a moment. A breeze rustled the leaves overhead, then the gap between them narrowed, and Morgan closed her eyes as Manny's lips met hers. His brief kiss was sweet and tender.

"I know this might seem sudden," he said, keeping his gaze locked on hers, "but there's something I would like to ask you."

He turned and lifted the lid to the picnic basket, giving Morgan a moment to ponder their discussion. It had gotten serious all of a sudden, and she didn't know what to think about it. She'd never had a relationship develop even this far.

From the basket, Manny suddenly pulled out a single red rose. "Morgan," he said, handing her the rose, "I've fallen in love with you. And I'd like to ask you to marry me."

Morgan's mouth dropped open. Tears stung her eyes. Her breathing stopped until it felt as though her heart would burst. She wanted to melt with joy, be thrilled and elated. Instead, confusion, fear, and panic filled her. What could she do? What should she say?

"I know this seems sudden, and maybe you need some time to think about it," he said, directing her gaze to the flower, where a diamond engagement ring was tied with a narrow ribbon. He untied the ribbon and slipped off the ring. "I hope you like it."

Woodenly, Morgan looked at the narrow band and small, sparkling stone. It was so dainty and beautiful. She didn't care that the stone was small; it was a lovely ring. She just didn't know if she could accept it.

"Try it on—just to see if it fits—then you can take it off and keep it until you make your decision."

She allowed him to slide the band onto the ring finger of her left hand. It looked beautiful, but out of place. Her heart constricted tightly in her chest, and she fought for air. Sheer panic set in, and she felt as if her head was about to explode with all the confusion tumbling inside of it.

What did this mean? Marrying Manny would certainly make her parents happy. They loved him. And why not? He was rock solid in the gospel, goal oriented, and focused on his future. His income would never amount to millions, but he would have the privilege of changing the lives of youth—helping them to learn and grow in the gospel. It was an honorable and commendable job, and as his wife she would have the security of knowing he would likely stay strong and faithful in his beliefs, honor his priesthood, and be a good father and husband.

But she couldn't honestly say she loved him.

She cared about him and she admired and respected him. But were those things enough? Would love follow?

Still speechless, she looked at the ring on her finger and blinked as tears fell to her cheeks.

Manny lifted her chin with his finger and looked at her. There was no doubt on his end; she saw the love he felt for her in his eyes.

"You don't have to answer now," he said. "I just want you to know that I love you, Morgan. I promise I will always take care of you and treat you like a queen. I've prayed and fasted about you and received an answer I can't deny."

She nodded, afraid to speak, unsure of what to say. She couldn't believe a diamond engagement ring was on her finger, and yet she couldn't get Justin's face out of her mind. But she also wasn't stupid. There were no guarantees with Justin. She didn't know anymore where his heart was. If she passed up Manny for Justin, then when Justin did finally come home, would there be anything lasting between them? What if it had all simply been the romantic Caribbean environment they'd shared, and nothing more meaningful?

Her head pounded. She couldn't think about it now. She needed time. And thankfully, Manny was willing to give her that.

They decided to finish their picnic and go on a bike ride, but more than anything Morgan wanted to run, fast and far. She had to get away, to think, to ponder, to somehow get answers. Justin was in Brazil, but it was time for him to come home. If he wanted her, if he cared at all, he needed to let her know. Otherwise, he was going to lose her.

Chapter Seventeen

She kept her secret for the next several days. Manny's ring was hidden in her jewelry box, but she never stopped thinking about it. Her head hurt from all the thinking, her knees hurt from all the praying, and worst of all, her heart hurt from not knowing what to do.

At times she actually found herself picturing being married to Manny. She didn't mind a simple life; she didn't need fancy cars and a mansion to live in. Manny wanted a large family, and she did too.

All the pieces of the puzzle seemed to be there; she just couldn't get them to fit together. There was no peace inside of her, and as much as she prayed for peace to come, it didn't. She read and reread the scriptures, searching for answers and exercising her faith.

She read the eighth chapter of the Doctrine and Covenants and focused on the second verse:

> Yea, behold, I will tell you in your mind and in your heart, by the Holy Ghost, which shall come upon you and which shall dwell in your heart.

As she did so, she pleaded with the Lord to help her know for sure if she should marry Manny. Finally, she couldn't stand it anymore. She had to talk to someone. So she called Samantha, and they arranged to meet for lunch.

They arrived almost at the same time and hugged in the parking lot. "I was so surprised you called when you did," Samantha told her as they walked inside. "Because I was going to call you to get together for lunch."

Morgan immediately picked up on the overly casual tone Samantha had used. They knew each other better than sisters, and Morgan knew something was up.

The hostess seated them in the back corner where it was more quiet. Morgan was grateful, because they could talk in private.

"So," Samantha said. "What's going on?"

It was all Morgan could do not to let everything tumble out onto the table at once. "Oh, Sammy," she said, as her emotions welled up inside her. "Everything's gotten so complicated. I don't know what to do."

Samantha squeezed her hand. "It's okay, we'll sort everything out. What's going on? What's got you so upset? Is it Justin?"

"No," Morgan answered. Then, "Yes! It's Justin *and* Manny."

"What's going on?"

Morgan opened her mouth to speak, but her tears erupted instead.

Samantha's face registered alarm, then she quickly slid around the bench seat and circled her arms around Morgan, holding her as she sobbed.

"Morgan, what's happened?"

"He . . ." Morgan choked out. "He . . ." Her voice quivered. "He . . . asked me to . . . marry him."

"What?" Samantha shoved Morgan away from her so she could look at her face. "Who did?"

"Manny," Morgan said in frustration.

The waiter brought their oriental salads, and Samantha motioned for him to just set them anywhere, which he did quickly, then hurried away.

"When did this happen?"

Morgan mopped at her tears with a napkin. "Saturday."

"What did you tell him?"

"I haven't given him my answer, yet." She pulled in a shaky breath. "He's giving me time to think about it."

"I'm assuming you haven't told your parents yet."

"Are you kidding?" Morgan exclaimed. "If they knew, they'd totally freak out. My mother would have the announcements out tomorrow. She thinks Manny walks on water. If she thought I was even hesitating to say yes she'd probably come unglued. I can't tell them. Not yet. Not until I decide."

Samantha's expression was full of compassion. "I'm sorry this is so hard on you. You must be so confused."

"I am," Morgan said as tears started again. She took a deep breath to calm herself. "I can't stop thinking of Justin. But he's so far away and I don't know when I'll see him again. Plus, he's down there with Marika and he's never even said anything about her to me, so I don't know what to think about that. And to be honest, I can't help wondering if those five days in Cancún with him were just some sort of bizarre romantic interlude that had no future. You know what I mean?"

"Sure I do. You've gotten to know Manny on a day-to-day basis. You know what he's like in normal everyday situations. With Justin, you were in paradise. I know he's a great guy—I love Justin. But being with Justin in Cancún is the stuff romance novels are made of, not real life."

Morgan felt her heart sink a little with Samantha's last comment. Maybe it was because she didn't want Samantha to say anything she didn't want to hear. But she knew she needed Samantha to be honest. She needed someone to help her see the situation clearly, no matter how painful.

"You don't think what Justin and I shared in Cancún was real?"

Samantha looked away, her face showing the strain of sadness. Morgan realized something else was going on, something with Samantha. This was what she'd sensed when they'd first walked in.

"What's going on, Sammy?"

Samantha's bottom lip trembled. She swallowed hard and kept her face turned. Morgan didn't like the uneasy feeling she had.

"Samantha?"

Her friend shut her eyes for a moment, then straightening her spine and pulling back her shoulders, she turned to Morgan and said, "My marriage is over."

Now it was Morgan's turn to be shocked. "What do you mean? What's happened?"

"I've tried to be patient with Trevor. I've put up with his drinking and his laziness and his *buddies*," she said with disgust. "He's been through two jobs since we got married, yet he spends money like it's growing on a tree in our backyard. He's negative about everything, and he puts me down every chance he gets. But that's not even the worst part."

Morgan didn't know if she was ready for the worst part.

"Do you remember the night on our honeymoon, when he was gone . . . ?" Samantha cleared her throat, obviously struggling to keep her composure. "He was away the entire night?"

Morgan nodded.

"I found out he was with another woman."

"Oh, Sammy, I'm so sorry."

"Yeah," Samantha laughed sardonically. "Imagine my surprise when I happen to intercept the phone bill and see calls to Mexico on it. He's actually still communicating with her."

"You're kidding!"

"No! That explains why he was so adamant about taking over the bill paying. He said he wanted to get a handle on our finances, but now I know he was just trying to cover up his little secret."

"Is he serious about her?"

"He says he's not, that he's just having fun, but that doesn't change the fact that he was with her on our honeymoon! Do you realize what a slap in the face that is for me?" Samantha's strong exterior began to crumble. "He didn't even have the decency to be faithful to me on our honeymoon." The tears began to fall, and it was Morgan's turn to hug her friend as she cried.

Morgan sadly realized that even though Samantha's news was horrible, it wasn't surprising. Trevor's actions were consistent with his past acts of selfishness.

As Samantha cried, they had to take napkins off the neighboring table, since they'd gone through all the napkins on their own table. Finally Samantha exhausted her tears and pulled herself together. Morgan quietly asked, "Have you two thought about going to a marriage counselor or getting some kind of help?"

"Trevor doesn't want to. He won't change. He likes how he is. He thinks the way he lives his life is perfectly fine, and if I don't like it then I can leave."

"That's what he said?"

Samantha nodded as she blew her nose.

"I'm so sorry," Morgan said.

"There's no hope for us. I cannot live this way. This isn't a marriage. There's no trust, no fidelity. He does what he wants, when he wants, and how he wants. I'm welcome to hang around if I'm willing to put up with it. Otherwise, he doesn't want to be bothered with me. You're not going to believe this," Samantha chuckled sarcastically. "I've been wanting to go back to church."

The news warmed Morgan's heart, despite her sadness for her friend.

"I've really been feeling a need to go back, but he won't hear of it. He wants nothing to do with it." Samantha looked her friend straight in the eye. "I wish I had married someone like Manny. Someone safe, someone I know loves me. Someone who would respect our marriage vows and be faithful, dependable, and caring. Looks, personality—all those things aren't important. And worse," Samantha's voice caught in her throat. "I'm pregnant."

These words came as more of a shock to Morgan than the revelation of Trevor's tryst in Cancún.

"Pregnant? I can't believe it. A baby?"

"Yeah," Samantha said. "A baby. How about that?"

Morgan's heart went out to her friend. "How are you feeling?"

"Tired, mostly. A little nauseated, but not too bad."

"And Trevor?"

"Doesn't want anything to do with it. He doesn't care, doesn't want to be bothered. He wants out. He said that after we got married everything between us changed. I changed. He can't handle how I expect him to spend time with me and not his friends."

"Wow," Morgan said, amazed at Trevor's selfishness. That was one thing about Manny—he constantly thought of her and her needs.

"That's why I say you should grab Manny and hold onto him with all you've got. He's good and kind and he loves you. You're so lucky. I'm sorry. I know I'm being painfully honest, but I think if Justin cared, he'd be doing more to show it. He'd be here instead of in Brazil with Marika."

Morgan felt all of her hopes dashed. The reality of it was, Sammy was right. No matter what Justin said in his letters or e-mails, his actions were speaking much louder. He obviously didn't care enough about her to show her.

Was this her answer? Certainly it had to be some sort of signal, some sort of arrow pointing her in the right direction.

❦ ❦ ❦

"Mom, Dad," Morgan said as their family sat down for dinner. "I have something to tell you." She'd called her mom earlier that day and asked if she could come over.

Her mother looked up from her plate with alarm, and her father's eyes narrowed in guarded interest. For some reason they acted as if they were expecting something bad. Had she really given them reason for concern?

She found herself wishing she were more excited to tell them, but the honest truth was that she wasn't. Maybe it was because she knew how ecstatic they would be at her news, while she wasn't. Once the words were out, her normal life would be over. She wasn't sure, but she knew she still had to tell them.

Steeling herself for their reaction, she said, "Manny asked me to marry him, and I said yes."

Her mother erupted like Mount Vesuvius. She jumped up from the table with a shriek of joy. With hands in the air she ran around the table to Morgan and bulldozed her with a hug. Then she did the same with her husband, hugging him with more enthusiasm than all the hugs she'd given him in the last five years combined.

"This is incredible," she said. "Where's Manny? Why didn't he want to tell us with you?"

"I wanted to tell you myself first," Morgan said, not really knowing why. There was some sort of hesitation on her part. She was holding back, and she knew it. She just didn't know why.

Morgan realized her father hadn't said even a word. "Dad?"

He gave her a fatherly smile. "Congratulations, sweetheart. I'm very happy for both of you. Manny's a wonderful man."

"He wants to make it official," Morgan said. "You know, come over and ask you for permission to marry me, before we officially announce our engagement."

"Engagement," her mother said, fairly swooning over the word.

"Mom," Morgan complained, already nauseated at her mother's intense joy over the news. She knew that if her mother had her way, arranged marriages would be practiced again. But if her mother could have handpicked someone for her daughter, it would have been Manny. Winning a million-dollar lottery wouldn't be any better than getting Manny for a son-in-law, as far as Laura Rose was concerned.

The news was out. There was no taking it back. And now that it was out, word would spread like wildfire.

ॐ ॐ ॐ

As she and Manny began sharing their exciting news, Morgan found herself going through the motions without consulting her feelings, feelings which were better off ignored. She'd made up her mind and accepted Manny's proposal. Her mind she could control; her heart she couldn't. So it was best to pretend her feelings didn't exist, because she knew what they were trying to say. And she wasn't listening anymore. Every time she did they got her into trouble. It was time to be smart about a relationship, and if that meant not getting emotionally involved, then so be it.

Manny had been wonderful about encouraging her to continue her educational dreams. Luckily there were on-line courses she could take to help her achieve her goal. It wouldn't be quite like she'd planned it, but the end result would still be the same, she often reminded herself.

One thing she couldn't do was turn off her thoughts and feelings about Justin. As much as she had prayed for a confirmation on her decision to marry Manny, she had also prayed for Heavenly Father to take away her feelings for Justin. Neither of those requests had been granted. Marrying Manny couldn't be wrong, but she hadn't had an overwhelming feeling that it was right. Still, waiting for Justin was a risk she'd decided she wasn't going to take, especially when everyone around her who loved her and wanted the best for her was voting for Manny. She trusted their opinions instead of her heart. She had to.

ॐ ॐ ॐ

Trying to slow her mother down was like trying to stop the space shuttle after the countdown. Laura Rose was unstoppable when her energy ignited for making wedding plans and arrangements. The biggest hurdle yet was trying to find a date that worked for everyone and was available at the temple.

"What about the last Friday in August?" Laura asked her future son-in-law. She'd invited Manny and Morgan over every night for dinner since the day their big news broke. Morgan didn't say anything, but there were times when she wished she could just have an evening to herself to relax in her apartment, read a book, watch television, or simply do nothing.

"That's getting too close to the beginning of school," Manny said. "Our mobile home is ready to move into any time after the tenth, so if we could find a date sooner we could get moved and settled before school starts."

"Okay, what about the eighth?"

"My parents get home from their mission on the seventh. I think it would be nice to give them more than a day after they get home, don't you think?"

"Of course," Laura agreed. "You're such a thoughtful son. They've got a long drive from Texas. I'm looking forward to seeing them again."

Morgan remembered Manny's parents. They were wonderful people, just like Manny. They were nearing the end of an eighteen-month mission in Dallas, then they'd be driving home to Salt Lake before coming to Sacramento for the wedding.

Feeling herself drift from the conversation as plans were made, Morgan pictured herself in Burley, Idaho, living in a mobile home, while Manny taught seminary every day. It wasn't a very romantic picture. She would have her classes and be working on her art, though, she guessed—that is, until they started a family. After that she didn't know how her classes would fit in.

"Morgan?" her mother's voice broke into her thoughts.

"Yes?" Morgan had completely drifted from the conversation and had no clue what was going on.

"The fifteenth. I think it's the best date for the wedding."

"Okay." Morgan nodded, still unengaged in the planning and choosing of crucial details regarding her wedding. Her body was there, but her heart wasn't. She had a hard time keeping her thoughts from drifting.

"I'll call the temple right now and see if that date is available," Laura offered.

While the call was made, Manny pushed aside the pile of papers and price quotes from florists, reception centers, and catering services and took Morgan's hand in his. "Can you believe how fast all of this is coming together?"

Mustering a weak smile, Morgan shook her head.

"Are you okay? You don't seem yourself tonight."

If she were to be honest, she would say she wasn't okay. But then he would ask what was wrong, and that was one question she didn't want to answer—partly because she didn't know herself, and partly because if she did figure it out, the answer might scare her.

"I'm just kind of tired. That's all."

Manny kissed the knuckles on her hand. "We're almost done here, then I'll take you home so you can get to bed early." He pushed a sheet of paper in front of her, a calendar page for the month of August. "Also, if we get married on the fifteenth, that will give us time for a short honeymoon before we move to Idaho."

Morgan raised her eyebrows to indicate enthusiasm and interest, but it was a motion devoid of feeling. She hadn't even thought about a honeymoon.

"I've thought a lot about where we should go. Have you got any place in mind?"

"Not really," she said.

"Well, I thought about somewhere tropical and exotic, but everything's pretty pricey and we need to stay within a tight budget, so I looked on the Internet and found some great deals for Vegas, or—"

"Not Vegas," she said, knowing immediately that she didn't want to spend her honeymoon in the desert. "It would be so hot."

He nodded. "True. Okay, how about . . ." He paused, as if to create suspense, " . . . Branson, Missouri?"

"Branson?" She could barely choke out the word. Not that she had anything against the place, but she wasn't a huge fan of country music, and it just wasn't a place she'd planned on for her honeymoon.

"Sure," he said enthusiastically. "If we take turns driving all night, we can save money on airfare and on a hotel room. That way we can take food with us—you know, like stuff for peanut butter and jelly sandwiches and cold cereal. Then we won't have to eat out as much."

Morgan didn't know what to say. *Branson? Driving? Peanut butter sandwiches?*

"Of course, if you have your heart set on going somewhere else, you know . . . like Cancún, maybe."

"No!" she exclaimed. "Uhhh . . . not there," she finished more calmly.

She could never go back there again. That place belonged to her and Justin. Nothing could ever measure up to her trip there in February. "Branson's fine," she said.

"Great." He turned to the paper and jotted down some notes. "We can find a place here in town for our wedding night, then I think we should wait to start our trip on Monday since we don't want to drive on Sunday. Don't you think?"

She nodded, looking blankly at the calendar, and then it struck her, like a ton of bricks. *August fifteenth! Wait a minute!* she nearly screamed. *I can't get married on that day.*

"It's set," Laura announced as she burst into the room. "We're lucky, too, because they're booked solid for weeks before and after that. In fact, it sounded like we were the last wedding to be scheduled for that day."

Morgan felt a wave of nausea come over her. She broke out into a cold sweat. "Excuse me," she said, pushing herself away from the table and hurrying for the bathroom, just in case.

With the door shut, she sat near the toilet and pulled in long, slow breaths. Tears stung her eyes. The nauseated feeling slowly disappeared, and she sat back on the floor, leaning against the wall. Tears leaked from the corners of her eyes and trickled onto her cheeks. *The fifteenth.* Just the mention of that date brought a world of memories to her mind.

Justin.

That was the day they'd agreed upon to celebrate—together—the six-month anniversary of their first meeting.

But that was when they shared the same feelings for each other and a promise of furthering their relationship. Those things didn't seem to exist anymore, which meant that date probably didn't mean anything anymore. Well, except that now it was her wedding day.

Her wedding day.

Resting her head in her hands, she let her tears fall. She needed to get herself together and stop this nonsense. Marrying Manny would be a wonderful blessing in her life. He was everything a girl would ever want in a man. Everything.

But it still didn't seem like enough.

What was wrong with her? Why wasn't she able to get her heart into this? She wanted to feel all those wonderful, exciting feelings a girl should have when she gets engaged and starts planning her wedding. Instead it felt like she was planning her funeral.

She knew what was wrong with her, but it didn't change anything. Justin was out of her life now. He was part of her past, and it was time for her to face that fact and move on to her future.

She just wished she knew how.

Chapter Eighteen

Justin woke up before the alarm sounded. His room was still dark, and a fierce wind blew outside.

"Not again," he muttered, wishing they could get one clear day so they could do repair work on the outside of some of the homes that had been damaged by the storm ripping through the town of Quarai.

Bracing himself against the cold, he climbed out of bed and shivered. The dampness in the frigid air went right through him. Hot chocolate. He needed hot chocolate.

Turning on the burner, he put on a pot of water and went into the bathroom. Cracks in the walls and around the windows kept a steady draft of cold coming inside.

He'd had some bad apartments on his mission, but this one was far worse than anything he'd lived in. When he'd been in Quarai as a missionary, he'd lived in a nice apartment with three other elders. That apartment was still there, and the elders were still living in it.

Still, he knew he shouldn't complain; his place was better than what some of the Brazilians were living in, especially since their homes had been destroyed.

A pounding at the door brought him running to answer it.

"Brother Justin," the elderly man said, "come quick. The roof has blown off the church. We must cover it before the rain starts."

"I'll be right there, Carlos."

Justin had slept in sweats, so he pulled on his muddy boots and donned a scarf, hat, gloves, and his damp winter coat. Nothing seemed to dry in this weather.

Rushing outside, he followed the path leading from his front door to the dirt road that was nothing more than a sea of reddish-brown mud.

Slopping along as quickly as he could, he saw several other brethren from the ward joining in the effort to save the church. If these dark clouds let loose like they had a few days ago, nothing inside the church would be worth salvaging. They had to hurry.

Several men were already on top of the roof while the men below handed them a large, black, plastic tarp to be nailed over the gaping hole torn out of the corner of the roof.

They had the right idea, but Justin could see what else needed to be done.

Grabbing the first person he came to, he ordered the man to find some long two-by-fours.

The man went running, taking several others with him.

Asking for a boost, Justin climbed onto one of the member's backs, then shoulders, and hitched his knee onto the edge of the roof, where he joined the other men.

The gusts of wind were strong enough to challenge his balance, and he prayed he wouldn't fall. There was no time for an injury for any of them.

A moment later, long boards were making their way to the roof, where the men placed them against the tarp and nailed them firmly into place. This prevented the tarp from tearing and held the plastic firm. It wouldn't keep out the cold, but for now, keeping out the rain was more important.

They continued working until the entire hole was securely patched.

"Hey," someone yelled. "What's that?"

He pointed down the street at a plume of smoke billowing into the sky and disappearing into the dark clouds overhead.

The man turned and looked at Justin. Justin's stomach churned. It was his place.

Practically jumping from the roof, Justin headed for home, praying now that the heavens would explode with rain. By the time the fire trucks arrived, the whole place would be in flames.

Cell phone service had been down for days, so someone ran to the nearest house to phone for help, while Justin and several other men arrived at his house, only to see it engulfed in flames.

It was his own fault. He'd left the pot boiling on the burner. The water must have boiled out and the pot overheated.

"I have to get inside!" Justin yelled, going for the front door.

Carlos grabbed him. "You can't go in there."

Justin thought of his few belongings. His important papers and documents, his laptop with all of his work, and everything he'd brought with him was going up in smoke.

Closing his eyes, Justin leaned against Carlos as the distant sound of sirens came closer.

☙ ☙ ☙

In a daze, Morgan went through the motions of going to work, shopping for a wedding gown, choosing flowers and a caterer, visiting reception centers, and spending time with her fiancé. She'd made the decision, and she prayed for the peace of mind that came with that decision, but it wasn't coming very quickly.

Thank goodness there were times when Manny turned on his old charm and helped her come close to feeling the excitement of being a young couple, engaged and full of anticipation for the start of a new life together. She couldn't deny he was a good man, one she admired and respected. She also knew that he truly loved her. There was something to be said for these things, proven by the fact that Samantha was miserable because her husband didn't possess these qualities. It was a stark contrast, and one that wasn't lost on Morgan.

Nighttime, after Manny went home and Morgan returned to her apartment, was the only time Morgan had to herself anymore.

Her dream of going back to college was on hold. Manny fully supported her in her decision, but until they got settled in Burley, she couldn't really begin to think about starting on her art degree. Her dream would have to wait a little longer.

She usually fell into bed physically drained and emotionally exhausted, but not until she checked her e-mail first, just in case Justin had sent her a message.

His messages had dwindled to nothing. She'd received a few quick notes from him, telling her he was still swamped with work, blaming the government and the weather for the project taking so long. In his spare time he was continuing to help rebuild the city where the storm had damaged so many homes and buildings. But it had been well over a week since she'd heard from him.

It just wasn't meant to be, she told herself over and over. And maybe somewhere down the road, her experience with Justin in Cancún would be a pleasant memory, one she could reflect on without heartache.

She snorted in derision at that thought. *Maybe, but she was going to have to live to be a hundred!*

Chapter Nineteen

Just as he'd expected, the townspeople of Quarai had come to his rescue. The people in the ward had taken him into their homes—at least, those who had homes. They'd fed him and given him a place to sleep. At times he slept in the church on the floor. It wasn't ideal, but he was stuck in Quarai until he was issued a replacement passport and visa. Who knew how long that would take?

Carlos and his wife and children were especially kind to him and invited him for lunch almost every day. He'd known them when he served in Quarai on his mission, and then, when he'd recently returned, they'd taken him in until he was settled into his own place. Along with the full-time missionaries, Justin had been able to help teach their daughter, Marika, who'd recently been baptized. He had a hunch that Marika liked him, but he'd made sure she understood he only liked her as a friend. She was much too young for him, and she was building a life for herself in Rio. He hoped that her convictions of the gospel were strong enough for her to withstand the temptations of that city, especially when she was pursuing a career as a fashion model.

They spent a lot of time together, but he felt more like her big brother, like part of the family—especially to Marika's little brothers, Antonio and Luis. He'd never been around kids until his mission, but then, as he spent time in the homes of families, teaching them the gospel and helping them find a better way to raise their children, he had grown to love children and appreciate the amazing spirits they had.

His mission had been a time of learning and growth. He'd seen families who had nothing, who lived in shacks with dirt floors and ate nothing but one meal of beans and rice each day, who were happier than the millionaires in his neighborhood back home. These families laughed together, loved each other, and didn't need material possessions to make them happy. As long as everyone in the family was safe and healthy, that was all that mattered.

These lessons in life had shaped and changed Justin forever. He was grateful for the time he could spend back in a town with people he'd grown to love on his mission. But as soon as his travel papers were replaced, he would head back to Santa Maria and finish up his work so he could return to the States. He'd been in Brazil much longer than he'd planned, and there were pressing matters for him to return to—one of which was Morgan.

With the phone lines down and all cell phone service gone, he'd been unable to contact her, but slowly the town was coming back together, and the local Internet café, where public computers were available, was up and running again.

He needed to contact Morgan. For some reason he felt anxious to get in touch with her. Maybe it was that he hadn't heard from her for so long, or that he missed her more with each day that passed. Either way, he was anxious to get in touch with her and get back to the States so he could see her.

❧ ❧ ❧

"So have you told Justin yet?" Samantha asked as she poured oriental dressing on her salad.

Morgan looked down at her own salad and stabbed at a piece of lettuce. "No."

"What?" Samantha's shocked tone surprised Morgan.

"What, what?" Morgan answered.

"You haven't told him?"

"No."

"Why?"

"Why?"

"Will you quit echoing me and tell me why you haven't told him?" Samantha scolded. "Morgan, you have to do it. It's only fair to Justin, and to Manny."

"Manny?"

Samantha gave her a look of warning; Morgan didn't realize she had an echo problem. "First of all, Justin needs to know. That's pretty clear. But Manny deserves to have your whole heart, and until you end your relationship with Justin, you still have part of your heart in Brazil."

It was true. Morgan knew that the final step in her commitment to Manny was telling Justin. But the thought of doing it made her feel faint and sick to her stomach.

"It's called closure, remember? You need to end your relationship with Justin so you can move on."

"I find it interesting that you, the person who was pushing Justin toward me in Cancún, are now so opposed to him."

Samantha took a sip of her raspberry lemonade.

"Why?" Morgan prodded.

"Why?"

Morgan smiled. Samantha had caught the echo bug.

With exasperation Samantha said, "Okay, I guess I've cooled on Justin because he's Trevor's friend, and any friend of Trevor's is an enemy of mine."

"But—"

"I know Justin's not like all of Trevor's other friends. But still, he has a past and he's still a 'buddy,' and—who knows—maybe deep down he's more like them than we think. I just don't want to see you involved with him anymore. I'm so relieved you found Manny, because if you were with Justin right now, I'd be scared for you."

Morgan laughed. "Sammy, that's a little extreme, don't you think?"

"No, I don't. After people get married, they change. Their true personalities surface. Things you noticed before you got married, little things that annoyed you or caused tension in your relationship, get worse. Love is blind, and marriage gives you twenty-twenty vision."

"That may be true," Morgan laughed, "but you're wrong about Justin. He's not like Trevor at all. In fact, I've never known a person who thinks more about others than he does. In all of his e-mails I hear about all the things he's doing to help the people. You'd think he was on a service mission, the way he's working to rebuild this city."

"Gee, I wonder if it has anything to do with the fact that Marika's parents live there," she said sarcastically.

"He's never said anything to me about Marika." Morgan found herself defending him.

"Surprise!" Samantha said with sarcasm. "Of course not. But they are together, and it's serious. He e-mails Trevor all the time, and he's mentioned her a lot. I think they're really serious."

Samantha's words stung.

"I'm sorry." Samantha reached over and clasped Morgan's hand. "I know you still care about Justin, but I just want you to see that you're better off with Manny. You're doing the right thing. Justin is charming and wonderful, but those things don't matter after you're married. Good looks, personality, romance . . . all that stuff isn't as important in a marriage. Commitment, devotion, security—that's what matters."

Morgan listened but couldn't believe that marriage was mostly a business arrangement, rather than an expression of love.

"You need to end it with Justin today. I'm sure you'll discover how much he really cares when you hear back from him. But I'll warn you now, I think he's more serious with this Marika than we think."

"What has he said to Trevor?"

"There aren't any hotels in Quarai, so he stayed at her parents' house until he found a place of his own. His work is in Santa Maria, which is about an eight-hour bus ride away, but he's staying in Quarai instead. Maybe if he'd go back to Santa Maria and finish his job he could come back to the States, but he's hanging out in this other town where she is. Maybe he hasn't come right out and said anything, but it's pretty obvious to me what's going on. He likes this girl enough to prolong his time in Brazil. I mean, he baptized her—they've shared something that important, so it makes sense that a relationship could develop. Especially if she's as gorgeous as he said she was."

"He actually told Trevor she was gorgeous?" Morgan felt a pinhole-sized leak develop in her bubble of hope.

"Yes. She's a model, remember?"

Morgan sighed. Whether she wanted to or not, she needed to face the fact that he was involved with someone else.

"Maybe he's as nervous to tell you about her as you are to tell him about Manny. If you let him know you've moved on, I'll bet anything that he tells you about Marika. It will hurt, but you'll feel better once it's all out in the open."

Morgan nodded slowly, feeling more and more deflated inside.

"I'm sorry," Samantha said. "I don't mean to be so cold about it, but I don't want you to have to go through what I'm going through. It hurts a lot worse after you're married than it does before. And it doesn't just affect me now. It's going to affect my baby's future. I love you too much to stand by and let you make the same mistake I did."

Morgan knew Samantha's words were based on sincere concern and love, but she just wasn't convinced that Justin was as bad a person as Samantha made him out to be.

Still, she knew Samantha was right about one thing. It was time to end it.

❦ ❦ ❦

"Morgan, we need to go get your dress fitted and meet with the caterer one more time to make a final decision on the refreshments."

It was Morgan's day off, and she and her mother had planned to spend the day together, but the last thing she felt like doing was wedding stuff.

"Your bridal photos are scheduled for Saturday. Did you remember to make a hair appointment?"

Morgan didn't say, "Oops," but her mother obviously sensed it in her silence.

"You'd better call right now and get an appointment. Morgan, I swear, getting you to help out with all of this is like pulling teeth. I can't do everything. It's your wedding . . ."

Her mother continued, but Morgan had tuned her out. She didn't want to hear it. She just wasn't in the mood today. Something inside of her was holding her back. Try as she might, she couldn't force herself to feel something that wasn't there. In her mind she felt like marrying Manny was the right thing to do, but still, in her heart, she wasn't sure.

Tears stung her eyes and she blinked to clear them, but it was no use. What started out as a trickle soon became a deluge. Covering her face with her hands, she slowly crumbled.

"Morgan, what is the matter?" her mother said with measured patience.

But Morgan couldn't answer. She wasn't even going to try. Her mother didn't understand—she would never understand. No one understood. Not even her best friend. She was on her own to figure this out. And if she didn't figure it out soon, it would be too late.

"Morgan." Her mother said her name again, but Morgan ignored her. She couldn't stop her tears, and frankly, it felt good to let out the emotions that she'd been holding inside for much too long.

The telephone rang and her mother answered it. Morgan gathered herself together enough to go to her old room that had become a spare bedroom, where she collapsed on the bed and finished shedding her tears. Thoughts and fears raced through her mind, but she couldn't sort out any of them, so she just cried until finally she fell into an exhausted sleep.

❦ ❦ ❦

"Morgan?" Her mother's voice came through the thick fog of sleep.

She forced her eyes open and saw her mother sitting next to her on the edge of the bed.

"What time is it?"

"Almost noon."

"Oh," she said, rolling over, ready to go back to sleep.

"Manny called."

"Okay." She shut her eyes and wished her mother would go away.

"I told him you were busy today and that you'd call him later."

That was new. Usually her mother expected her to drop everything when he called.

"I thought that maybe we could go to that spa this afternoon. You know, the one you gave me a gift certificate for."

Morgan couldn't help herself. She had to turn and look to ensure it was really her mother talking.

"Why?" Morgan asked.

"I think you need a break, a little 'you' time. And I wouldn't mind a little 'me' time, either. I haven't had a pedicure in years, and frankly, I wouldn't mind a massage either."

Was her mother actually being understanding? Morgan was touched. Especially when she knew her mother never indulged herself. But she wasn't doing it for herself; she was doing it for Morgan. And it meant the world to Morgan.

"Sure. I think that's a great idea, Mom."

§ § §

Morgan couldn't remember the last time she and her mother had actually spent time together having fun, laughing like friends. The topic of the wedding and Manny didn't come up the entire afternoon. They each had a relaxing massage, then they had facials and pedicures, lounging luxuriously in pampered comfort.

But the best part still was seeing a side of her mother Morgan hadn't seen before, a side that was carefree and enjoyable to be around. Her mother was usually so driven and focused on what needed to be done that she didn't allow herself time to relax and just have fun. It was a side of her mother Morgan wished she could see more often, because for the first time in their adult lives, Morgan actually felt like they had connected.

On the way home from the spa they stopped at the mall and went shoe shopping. They both wanted a pair of sandals to show off their lovely, pedicured toes. Morgan talked her mother into splurging on a new skirt and knit top that was stylish and fun. Her mother was slim and attractive, and the outfit looked spectacular on her.

"We should go shopping more often," Morgan said as they carried their packages to the car.

"Your dad will be amazed when he sees all this. He wanted to take me shopping for our anniversary, but I just wasn't in the mood. But this was so fun, I think I'll see if he's still willing to go. My wardrobe could use a little updating."

Morgan exercised all her willpower not to comment. Her mother's wardrobe needed a complete overhaul, but Morgan knew to take it a little at a time. This was a huge step for her mother, and hopefully the start of more fun times together.

ॐ ॐ ॐ

Why was her e-mail getting returned?

She checked Justin's address one more time to make sure it was correct. It was the same e-mail address she'd been using the entire time he'd been in Brazil, but her e-mail to him had been returned and deemed "undeliverable."

Her calls hadn't been successful either. Even though he hadn't answered the phone when she called, at least his voice mail picked up. She called again and left an urgent message, telling him that she had something very important to talk to him about and asking him to call.

After leaving the message, she was startled when the phone rang just seconds after she had hung up. For a split second she thought it was Justin but knew it was just wishful thinking.

"Is there a Mr. Greg Rose or Morgan Rose available?"

"This is Morgan," she answered.

"Hi, this is Mike from Sacramento Scuba. I just wanted to make sure you were still planning on the open dive this Saturday?"

"Yes," she replied.

"It's a three-hour drive to Monterrey, so you'll need to arrive by eight in the morning so we can get your gear together and be there by noon."

"We'll be there, thanks," she told him, wishing she didn't feel a nervous twisting in her stomach. She knew once they got into the water she would be fine, but she wasn't confident enough about her diving skills to banish all fear.

She hung up the phone and it rang again.

"What is going on?" she said aloud as she picked up the phone and said hello. It was Manny.

"I just called to see how your day was," he said.

Morgan told him about the fun she'd had with her mom and tried to share with him how much it had meant to her that her mother had actually made the effort to spend time with her. She couldn't really tell him why she had needed a break at a day spa or why her mother had felt a need to give her that break, so she made it sound more like a "mother-daughter thing" than a "nervous breakdown thing."

The break had helped. But a few hours away from her problems hadn't solved them. She still felt turbulent inside. And she knew that somehow she needed to find peace.

"So, what's going on?" he asked.

She knew he wanted to come over, but she just didn't feel like it. She needed to have her space, to continue the "break" just awhile longer.

"I just got off the phone with our dive master," she told him. "We have our open dive on Saturday."

"What's that?"

"Now that we've passed our written test and completed all our skills in the pool, we need to go on a dive out in open water and practice and pass off the skills one more time. After that we're considered certified. Of course, I would still never go diving without a dive master, but I could take care of myself under the water. Dad and I want to plan a trip sometime so we can dive. Maybe in Florida or somewhere warm."

"Florida? When are you planning on doing that?"

She didn't like the alarmed tone of his voice. "I don't know," she replied. "We were just talking. I mean, it's silly to get certified then not go diving."

"Once we get married I don't know how we'd be able to manage a trip like that. Financially we aren't going to be able to go on any big vacations for a while. We'd have to work some kind of savings plan into our budget."

"I understand that," she told him, getting a sinking feeling that made her wonder if there would be enough money in the budget to go back to college. "But I'm going to be working too. It wouldn't be hard to save enough for a trip."

"Of course, the money we spend on a vacation is money we could use toward a down payment on a home. And besides, if we're going to plan a vacation, I don't know if gearing it toward diving would be my first choice."

"Don't you have any interest in diving? They have courses where you can learn just enough to dive without going through the certification."

"I'm not a big fan of water."

"You're not? I thought you surfed and stuff in high school."

"Not really. When I was thirteen I went on a Scout trip. We were kayaking down this river and my boat overturned and I got trapped underneath. I nearly drowned. Ever since then I haven't had much to do with water sports. I only went surfing because of the peer pressure from my friends, but I didn't spend a lot of time in the water. I usually found some excuse to stay on the beach. I doubt I'll ever dive."

Even though Morgan understood his trauma—and she truly did understand—she found herself wondering what the point of her even getting her certification was if she was never going to go diving again.

"But that doesn't mean you can't go," he said, sensing her discomfort. "I mean, you have your dad to go with. And your friend Rhonda."

"Yeah," Morgan said with disappointment.

"Anyway, I just thought I'd call and see if you wanted to go get an ice cream or something," Manny said, changing the subject.

"You know what?" she said. "I think I'll pass. I'm kind of tired, so I'm just going to go to bed."

"Oh." It was Manny's turn to be disappointed. "Okay. Don't forget we're calling my parents tomorrow."

Since Morgan and his parents hadn't had a chance to really talk since the engagement, they had decided to call them together so they could all have a chance to get to know one another again before the wedding.

"I haven't forgotten," she said. "I'll see you tomorrow, then. Good night, Manny."

She hung up the phone, hating how she felt inside. Something wasn't right. Whatever it was, she had to figure it out, and quickly. There was someone else she could call. Maybe he could give her some insight.

ॐ ॐ ॐ

"Thanks so much for seeing me on such short notice, Bishop Terry."

"I'm glad you called. I've been meaning to meet with you and your fiancé one more time before your big day. It's getting close, isn't it?"

He asked her as if he expected her to be excited. Of course, why wouldn't he expect that? Brides were supposed to be excited, Morgan thought in annoyance.

"So, what can I do for you, Morgan? How is everything?"

"I can't seem to sort out all the feelings I'm having," she told him. "I feel like I'm all bruised inside from all of these emotions bumping and colliding together."

"Why don't you tell me what's going on and we'll see if we can sort things out together?"

For the first time in weeks, Morgan felt hopeful that she was finally going to make some progress.

"There's this guy I met last February, in Cancún . . ."

She explained about Justin, the strong connection they'd shared, and the way he'd helped her feel better about herself. Then she told about her feelings for Manny, making sure to acknowledge the fact that she respected him and admired him.

The bishop nodded as she laid her feelings out before him, allowing her to tearfully unload everything, to share her most private feelings that she'd held in for so long because no one else seemed to understand or want to hear them.

Five tissues later, she stopped. "So, that's it. I'm so filled with confusion I don't know what to do."

Before speaking the bishop paused, as if choosing his words carefully.

"It's understandable that you're confused since you have feelings for two men. It's obvious that you need to resolve your relationship with Justin before you can completely commit to Manny."

"Yes," Morgan said. "I agree."

"Do you see any future with Justin?"

She looked down at the wad of tissues in her lap and shook her head sadly. "I used to think so, but I don't know anymore. In his e-mails and letters he says that he thinks of me and doesn't want me to forget about him, but I don't think I can expect any kind of commitment from him. We only knew each other five days before we flew in opposite directions."

"That makes it hard to develop a relationship."

"If not impossible," Morgan said. "I just don't know if it's worth the risk of losing Manny to hold out until I see what happens with Justin."

Again the bishop nodded. "I won't lie to you," he said. "Manny is the type of man I would like all the young men in my ward to be like and that I'd want any of our young women, including my own daughters, to marry. I don't know Justin. Having him gone so long with no idea of when he will return presents a very difficult problem, and an even more difficult decision for you. I can't tell you what to do, Morgan. I know it's possible to love two people at the same time, but it is time for you to make a decision, for your sake and for Manny's. Keep in mind that the man you choose to marry should give you a home full of love and security—a place where trust and joy and the Spirit of the Lord can always dwell. But it has to be your choice. You need to prayerfully consider your decision. You might want to ask your father for a priesthood blessing and then fast before you approach your Father in Heaven. You will get an answer, Morgan. And once you do, you need to move forward and have faith, and never look back."

Morgan's eyes filled with tears again. She was ready to do anything to find out. It was time to know, one way or the other, and then, just as the bishop said, never look back.

Chapter Twenty

"Undeliverable!" Justin exclaimed. What was wrong with this crazy Internet? Why wouldn't his messages go through? He wasn't getting any messages from home or from Morgan.

With a groan he pushed himself away from the computer, thanked the owner of the Internet café, and went outside.

Sunshine greeted him, along with the happy smiles of many of the townspeople on their way to the market or to work. Finally, after the long stretches of bad weather, things were looking up for this small community. Justin marveled at the resiliency and patience in affliction these people possessed. They were admirable in their faith, not wavering in the face of trials. They handled loss and devastation with the ability not to lose perspective. Things that they considered an inconvenience, like no roof on their house, would devastate most people back in the States—at least the people he knew. Yet these wonderfully humble people rolled with each punch, making the best of every situation. And when Justin asked them how they did it, they only said, "We have no choice—this is life."

Stopping by the post office on his way back to the church, Justin was disappointed to find out his passport and visa still hadn't arrived.

His plan was to stay long enough to finish repairs on the roof of the church, tie up a few loose ends in Quarai, and be on his way back to Santa Maria. Hopefully his passport and visa would arrive soon. Then his next stop would be Sacramento.

❧ ❧ ❧

"That's the saddest-looking bride I've ever seen," Morgan overheard the saleslady whisper to her co-worker as they walked away from the fitting room. Morgan was in for the final fitting of her wedding gown, and they were having to call a seamstress because the dress needed to be taken in at the waist. Morgan had lost quite a bit of weight during her engagement, and the dress hung on her like a gunnysack.

Taking a hard look in the mirror, Morgan examined her reflection. All the hours in the gym had helped her trim down and become more flexible, also giving her some nicely toned muscles. But in this dress, none of that showed. She wondered if it was too late to change her mind and get a different dress.

Forcing a smile, she pulled her shoulders back and stood tall. That helped; but no matter what she did to the outside, she couldn't change what was going on inside. No amount of tailoring could make her feelings fit the expectation everyone else seemed to have placed on her.

Expelling her breath in frustration, she turned from the mirror. She'd have to start ignoring her reflection, just like she was ignoring her emotions. That was going to be the only way she got through this, unless she finally did what she had to do.

❧ ❧ ❧

"Dad." Morgan knew her father didn't like to be interrupted while he was reading the paper, but she wanted to talk to him while her mom was out. She was on her way to Manny's to call his parents. Time was running out.

"Yes, sweetie." He put the paper down and looked at his daughter.

She cleared her throat, feeling on the verge of tears again. "I . . . um . . ." she started but found it difficult to ask her question.

"What is it, Morgan?" he asked. His voice reflected his concern.

"Dad, do you think . . ." The tide of tears continued to rise and her throat felt clogged. "Could you give me a blessing?" she finally managed to say.

Folding his paper and putting it aside, Greg Rose looked at his daughter and smiled with compassion. "I was wondering when you were going to ask."

Morgan crumbled and knelt down by her father's chair. He leaned over and pulled her into a hug, holding her and giving her strength through his embrace. She'd been fasting all day, and she'd prayed many times, even taking breaks at work to go into the bathroom to pray. Rhonda thought she was sick—and Morgan let her believe it, because in a way she was sick, certainly sick of feeling the way she felt.

Finally Morgan's well ran dry. She wiped her tears and sat back on her heels. "I know it's not necessarily the wrong decision to marry Manny. In my head, I know he's a good choice. I just don't know for sure in my heart. Shouldn't it feel right in both? Shouldn't I feel peace? Because right now it's like a tornado in here." She pointed to her heart.

He nodded and ran his hand down the side of her face. "You've looked pretty miserable the last few times I've seen you," he said. "I had a hunch you were getting cold feet, but I didn't want to pry."

"You can always pry, Dad."

He smiled. "I wasn't sure yet what to tell you. I wanted to make sure I had the right advice to give you."

"And do you?"

"Oh, I don't think I have anything to say that you haven't already heard or that you don't know yourself. Everyone gets cold feet before they get married."

"They do?"

"Sure. It's a big step—you want to make sure it's the right decision."

"Is it, Dad? Is it the right decision?"

"Well, I know Manny will be a good husband and a good father. He loves you and I know he'll give you security and take good care of you. As a father, I think this is important. I want the man who marries you to take care of you as well as or better than I'd take care of you. I think Manny will do that."

Morgan agreed. Manny had everything going for him. Sure, life with Manny might get a little monotonous, predictable, and even dull at times, but she was used to living her life that way—it wouldn't be much of a stretch for her. Except that she'd had a taste of adventure, of the wonderfully exciting experiences and richness that life had to offer. It was hard to go back to the plain potatoes Manny had to offer when she'd feasted at a buffet of experience such as Justin had shown her.

But if that was what she needed to do, then she would do it. She didn't care, just as long as it felt right inside. That's all she needed.

The house was peaceful and quiet. Taking the phone off the hook, Morgan's father placed his hands on her head and gave her a father's blessing. He expressed his great love for her and the love Heavenly Father had for her. He told her that she had a great and glorious purpose in life and that she would have opportunities to touch people's lives and devote herself to giving service, not only to her family, but to those around her.

Tears Morgan thought had long since dried up trickled down her cheeks as her father spoke of the good decisions she'd made in her life, how proud her Father in Heaven was of her, and how blessed she was for her obedience to the teachings of the gospel. He blessed her that answers would come and that she would know in her heart and mind that her decision was Heavenly Father's will.

After the blessing, Morgan and her father hugged, sharing a spiritual moment that would be close to their hearts for eternity. Her earthly father was a link to her Heavenly Father, and she knew, without a doubt, that the answer would come. Peace filled her heart and her fears fled. She knew she would recognize what to do when it was the right time.

৺ ৺ ৺

"Dad, I'm scared." Morgan checked the connection of her air tank and turned on the valve. The hoses connected to her Buoyancy Control Device inflated with a whoosh. The BCD was the vest divers wore, and Morgan found herself dreading to put it on in order to jump into the deep, blue-green water off the shore of Monterrey, California. She had a seven-millimeter suit, which was the thickest the dive shop had, but with fifty-five-degree water, it could still get cold. But it wasn't the cold she worried about. It was drowning.

"Honey, we've practiced every skill a dozen times. You've got everything down perfectly. I'll be right there with you and so will Mike. You just wait—the minute you get under the water you'll have so much fun, you won't want to get out."

"Don't hold your breath, Dad."

"That's right! The first rule of diving is never hold your breath." He winked. "See, you're a great dive buddy."

"Buddy, schmuddy, I'm concerned for my life."

"Okay, folks," the dive master said loudly. "It's time to put on your BCDs, and one by one we'll enter the water. I want you to establish positive buoyancy once you're in the water, and wait over by the buoy until everyone gets in."

Morgan wasn't even cold, yet she was shivering. Her nerves were taut and her concerns caused her breath to come in choppy gulps.

"Help me get my BCD on, then I'll help you with yours," her father said.

Over on the other side of the boat, Rhonda received help from Mike, since he was not only her dive buddy but her steady boyfriend.

Morgan watched them for a moment—the way they interacted, their lingering gazes, meaningful smiles, tender touches, and stolen kisses. They seemed closer and more intimate and comfortable than she and Manny did. Not that she wanted Manny constantly touching her or anything, but the difference was evident. Rhonda and Mike were blissfully head over heels about each other. Morgan and Manny were bound by common goals and good sense.

She watched as the others in the group lumbered to the back of the boat, their walking difficult because of the weight of the air tanks and the fins on their feet.

"You two ready over there?" Mike asked as he observed everyone's entry into the water.

"All set," Greg Rose replied, helping his daughter to her feet. The rocking of the boat and the difficulty in walking made Morgan's legs wobbly and her stomach queasy.

I can do this, she told herself. *I'll be proud of myself for going through with it. Dad will be proud. Justin will be—*

She stopped as the thought of Justin broke her concentration. It was true, though. Justin would be proud of her right now. He would encourage her and assure her that she'd be fine and that she was going to love what she was about to do.

Somehow, the thoughts of Justin encouraging her, just like he'd done in Cancún, gave her the strength and courage she needed to take a deep breath, face her fear, and not back down. She was going into that water if it was the last thing she did.

"Okay, Morgan, just like we did in class. Big step off the platform. Ready?" Mike looked at her with a steady gaze, helping her to calm down and focus. Then, without another thought, she took a step and plunged into the cold, shimmering water.

Quickly, she put more air into her vest and paddled her feet toward the buoy. Once the shock of the chilly water wore off, she found she was comfortable in the thick dive suit.

Rhonda reached out for her when she got near, and they shared nervous excitement. Rhonda had her own phobias about diving, but Mike had helped her work through them, and she had taken to it so easily.

"We're ready to go under," Mike said when he joined them. "I want you to descend slowly by releasing the air from your BCD. Remember to equalize all the way down. We'll stop at about forty feet and go from there. Any questions?"

No one seemed to have any, so without further instruction, the descent began.

Morgan's heart sped up as she began to sink, and she felt the urge to fight against submerging. Forcing herself to calm down, she slowly went under the water and took her first breath. From then on she became fascinated with the underwater paradise before her eyes.

The visibility was amazing. They could see nearly a hundred feet around them. The sun's rays penetrated the deep water, illuminating the silvery fish that darted around them.

Keeping an eye on Mike, the small group followed him as they began their series of skills in finishing certification.

This would be their deepest of the three dives that day, since any subsequent dive couldn't be deeper than the first for safety reasons. They would be under the water about twenty minutes each time.

They were near a barrier reef that teemed with dozens of varieties of fish and displayed an undersea garden of plant life. Occasionally she would catch her father's eye and open her own eyes wide to indicate just how amazing it was. Her father had been right. Just getting beneath the water was all it took; all she cared about was enjoying the weightless feeling of floating through the water and observing the amazing beauty before her.

A tap on her shoulder caused her to turn and find Rhonda, who was pointing in the distance. There, about the size of a regular-sized bed pillow, was a sea turtle, his little feet and tail flipping gracefully through the water. It was one of the most amazing things Morgan had ever seen. And just like her father had said, she was one of the last to surface after that first dive. She just hadn't seen enough.

The rest period between each dive allowed any nitrous elements that had built up in their bloodstreams to get released so they could go back down again. By their third time down, Morgan was first in line to get back into the water. Her father nicknamed her "mermaid" and did his best to keep up. She was determined to see another sea turtle and anything else that was down there.

One by one Mike helped each member of the group pass off each of the skills they'd learned in the pool. The only thing that had Morgan worried was the skill that had caused her so much trouble in class—filling her mask completely, then clearing it. She was doing her best not to dwell on what had happened in the pool. She was determined not to lose her cool this time and inhale a lungful of water. But part of her hoped that Mike would forget about the skill, even though she knew that if he wanted *anyone* to pass it off, it was her.

Sure enough, just as she was having fun hovering in the water, amazed at being surrounded by marine life, Mike tapped her on the shoulder. Giving her the signal to fill her mask, Mike floated in front of her, ready to observe her execution of the skill. She shut her eyes, offering a prayer requesting that she remain calm. She could do this; she knew it.

Mike tapped her again and gave her the "OK" sign with his hand, asking if she was all right. She nodded and took several steady breaths while she mentally reviewed the steps: fill mask, breathe through mouth, push on top of mask, blow out air through nose, breathe in through mouth. The last part was where she'd messed up. She knew it was dumb, but she'd always been a nose-holding swimmer and therefore couldn't change back and forth from mouth to nose very easily. But she'd done it before and she could do it again. And Mike was going to make sure of it. Out of the corner of her eye she caught both her father and Rhonda watching her. They flashed a thumbs-up signal her direction. She didn't motion back but appreciated their support; they knew how hard this was for her.

She lifted her hand to her mask and felt her breathing rate escalate. Mike took her wrist and pointed to her eyes, then his eyes, then back to hers. He wanted her to watch him.

Slowly, he lifted his mask, filled it with water, pushed on the top and cleared it by blowing out through his nose. Nothing to it. It took all of five seconds. Then he pointed at her, and she nodded. It was time.

She shut her eyes, something she was grateful he allowed her to do, and lifted her mask. Water flooded it, and she concentrated on breathing through her mouth.

Step one completed. Next was to continue breathing, and then, after taking a breath in through her mouth, she need to breathe out through her nose to clear the mask, then in through her mouth again. That was the key. *Breathe in through your mouth,* she reminded herself.

With steady breathing and concentration she pulled in one more breath through her mouthpiece, pushed on the top of her mask, and blew out through her nose. She didn't get it completely cleared.

She took several more breaths, pushed on the top of her mask, and cleared it one last time, then continued breathing through her mouthpiece. When she opened her eyes, Mike, her father, and Rhonda were in front of her, silently and slowly clapping their hands under the water. She'd done it!

She was now officially certified and had completed the one skill that she'd never thought she'd conquer. And it wasn't even that hard. It just took having faith in herself and the courage to go through with it. She was so happy she could hardly stand it.

With everyone now passed off, Mike allowed the group to take the last ten minutes of the dive to explore. Morgan began to think of all the awesome places in the world to dive, all the incredible things to see under the ocean. The island of Cozumel, near Cancún, was supposed to be one of the most amazing places. She would love to go somewhere warm and tropical, where the water was turquoise blue and clear for miles.

Thinking of Cancún and warm, tropical water made her think of Justin. He would be so proud of what she'd just done. And she was so glad she'd done it, even though she might not ever get to dive again, at least for a very long time.

Then she thought of Manny. She wished he would just try to scuba dive one time. She was certain that if he would try, he would love it too. Maybe she could talk to him about it and get him to reconsider. He could try once, just for her sake, couldn't he?

It made her wish that they were going on their honeymoon somewhere tropical so they could go on a dive. She'd much rather do that than drive to Branson, Missouri, to watch country-music acts. Her parents had told her that Branson was a great place to visit and assured her she would enjoy her honeymoon there. But every time someone asked her where she and Manny were going on their honeymoon, she was almost embarrassed to tell them. It just wasn't her idea of a romantic honeymoon destination.

Now that she was thinking about it, she was also embarrassed to tell people that they were going to live in a mobile home for a while until they could save money for a down payment on a house. Manny was convinced it was much more practical to buy a mobile home than to throw money away on an apartment. *But really, a trailer?* Rhonda tapped her on the shoulder, shaking her from the thoughts that had begun to depress her. The sea turtle was back, and Mike had a waterproof camera which he was using to snap photos of each of his students. Rhonda and Morgan posed for a picture with the turtle in the background. She was glad she didn't have to smile for the picture because she wouldn't have been able to.

This isn't right, she told herself as they began to ascend slowly to the surface. Manny was a wonderful man, and she should count herself very fortunate to be marrying him, but it just wasn't normal not to be excited about marriage. It also wasn't right to be embarrassed to tell people about their honeymoon and their little twelve-by-sixty mobile home. But she was. Manny deserved someone who loved him enough that little things like that wouldn't bother her.

And as she burst through the surface of the water into the bright sunlight, it finally dawned on her like a powerful awakening—it was time to either make it right or make a change.

Just as she had to have faith in herself and courage to go through with the skills beneath the water today, she needed to have that same faith and courage to follow those feelings inside, to know without a doubt that she was supposed to marry Manny. Not only for her sake, but for his, too. He deserved to be married to a wife who adored him as much as he adored her.

Feeling a strength and a resolve inside herself, an unwavering determination to take control of the situation, to get it figured out and make it right, Morgan once again felt peace rest upon her. Everyone she knew—her parents, her bishop, Samantha, Stephanie, and Rhonda—all agreed wholeheartedly that marrying Manny was absolutely the right thing to do. The only person who didn't know was the bride. But that was about to change.

Chapter Twenty-One

⟡

She was on a quest to get ahold of Justin. She left messages on his phone and e-mailed him a dozen times, but still no reply. Even Samantha and Trevor hadn't heard from him. Trevor had been trying to track down Justin himself. Now that Samantha and Trevor had separated, Trevor had wanted to talk to Justin about what was going on. Samantha and Trevor were getting marriage counseling after all, and Samantha was encouraged that Trevor had admitted he needed to grow up and focus on his marriage. Still, it was one thing to say it and another thing entirely to do it. Samantha was skeptical but hoped for the best. She loved her husband, but she wasn't going to stay in their marriage unless there were big changes.

Morgan was glad to know Justin wasn't ignoring her only, but what was going on with him that he wasn't returning any phone calls or e-mails? Morgan wondered if something had happened to him, because something had to be wrong for him to completely stop any communication with her and Trevor—especially in Trevor's time of need.

Trevor had Justin's parents' home phone number, but they were traveling abroad and wouldn't be back in the States for another month. Morgan didn't have a month to wait. She had exactly two weeks until the wedding. Two very short weeks.

ॐ ॐ ॐ

"Morgan!"

Her mother's voice vibrated through the phone like a high-pitched alarm.

Clutching a towel around her, Morgan held the receiver away from her ear, then answered, "Mom, what's the matter?"

"You haven't mailed the invitations. They were supposed to go out last Friday." Her mother's panic made Morgan wince with regret that she'd been caught. Laura Rose had wanted the invitations mailed three weeks before the wedding, but Morgan just couldn't get herself to do it yet.

"I'm sorry. I just . . ." She attempted to come up with a viable excuse but found herself stumbling.

"I'm running them to the post office right now. Maybe there's still time to get them there before they close." Her mother was clearly frustrated with the situation. "Honestly, Morgan. I don't understand you. Usually you're so dependable, especially with something this important."

"Mom!" Morgan blurted out, not wanting to get into this discussion but realizing that she had to say something. "Wait."

Her mother didn't answer, but her silence was cold.

"Mom, I'm . . ." she searched frantically for the right words. "I'm not sure . . ." She waited for her mother to demand an explanation, but silence remained on the other end. "I can't send them out yet."

"Why?" her mother asked, with measured patience. Morgan imagined her mother checking her watch to see if she could still get to the post office on time.

"I just don't feel . . ." She wanted to pour her heart out to her mother, to share her deepest feelings, her concerns and worries, but she knew her mother didn't want to hear them. "My heart's not . . ."

"You're heart's not what?" her mother prompted.

Shutting her eyes for a moment, Morgan gathered her strength and courage, but the tears came anyway.

Blinking quickly, she unsuccesfully tried to dry the moisture that stung her eyes.

"Morgan?"

A few tears trickled onto her cheeks. "I know everyone thinks I'm doing the right thing by marrying Manny," Morgan said, her voice thick with emotion.

"That's because it is right," her mother said.

"Then how come I don't feel like it is?"

Her mother chuckled. "Morgan, that's because everyone gets cold feet. It's normal. If you didn't have second thoughts I would be concerned."

"It is?"

"Of course it is."

"But I don't think this is normal 'cold feet,'" she told her mother. "It's more like a cold heart. My heart just isn't feeling what it's supposed to be feeling. Mom," she said in a final statement of her feelings, "I don't know if I love him like he loves me."

Her mother sighed. "Honey, sometimes it's easy to confuse love with romance. Manny is a wonderful young man who adores you. He's a spiritual giant and will be a great husband. You will have a happy, stable, rewarding life with him. Romance isn't all it's cracked up to be. It fades and there's usually nothing left when it's gone. But love is something that will keep a marriage together through good times and bad. It's something that can grow stronger and deeper with each passing year. I love your father more now than I did the day I married him."

Morgan had never heard her mother confess her love for her father in such a way before. It was sweet and touching.

"You know this is a good decision, sweetie. How could it be wrong? He's everything a mother would want for her daughter."

"Wouldn't it be more fair to both of us if I figured out my feelings first?"

"But that's what I'm saying," her mother explained. "The love you have for him will grow because you have all the right things in place for that love to grow. You enjoy being with him and you both want the same things out of marriage. I'm sure if you pray about it you'll feel better. You've got cold feet, that's all. Everyone gets cold feet before they get married. It's normal."

Morgan found herself feeling a little more assured. Her mother was right. Everything was going to be okay. She was already praying and she just needed to be patient. The answer would come. Then she would have the peace and assurance she needed.

"Can I still have one more day?" Morgan asked.

Her mother didn't answer right away, but Morgan didn't want to relent. She needed to try to reach Justin one last time.

"All right, we can wait until tomorrow."

They both said good-bye, and Morgan stared at the receiver for several minutes after she had hung up the phone.

Then, going to her bedroom, she knelt by the side of her bed and prayed like she'd never prayed before.

❦ ❦ ❦

Luckily, that evening Manny had some kind of meeting to go to so she had the night all to herself. It was time to track down Justin. Dialing Samantha's phone number, she was surprised when Trevor answered instead of Samantha.

"Hi, Morgan. How's it going?" Trevor asked.

"Okay," she answered. "Am I calling at a bad time?"

"I'm just waiting for Sam to get dressed. I'm taking her to the city for dinner."

Morgan smiled in hopes that they would work things out between them, especially with a baby on the way. Then she realized that maybe talking to Trevor was better than Samantha. He probably knew the answers to her questions more than Samantha would.

"Trevor, I need to get in touch with Justin. Do you have any idea how I can reach him?"

Trevor let out a frustrated sigh. "I've been trying to reach him myself. I don't know what's up with that guy. He's not answering his cell phone, and I've even got a work number, but when I call the message says his voice mail is full so I can't even leave a message."

"Same here. What about e-mail?"

"My messages get returned. How about you?"

"I haven't had any luck either," she replied. "Do you know the name of his company? Maybe I could call the company and have him tracked down."

"I don't know," Trevor said. "And other than his parents, I don't know who else we can call. I've never not been able to reach him, so I've never needed to know all of this. Sorry."

Morgan didn't reply. There was nothing she could do. Her hands were tied.

"Listen, Morgan," Trevor said. "Maybe it's none of my business, but Samantha told me about what's going on, and I just thought I'd tell you that even though Justin's like a brother to me, if I were you I wouldn't wait around for him or postpone your wedding for him."

"You wouldn't?"

"He's got a lot going on down there in Brazil with this company and his career. And to be honest, even though he hasn't come out and said so, I think there's a lot more going on between him and Marika. I think the reason we're not hearing from him is because he's too involved to be taking phone calls and checking his e-mail. He may not even be at work right now. Sometimes he does some traveling while he's there. For all we know he could be in Rio right now."

"Oh." Disappointment deflated the hope inside of her. That was where Marika worked as a model. Was he in Rio with her? "Trevor, do you think he's with her? With Marika?"

"Yeah," he answered. "I'm really sorry, Morgan. But I do."

Her bottom lip trembled. She forced her breathing to remain steady, but tears threatened, and her heart ached in her chest. "Okay." She had to whisper. "Thanks, Trevor."

She didn't give him a chance to say good-bye. She barely got the phone hung up before she burst into tears. It was time to accept reality. Justin was gone from her life. She'd done everything she could to reach him, with no luck.

It was over.

☙ ☙ ☙

Morgan had promised her mother she'd come over for lunch on her day off, but she wasn't hungry. All she needed was a pain reliever. Her head was throbbing. Holding her head in her hands, Morgan sat at the kitchen table, wishing she could just curl up in a corner and disappear. She didn't want to face anyone or anything today—especially reality.

Her mother came in through the back door with a handful of flowers cut from her garden. "I didn't hear you come in," she said as she held up the flowers. "My roses have never looked this good. Don't you think, Morgan?"

Morgan didn't answer.

"Morgan? Honey, what's the matter? Are you sick?"

Morgan nodded. That word worked just fine. Sick, depressed, disappointed, frustrated . . . the list could go on, but for now, sick was close enough.

"Can I get you something? Have you got a bug? I hear something's going around. Have you got a fever?"

Morgan shook her head.

"What about the temple tonight? Should I call and reschedule?"

Morgan was going through the temple for the first time that night. It was something she didn't want to miss. She believed it would help her draw closer to the Spirit and that she would get the peace she needed.

"I'll be okay."

"Maybe you should stay home from work this afternoon, get some rest." That was the first thing that made sense to Morgan. Maybe she should crawl back into bed and escape life for a while.

She lifted her head off her hands. "Yeah, maybe I will."

"Honey, you have rings around your eyes. You look horrible. Do you want me to call the library for you?"

"Sure," Morgan said, appreciating her mother's gesture of kindness. She pushed herself up from the table. "Can I just go upstairs and rest? My head hurts too badly to drive to my apartment."

"Sure, I'll come check on you in a minute, sweetie," her mother said.

"Okay." Morgan turned to leave, then she stopped. "Oh, and mom, you can go ahead and mail the invitations if you want." Her talk with Trevor had helped her face the fact that Justin had moved on, just like she needed to do. Still, that didn't mean it would be easy to get Justin out of her heart.

Her mother's reaction was more skeptical than surprised. "Morgan, are you sure?"

Morgan nodded as tears threatened. If she hung around much longer she'd fall apart right there on the kitchen floor. "I don't feel well. I have to go lie down."

She didn't wait for her mother to comment. Instead, she hurried up the stairs to her old room where she crawled into bed, pulled a blanket over her head, and prayed for sleep to come. It was her only way to escape.

ॐ ॐ ॐ

"Mom?" Morgan called when she finally came downstairs. It was late afternoon and her stomach was complaining. Her father was at work and her mother was probably at the grocery store. Morgan grabbed a cinnamon-raisin bagel, then went outside on the porch to sit in the sun. Maybe absorbing some warmth and light would perk her up and help her get recharged again. Something had to help.

Chewing a bite of bagel, she laid her head back and closed her eyes, letting the sun's rays bathe her in a golden glow. Her headache was gone and she felt much better. She was actually looking forward to going to the temple. Maybe this experience tonight would be the pivotal point in helping her focus on her problem so she could put her heart and soul into her future.

Resting there in the sun, hearing the birds chatter in the trees, and feeling the gentle breeze on her face reminded her of a time several months ago in Cancún when she'd basked in the sun and been surprised to have Justin join her. It had been their first real introduction.

The memory came with pain, which she hoped would someday fade so she could look back on her vacation with fondness instead of agony.

Pushing the memory from her mind, she got up from the chair and went inside. The best thing to do was eliminate anything that triggered any recollection of her time with Justin—at least for now. Those memories distracted her from what she needed to do. It was time to exercise control over her heart and her mind.

She wanted this day to be special. She'd looked forward to going through the temple her entire life, and finally tonight it was going to happen. Much preparation had gone into this day. She'd read everything she could to help her understand the things she would be taught. More than anything, she wanted to be prepared so she could have the Spirit with her.

An unexpected peace warmed her heart. Everything was going to be okay. She didn't know what was going to happen, but she was turning her life over to the Lord. It was in His hands, and she knew that no matter what, she would be okay with whatever happened.

ॐ ॐ ॐ

"So," Manny said, taking her hands in his as they stood at the entrance to the temple. "Are you ready?"

Morgan nodded. "I've been looking forward to this for a long time."

"We haven't had a lot of time together lately. How are you doing?"

"I'm fine," she said. "Everything's good."

He smiled. "I'm glad to hear that. You've seemed distant."

"I know; I'm sorry. But I'm okay now," she told him.

He smiled broadly, then pulled her into a hug. "Just think, the next time we're here will be to get married."

"Yeah," she said. "Less than two weeks."

"I wish it were today. Two weeks seems like forever."

Morgan had the thought that she wished it were forever, but she quickly pushed the thought from her mind. It was time to be positive and focus on what was important. And that started by controlling her thoughts.

"I think they're waiting inside," she said. "Maybe we'd better go in."

Before he let her go, he gave her a kiss. "I love you, Morgan."

A gush of emotion came unexpectedly. She gave him a tremulous smile and tears filled her eyes. She couldn't speak. Manny chuckled and gave her a big hug. "Don't cry. I know this is a big day for you, but you're going to love every minute inside the temple."

Morgan let him think that she was just nervous about going through for her first time. But she wasn't; she was excited about being inside the temple. She couldn't tell him the real reason why she was crying. She couldn't tell him that it was because she couldn't tell him she loved him back.

Chapter Twenty-Two

Morgan helped her mother clean the kitchen after Manny left. They'd come back there after the temple and had a wonderful meal her mother had prepared in advance. Stephanie and Leo, and the bishop and his wife had joined them at the temple and come over for the meal.

It had been enjoyable, but it was nice to have everyone gone. Morgan hadn't really had a chance to think about everything that had just happened—all the wonderful things that had gone on inside the temple—and she wanted to contemplate and reflect upon the feelings she'd experienced while she'd been there, most importantly the feeling of peace that had encircled her throughout the entire session.

Finally, she was blessed with the peace and joy she'd been craving for such a long time. It seemed as if her concerns and worries had been left outside as she walked through the temple doors. All that existed was joy.

There was only one problem. She'd also received an answer, an undeniable, without-a-doubt answer that left her with no choice but to follow through on the answer—no matter what it took.

"I'll wipe the counters," her mother told her. "Thanks for helping me clean up."

"And thanks for the great meal, Mom."

Morgan left the kitchen and found herself joining her father in the living room. He was in his favorite chair. She sat on the couch nearby.

He put down the paper and said, "So, how're you doing?"

"I'm good," she answered.

"You enjoyed the temple?"

"It was amazing. I'd like to go back tomorrow."

Her father chuckled. "That's good. You should go as often as you can."

"It's very peaceful there."

"Yes, it is. Sometimes it's the only place to find true peace."

"Everyone was so nice. I felt such love from the workers."

"Kind of makes you see what heaven's going to be like, doesn't it?"

"I thought the same thing," she said.

Her father didn't reply but seemed to sense she'd come in the room for a reason. And she had.

"Dad?"

"Yes, sweetie."

"I need to talk to you."

"Okay."

"This is going to be pretty serious."

"Oh?" He smiled with surprise. "Should I strap myself into my chair?"

"No, really. I've been struggling with something for a long time and I've been ignoring the impressions in my heart. But tonight I received a very strong answer to my prayers. I need to talk to you and mom about it."

"This does sound serious. Let's get your mother in here, then." He called for his wife, who came into the room after a moment.

"What is it?" Laura Rose finished rubbing lotion on her hands, then removed her apron.

"I think you'd better sit down, dear."

Laura's face went pale.

Morgan knew that what she was about to do was going to cause her mother great heartache and probably ruin their relationship for a long time, but she didn't falter. She knew what she needed to do, and she wasn't going to let anything stop her—she'd come to understand her Father in Heaven's will. She realized that she'd known the answer all along; she had just let everyone else's opinions become more important than what she knew in her heart.

"Go ahead, sweetie," her father encouraged.

"Mom, Dad," she began. "I think you both know I've been struggling with my decision to get married."

Laura's mouth opened, but Morgan quickly held up her hand to let her mother know she needed to talk without interruption.

"I'd like to ask you both a question. Maybe you can each take a turn answering it."

Her mother fidgeted uncomfortably but Morgan didn't stop. She knew her mother had hoped that her daughter had finally worked through her "ridiculous" reservations about marrying the most wonderful boy in the world. But it wasn't going to be that easy, and Morgan needed both of her parents' help.

"What do you think the most important thing is in a marriage?"

Her father nodded, contemplating her question. But her mother's face grew pinched with anxiety. Morgan wasn't giving up. She'd made a decision and they needed to hear it tonight.

"Dad, maybe you could go first," Morgan requested.

"All right. Well, I think you need the basics like common goals and the same beliefs. But I also think it's important to be best friends. I also think it's important to laugh together."

Morgan nodded. She'd always trusted her father's counsel and advice. Even as a teenager she'd listened to him, knowing that his guidelines and rules for dating and curfew were based on his love for her.

"Mom?" Morgan knew her mother wasn't going to willingly add to the conversation. As far as her mother was concerned, marrying Manny was a no-brainer. But Morgan was determined to help her mother understand what she was feeling. Somehow.

"I agree with your father," her mother said quickly.

"What else?" Morgan asked her father, since her mother apparently wasn't going to add to the list.

"I think it's important that you understand that as individuals you'll grow and learn and change, and this is good, but make sure you stay close to each other and do things together so it can strengthen you as a couple and you can grow together. Plus, you need to communicate and spend time with each other. This can get tricky when you have children, jobs, and Church callings, but it is very important for your relationship with your spouse."

Again, Morgan felt his advice was inspired. How many marriages had fallen apart due to this problem? Many times the couples involved weren't even aware that they were growing apart until it was too late.

"What do you think, honey?" Greg solicited his wife's opinion.

"I agree," she said.

Morgan sensed her mother's demeanor softening, but not enough. Morgan wanted more; she wanted her mother to actually see where she was coming from—and, even though it was a mighty stretch, to actually agree with Morgan's decision.

"That's good, Dad. What else?"

"Well . . ." He thought for a moment. "I certainly don't have all the answers, but I think one thing kids tend to do is think they can change a person, or think that the person will change for them. This is a setup for problems. First of all, you have to be able to be yourself around the person you marry, and second of all, the person you marry needs to love you for who you are. Now that doesn't mean that being around this person can't inspire you, because I think a good marriage does that. Just being with that person makes you want to be a better you. But this notion kids have that they can change the other person isn't good. It just doesn't work out that way. Right, Laura?"

Laura nodded. "It's true."

Morgan pondered her father's comments. Everything he'd said supported what she was about to do. Manny was a good man, but he wasn't her best friend. He didn't seem to be truly interested in her feelings. He asked questions, but when she tried to share her feelings, he didn't listen—not with his heart, anyway. They just didn't have the connection she needed in a relationship. And his plans for the future were so set in stone that she knew her desires would never see fulfillment.

And as for being herself around him, she wasn't. She didn't feel like she could just relax and be herself. She always felt like she had to be guarded about the things she said and did. Just like when she'd wanted to sing karaoke with Stephanie at the restaurant. Ultimately it was her decision to back out, but she had felt she would embarrass him or something. No, she'd realized, going through the motions wasn't enough. A person's heart had to be there. It just had to.

She was finally ready to tell them. "Thanks for your advice. I believe everything you've said and want those things for myself when I get married." She cleared her throat and gathered her courage. *Here goes,* she thought. "I know how you feel about Manny. I know how everyone feels about him. He is a wonderful man and will make a great husband and father." She looked down at her hands in her lap, then added, "But not for me, because I can't marry him. I'm sorry. I just don't love him." She looked at her parents, waiting for the explosion.

Her mother opened her mouth to speak, but clamped it shut. Her father raised his eyebrows and pulled his we-have-a-challenge-before-us face, but he also said nothing.

Morgan decided to give supportive evidence of her statement. "All those things you said—I don't have those with Manny. And I don't love him the way he loves me. It's not fair to him or to me. When he tells me he loves me, I can't say it back. That can't be good for a marriage. And I can't make myself feel something that's not there. I've tried to love him. I've tried for everyone's sake—everyone's but my own. But I don't. And I can't fake it anymore."

Morgan's mother finally spoke up. "Does this have something to do with this boy in Brazil?"

"Yes, kind of. But no. I mean, I connected with Justin in a way I've never connected with anyone in my life. Everything you said tonight, Dad, is how I felt with Justin. I could share my deepest thoughts and feelings with him. We laughed together. I could be myself around him and he liked me for who I was. I wanted to be the best me I could be. It was a very inspiring and fulfilling experience."

Laura Rose's eyebrows arched in skepticism.

"I know you can't understand this, Mom, because I know how much you care about Manny. The bottom line is this: I don't even know where Justin is. I haven't heard from him for a while and there may not ever be a future with him, okay? Even though I plan to find out what's happened to him, right now this isn't about him. It's about Manny. He isn't right for me. You both know me better than anyone in the world. Can't you see it?" Her tone was pleading. They had to understand; they just had to.

Her parents looked at her for a minute, then her mother spoke. "Yes, I can."

Morgan's eyes opened wide with surprise. "Mom?"

"I think Manny is the most wonderful young man in the world, but it's true that you two aren't a perfect fit—at least, not these last few months."

"Laura?" Greg's mouth hung open with his own surprise at her revelation.

"Why didn't you say something?" Morgan asked her mother. "Why didn't you help me more, or . . . I don't know, something . . . " Morgan's heart filled with disappointment. Her mother knew they weren't right for each other, yet she encouraged them to get married.

"Because I thought that by now you would have fallen in love with him. I had hoped you would."

"And you were willing to let me marry him, even though you knew I hadn't?" Morgan felt completely betrayed by her mother.

"Actually, no."

"Laura, what do you mean?" her husband asked the question Morgan was too amazed to ask.

"I had my doubts. Enough that . . ." Laura gave an exasperated sigh. "That I didn't mail the announcements."

Morgan gasped. Greg looked at his wife with complete shock.

Laura quickly spoke up. "Something told me to wait until after we went to the temple tonight."

"Well," Greg said. "I don't know what to say."

"I tried to ignore it," Laura said to her daughter. "I tried not to see the pain in your eyes or hear the heartache in your words, but it was there, and frankly, I don't know how Manny hasn't picked up on it. Of course, maybe that's one of the things that's wrong; you need someone who is more in tune to your feelings. Communication is vital to a marriage, just like your father said." Laura looked at her husband, her expression filled with love. "I could have never made it through your sister's death without your father. He was so patient to listen to me every time I needed his shoulder to cry on. He let me grieve. He shared the pain with me. I think it made our marriage stronger, even though it was the worst thing we've ever been through. I want that for you. I want you to have a husband who will listen when you have something to say, whether he's interested or not. Someone like your father. I guess Manny isn't that person."

Tears streamed down Morgan's face as the three of them finally arrived at the same point of understanding and realization. Not only did her parents understand, but they supported her. "Thank you," Morgan said as she got up from her chair. Both of her parents stood, and the three met in the center of the room and embraced. Peace settled upon them, helping them know that all was well. It wouldn't be easy. Telling Manny would be one of the hardest things she'd ever done, but the peace in her heart and resolve in her soul let her know her decision was right. For the first time in weeks, the heaviness she felt was gone.

"I might as well not put it off any longer," she said. "I think I'll call Manny right now."

❦ ❦ ❦

Manny's expression went blank. They sat on the couch in her parent's living room, facing each other.

"What did you just say?" he asked.

Morgan felt the queasiness in her stomach grow stronger. Her palms began to sweat.

"I said I'm calling off the wedding."

His eyes narrowed and the muscles in his jaw clenched with tension.

"I'm sorry," she added, wishing there was some way not to hurt him. She reached for his hand but he jerked it away.

She recoiled at his sudden burst of anger, but she wasn't surprised. He had every right to be upset.

"You mean you want to change the date?"

"No, Manny. I don't want to change the date. I just can't marry you."

"Why?" he shot at her. "Why can't you marry me?"

"Manny, you are a wonderful man. I admire—"

"Stop!" he interrupted. "I don't want to hear it. Just tell me why."

His level of intensity made her nervous. She scooted away from him a few inches. "I don't . . ." She swallowed, afraid of fueling his anger. "I don't love you."

He stared long and hard at her, like her news was the last thing he'd expected her to say. Was he so sure of himself that this revelation was out of the realm of possibility?

"Manny, please say something."

"You don't love me." He stated the words and nodded his head slowly. Then, raising his voice and narrowing his gaze, he stared at her and said, "You'd better be sure this is what you want."

She nodded. "I've thought long and hard—"

"You're making a big mistake," he interrupted. "I've had plenty of girls to choose from. And I won't take you back. You'll change your mind and realize what a big mistake you've made, but it will be too late."

He's had plenty of girls to choose from? She couldn't believe it. She hadn't seen much of it until now, but his ego was still there. "That risk is what has made this decision so hard," she told him evenly—trying not to be offended at his behavior, since she knew he was probably acting out of hurt.

"Oh really?" he mocked. "Well, you've certainly had a funny way of showing me you *don't* love me."

"But don't you see? I tried. I wanted to fall in love. Everything looked right. It seemed natural that love would follow. But I just can't make myself feel something that's not there."

"So that's it? We just call it off? Well, that's just great, Morgan. It's not like everything hasn't been arranged, you know? Schedules have been changed, plans have been made. What about the invitations? The gifts? I've already paid for our honeymoon and put a deposit on the mobile home," he fumed. "And what do we tell people? Do you realize how embarrassing this is, especially for m—"

He stopped himself, but she knew what he was going to say. His pride was wounded and since he'd never been rejected, he didn't know how to handle it.

"Especially for you?" she said. "I guess you don't think this is hard for me?"

"Hey, you're the one calling it off. Not me."

"You know what?" she said, feeling a flicker of anger ignite in her heart. "Just tell everyone that you changed your mind and decided you didn't want to marry me."

Manny bolted to his feet and paced across the floor, then he spun around. "You're a piece of work, you know that?" he spat at her. "You've always been a little weird. I guess I thought you'd changed. But just because you look good doesn't mean you've got everything up here." He tapped his finger on the side of his head.

"What do you mean by that?"

He shrugged. "If you can't see what you're giving up, then you prove my point exactly."

"You mean, that out of all the girls you could have chosen, I was the lucky one?"

"You said it; I didn't."

"But that's what you mean, isn't it?" She didn't want it to turn into an argument, so she tried to stay cool and calm. "You don't have to worry about anyone knowing, because we didn't send out the invitations," she told him.

His expression melted from his face.

She shut her eyes, wishing that it didn't have to hurt him. But in the long run, wouldn't they both be happier?

"How long have you had this planned?"

"Manny, aren't you listening to me?" she asked. "I wanted this to work out, but I realized tonight, in the temple, that it just wasn't right. It doesn't mean I don't care about you. I do. I care enough to back out before it's too late. You need to find the right person, someone I'm sure you'll be much happier with."

"So is that what you've done, found someone you're happier with?"

"No. This isn't about anyone else. This is about us."

"What about that guy you met in Cancún? You still have a thing for him, don't you?"

She knew that even a week ago she couldn't have honestly answered that question, but now she knew her feelings for Justin weren't standing in her way of loving Manny. Nothing was. It just wasn't there. They weren't suited for each other. It was as simple as that.

"Manny, this is just about us. I'm so sorry. I really am." She removed the ring from her finger.

"I'll bet you are," he said as his face reddened, his words coming in angry, measured tones. "You will never do better than me."

She knew that to say more would only give him more ammunition to launch back at her, and she wasn't up to a fight. She truly was doing this out of sincere concern for his feelings and happiness, and for both of their futures. He deserved a wife who adored him and worshiped the ground he walked on—which he clearly wanted, she thought, still surprised at his pride and aggression. He needed someone who would let him plan and control her life and not feel trapped by it. That person wasn't her. She couldn't be who she wasn't. She couldn't pretend any longer.

He snatched the ring out of her hand, spun on his heel, and started for the door, then turned and said, "Someday you'll regret doing this."

Her reply was quick and without malice. "And I believe that someday you'll thank me for doing this."

With an angry huff he yanked open the door and slammed it shut, giving the windows a rattle that would have measured on the Richter scale.

Morgan stood in stunned silence, taking in shaky breaths. It had gone as well as it possibly could have. She'd hoped he wouldn't be quite so hurt and angry and that maybe they could have parted on civil terms—maybe not friends, but certainly not enemies. But he'd made it clear that wouldn't be the case.

She didn't hear her mother come up behind her until she spoke. "I didn't think it would go over too well with him," she said. "But I sure heard a different side of him tonight."

"You hurt his pride more than his heart, I think," her father said, coming up on the other side of her. "He'll be fine. You watch, he'll have someone else wearing that ring in no time."

"I hope so," Morgan said. "I felt terrible hurting him like that. I really do want him to be happy."

"You handled that with real class, sweetie," her mother said, wrapping an arm around her daughter.

"You sure did," her father said. "We were proud of the way you explained everything to him. You could have gotten defensive and mean, like he did, but you didn't. And you're right—he'll realize one day that it was for the best."

"Are you okay?" her mother asked.

Morgan nodded. "Yeah. I think so. Of course, it is going to be awkward telling people what happened when they ask. Maybe I should change wards for a while."

Her father chuckled. "It'll be fine. We'll help you through this."

A sudden rush of emotion knotted in her throat. "Thanks, Dad, I know you will," she managed to say. "You too, Mom. I don't know what I'd do without either of you."

Chapter Twenty-Three

Luckily, church on Sunday was a special area conference so she didn't have to go to their regular ward, which spared her a few more days until the backlash hit. Morgan relied upon her inner strength and resolve, knowing that she had done the right thing.

She'd called her closest friends to tell them of the news. Surprise and shock were about the only words to describe the reactions. Samantha accused her of being brainless. Rhonda, on the other hand, had been understanding and had said that going to Branson on a honeymoon was about the worst idea of the century.

Morgan wasn't surprised that the bishop already knew when she called him. He'd already spoken with Manny, and the account the bishop heard was surprisingly close to the truth. Not that she'd expect Manny to lie, but she'd thought he'd slant the story a little his direction. The bishop set up a time to meet with her during the week and said he'd keep her in his prayers.

So that was that. It was over.

Now what did she do?

Risking her job but needing the break, she took the week off. The first few days she spent either sleeping or watching television. The next few days she ventured outside and sat in the sunshine, reading magazines and sipping on raspberry smoothies. By the weekend she actually ran a few errands and went to the gym.

And instead of going to work on Monday, she decided to play hooky one more day and drive to San Francisco State University to meet with James Halladay, a professor in the art department there. She was deciding between SFSU and UC Davis and hoped that a visit to each of the universities would help her make that decision. With her future free and her schedule blank, there was no reason to put off going back to college. She would start classes in the fall.

As Morgan searched for something to wear for the trip, she started pulling items out of her closet that were either out of date, didn't fit, or were in the category of what-was-I-thinking-when-I-bought-this ugly. She ended up with more clothes in a pile on the floor than she had in her closet, but she was in the mood for a fresh start and a new beginning. The problem with cleaning out her closet was that some of the clothes brought back memories, and as much as she'd been through the last few days, anything that triggered her emotions brought unwanted tears.

Looking in the mirror, she wrapped the beautiful turquoise sarong Justin had given her around her waist, and in a flash she was recalling every feeling, every smell, every sensory memory of Cancún, Justin, and five days in paradise.

It was a stupid move, but she couldn't stop herself from grabbing her photo album and looking through the pictures that now seemed unreal. Was that really her, standing there next to Justin? Had she been the only one affected by their time together? Obviously so, because his feelings had faded away into nothing. Hers had faded away into memories that created a painful ache in her heart.

She almost didn't answer the phone when it rang, since she noticed the library's number on the caller I.D., but it wasn't the main number, so she knew it was Rhonda.

"So what's going on?" Rhonda asked.

Morgan slammed the photo album shut, as if Rhonda could see it. "Oh, not much," Morgan answered. "Just going through my closet."

"I hate that 'no solicitor' message I get when I call you. Does that thing really work?" Rhonda asked.

"I don't get any calls from salesmen," Morgan replied, untying the sarong and putting it back on a hanger. She couldn't part with it or any of the clothes she'd worn on her vacation.

"You getting rid of anything good? Not that it would fit me."

"Just junk. Winter clothes I've had for years and stuff I wouldn't be caught dead wearing."

"Hey, that describes everything in my closet. We need to go shopping."

"Just name the day. I'll be there," Morgan said.

"So, how are you? We haven't had much of a chance to talk."

"I'm okay. It's kind of weird to think I would have been married in two days."

"Yeah, I bet that is weird. Aren't you glad your mother didn't mail those invitations? Can you imagine how hard it would have been to contact everyone about the wedding being called off?"

"I know. Mom's making me pull all the stamps off so she can reuse them. I guess that's only fair, though."

"So you haven't had any second thoughts about calling off the wedding, have you?"

"Actually, those would be third thoughts," Morgan told her. "The second thoughts were the ones that made me realize I didn't love Manny. And no, I haven't had any regrets. I mean, now that I can be honest with myself and everyone else, I can see so clearly how wrong Manny and I were for each other. We didn't share that many common interests or even enjoy doing the same things. And his ego and unchangeable plan for the future really didn't help matters."

"You were smart to end it, then." She paused. "So . . . I guess you haven't heard from your other friend, then, have you?"

"Justin? No, but it's funny you'd ask—I was just thinking about him."

"I wonder what happened to him?"

"Me too. I may never know, but someday I'd like to thank him."

"For what?"

"Up until I went on that vacation in February, the world seemed flat and one-dimensional for me. Justin helped my view of the world become three-dimensional. He helped me appreciate how wonderful God's creations are. Of course, maybe in a way it wasn't good," Morgan added as an afterthought.

"What do you mean?"

"If Justin hadn't shown me what I had inside of me and how much I was missing, the life Manny offered might have been more appealing. But the way I am now, I know I would always wish for more. It's like the difference between snorkeling and scuba diving. Snorkeling is like someone on the outside, looking in. But scuba diving lets you become part of the experience, to actually feel, touch, and live the experience, instead of observing it from the surface. Does that make sense?"

"It makes perfect sense, kiddo. And it's much better to find out these things now, rather than after the wedding. I mean, especially how you guys believe in eternal marriage and stuff. I mean, when it's the right guy, eternity sounds pretty good. But with the wrong guy, that could be a really long time."

Morgan chuckled. "Yeah, I guess it could." The phone beeped twice, telling her that another call was coming through. A series of strange numbers came up on the caller I.D. display. She'd seen this number come up before, but every time she'd answered there was never anyone on the line. "Hang on just a sec so I can see who this is."

Just as it happened every other time, a few beeps sounded, then the line went blank.

She got back on the line with Rhonda and said, "Sorry, no one was there. What were we saying?"

"By the way, what's up with your cell phone? I tried to call you on it."

"My dad's getting us a family plan so we can have more minutes, so I don't have service right now. I'll let you know what my new number is as soon as I get it."

"Okay. Well, I need to go. Don't worry about things here at the library. Nothing's new—we're still using the Dewey decimal system."

Morgan laughed. "I'll see you at work tomorrow."

"All right, and we'll plan a big shopping day."

Morgan was so grateful for her friend's thoughtfulness. The phone call meant a lot to her, and she realized now more than ever just how much friends and family support meant, during both good times and difficult times.

❧ ❧ ❧

She'd finally organized her closet and was going through her drawers when the phone rang again. She smiled as she answered it.

"Hey, Sammy," she exclaimed, glad to hear from her friend. It had taken a while, but she knew Samantha would finally come around and accept her decision about calling off the wedding.

"Are you still talking to me?" her friend asked.

"Of course I am."

"I'm so sorry I wasn't more understanding when you called. You have no idea how hard it is with these hormones. I feel like my personality has been altered along with my stomach. I'm getting so fat."

"No, you're not. You don't even show yet."

"I can't button my pants anymore."

"Maybe you need some new clothes. Rhonda and I are going shopping soon. You want to come?"

"Could I? New clothes would definitely help," Samantha said. "So, how are you?"

"I'm fine. I've had a few awkward moments with ward members, but other than that I'm fine."

"I guess you haven't talked to Manny, have you?"

"No. I doubt I ever will. In fact, I'll be surprised if I ever see him again. He was coming to our ward, but he's going to his uncle's ward again."

"So what are you doing—hold on, someone's trying to call," Samantha said with a click of the phone.

While Morgan waited for her to come back on the line, she pulled open her sock drawer and began pulling out orphaned socks and socks with holes in them. A moment later Samantha came back.

"I swear, these weird numbers keep coming up, but when I answer the call no one is there."

"That's been happening to me—" Then a thought occurred to her. Morgan dropped her handful of socks. *What if . . . ?*

"Sammy, when you answer are there a couple of beeps, then nothing?"

"Yeah, that's exactly what happens."

"What number is coming up?"

They compared phone numbers and both of them nearly simultaneously had a heart attack. It was the same number.

"Sammy, the same person is trying to call both of us and isn't getting through."

"Do you think it might be Justin?"

"Who else would be trying to call us from a weird number?" Morgan said.

"Well, hurry up and call the number and see who it is, then call me back."

"Okay," Morgan said, her nerves sparking wildly. "Stay by the phone."

Morgan hung up and pushed several buttons to call the number in question.

There were several clicks and a beep, followed by a fast busy signal, not like the normal busy signal she was used to.

She tried again, but the same thing happened.

She checked the number on the phone with the regular number Justin had given her, but none of the numbers matched up.

Quickly she called Samantha back. "I don't get an answer. I don't know what's going on. It seems like it's busy, but the signal is weird."

"Same here. We need to keep trying; maybe one of us will get through."

"Okay. Call if anything happens."

They both hung up, and Morgan tried the number again. Her heart pumped wildly and she could barely dial the phone. Once again she got the strange busy signal.

She nearly jumped a foot off the floor when the phone rang just as she hung it up.

"Hello?" she answered breathlessly, daring to hope it was him.

"You know, I thought we were better friends than that."

"Stephanie? Is that you?" Morgan said quickly. Her friend sounded upset. "What do you mean?"

"I mean, I thought we were better friends than just getting a phone call from your mother telling me your wedding was off. You could have talked to me about what was going on before then, you know."

"Steph, I appreciate that. I do. But I did try to talk to you. You didn't understand."

"What do you mean?"

"It's okay. I know you're one of Manny's biggest fans, so I don't expect you to understand why I did what I did. And frankly, it's hard to explain, but . . ." She thought for a moment. "Okay, let me ask you this; what if Leo wouldn't let you sing karaoke anymore?"

"What?" Stephanie exclaimed.

"Just tell me—what if he said you couldn't sing karaoke anymore?"

"But he wouldn't do that. He knows how much I like to sing and perform. Besides that, he likes to sing too, so he would never ask that of me."

"That's the problem. Manny would. He wanted our marriage to be the way he wanted it, not the way I wanted it. He wanted me to be the person he wanted me to be, not the person I really was. He had our lives planned without even asking what I wanted. I'm sorry, but I decided I couldn't go through my life knowing I could never sing karaoke. Even if I never do get up in front of an audience and sing, it should be my decision, not because he disapproved of me doing it. Does that make sense?"

Stephanie didn't answer for a moment, then, with a gentler tone to her voice, she said, "You know what? It does make sense."

"Good. I'm glad you understand." Morgan glanced at the clock on the microwave. She was running out of time to get to her appointment. "Steph, I'm late for an appointment. I'll call you later, okay? I've missed you."

"I've missed you too."

Morgan hurried to get dressed, then flew to her car and raced from the parking lot, pushing the speed limit all the way to the university. She felt elated, anxious to take the first step to a new experience and hopefully a new life.

Weaving in and out of traffic, she prayed she could make her appointment on time. Driving into San Francisco always made her nervous. She didn't know her way around and had gotten lost there many times, but she had good directions today, and she felt unusually brave with the thought of starting a new phase of her life.

She checked the clock on the radio and noticed the flashing date. She was supposed to meet Justin in two days in San Francisco. Her used-to-be wedding day. A day she would probably always remember with some degree of nausea.

Justin wouldn't be there. He was in Brazil, probably in Rio. She didn't even consider the possibility that he'd be there. Nothing could convince her that he'd be in the United States, let alone in San Francisco, in two days.

Or would he? Had he been the one trying to call her?

Besides that, they'd promised, hadn't they?

With her thoughts preoccupied by the question, she signaled to change lanes to get around a semitrailer. Just as she moved into the other lane, the car in front of her got the same idea and, without any advance warning, barreled into her lane.

Morgan swerved to miss the car but nearly struck a barrier on the side of road. Quickly she steered back into the lane of traffic as her back wheels squealed and skidded, propelling her car directly toward the other car. The last thing Morgan remembered was screaming as the two cars collided. Then everything went black.

ॐ ॐ ॐ

"How is she?" Samantha asked as she met Morgan's parents in the waiting room the UCSF Medical Center.

"The doctor hasn't come out yet. We don't know," Morgan's father answered.

Laura Rose reached out to Samantha and gave her hand a squeeze. She wiped at her red, tear-filled eyes with a tissue.

They sat on some chairs and watched for the first sign of the doctor.

"Is her car—"

"Totaled," Greg Rose answered. "The EMTs were amazed she made it out alive."

"I can't believe this," Laura Rose said. "She didn't even tell us she was going to the city today. I would have come with her. This wouldn't have happened."

"Honey," Greg Rose said as he patted his wife's hand, "she's going to be okay."

"I know." Laura sniffed into her tissue, then buried her head in her husband's shoulder as he circled his arms around her and held her close.

Samantha looked at the couple clinging to each other for strength and courage to face the outcome, whatever that would be. She thought of herself down the road. Would Trevor be there for her, weathering the storms with her?

Life was hard enough without having to face it all alone. She needed the strength of a devoted, loving husband and faith in God to help her. What if something happened to this child she carried inside her? Already she loved her baby. Feeling the stirrings of the growth of new life inside caused her to look deeper at life and its meaning. She'd been taught long ago about the purpose of life—where she'd come from, why she was here, and where she would go when she died. For the last few years she hadn't thought of anything but what was going on at the moment. Where she'd come from had seemed to make no difference, and where she was going seemed to be a silly thing to worry about, until now.

Her life held a much greater meaning as she thought about taking care of a child, a child who was completely dependent on her for everything. More than anything, she wanted to be a good mother. She wanted to be a good wife and have a happy marriage and family. Seeing Morgan's parents in front of her, overwhelmed with worry but getting through the crisis together with a unified faith in God, convinced her that there was only one way she wanted to live her life and raise her child.

"Excuse me, are you the Roses?" They all looked up to see a doctor in green scrubs.

Mr. Rose jumped to his feet. "Yes, sir. We are."

"Your daughter's been wheeled into the recovery room, and she's resting peacefully. There was no internal bleeding. Her neck is sore from the impact and could be sore for several weeks. She took quite a jolt. She's bruised some ribs and has scrapes from the seat belt and air bag, but those things saved her life. You're daughter's sore, but she's going to be fine. I'd like to keep her in the hospital a few days for observation, though."

"When can we see her?" Greg asked.

"I'll have the nurse come and get you when she wakes up."

"Thank you, doctor," Laura managed to say.

"I'm always happy to deliver good news to families." The doctor smiled and was on his way.

Laura collapsed into her husband's arms and cried again, this time with tears of joy.

ಠ ಠ ಠ

"You want some tapioca?" Morgan asked Samantha, who was sitting next to her bed.

Samantha pulled a face. "Ugh, no. I hated that stuff as a kid."

"So did I, but the hospital's food is surprisingly good." Morgan took one last spoonful, then pushed the tray away. She was stuffed. "And thanks again for the flowers. You didn't need to bring them. Especially since I'm probably going home this afternoon."

"I wanted to bring them yesterday, but your mom said you slept most of the day, so it was good I waited until today to come. By the way, they're from Trevor too. In fact, they were his idea."

"Really?" Morgan couldn't hide her shock.

"Yeah. Normally I'd be surprised too, but we had a really good talk the night after your accident, and I think I'm going to be seeing this side of him a little more often."

"Wow, that's good to hear. What's going on?"

"I hope you don't take this wrong, but your accident was kind of a blessing for us."

"It was?"

Samantha nodded and cleared her throat. "At first, when your parents called and we didn't know how badly you'd been hurt, it was horrible." She cleared her throat again and blinked her eyes quickly as emotions surfaced. "The thought of losing you was terrifying. I can't imagine how your mother felt."

Morgan felt her own emotions falter as she thought about her mother's anguish. After losing one daughter in a car accident, it wouldn't be fair to lose her only other daughter the same way. But then, who said life was fair? Morgan had realized this fact with complete clarity lately.

"It's been hard on her," Morgan told Samantha. "She still can't see me without crying and hugging me every five minutes."

"I don't blame her. I'd be the same way," Samantha confessed, then she went on. "Trevor was really worried and wanted to come to the hospital with me Monday, but he couldn't because of work. So he called me every hour until we finally found out what was going on. Then, that night when I got home, we had a serious talk. I told him how I felt about everything—about our marriage, our baby, and going to church."

Morgan didn't say anything but felt a warmth in her heart as she saw the revelations of truth growing inside her friend. As Samantha talked, the power in her voice became stronger, and her eyes seemed to glow as her convictions became solid.

"I told him that I wouldn't go through life married to someone who didn't share the same goals and values as mine. I wanted to be married to a husband who stood by me through everything—the good and the bad—one I could always count on and who was devoted to me. I told him I wanted to raise my baby in the Church, going to Primary and Sunday School, and having family prayer and scripture reading. I told him I wanted God to be part of our family."

"What did he say?"

"He said—" A sob caught in her throat and tears filled her eyes. She struggled to get hold of her emotions, but it took a moment. Morgan reached out and took Samantha's hand in hers. "Morgan, he told me he's ready to change. He wants to make our marriage work, and he knows it's time to grow up and to put me and the baby first instead of his friends. He even tentatively agreed about going to church." Samantha wiped away her tears. "I know it's going to take a lot of work and I'll need to be patient and not expect big changes all at once, but to have him show the desire—well, you know . . ."

Morgan nodded. This was big for Trevor. More than anything in the world, Morgan prayed that Samantha and Trevor could make their marriage work.

"So," Samantha said, reaching for another tissue. She glanced outside at the cloudy sky. "What time do you get out of here?"

"Sometime this afternoon," Morgan answered. The doctor had checked on her earlier that morning and found no reason to keep her at the hospital any longer. She'd need some strong pain medication for neck pain and would need to follow up with physical therapy, but she could recover at home just as quickly.

"How do you feel?"

"I feel good," Morgan replied. "I'm ready to go . . ." Her sentenced trailed as she tried to keep her thoughts about the date from surfacing.

"Where? You're ready to go where?"

Morgan swallowed, gazing outside. "Home. I'm ready to go home."

"What about . . . ?" Samantha didn't finish. Morgan knew what she wanted to say, but Morgan wasn't going to go there. The thought was ridiculous.

"Morgan?" Samantha persisted.

Samantha wasn't going to make it easier. "I'm not going," Morgan said.

Releasing a frustrated sigh, Samantha got to her feet. "Why not? I know what I've said about Justin, but I've changed my mind. How can you not go and at least see if he shows up? It's right down the street. You can practically see the restaurant from here. What if he shows up and you're not there?"

"He's not going to show up," Morgan told her. "No one wanted this to work out more than I did, okay? But I'm not going to put myself through that. I'm in enough pain right now, thank you."

"Morgan, I won't let you miss this chance."

"If he wanted me, he would've contacted me somehow. All I needed was a short e-mail, a voice-mail message even, two short words . . . 'I'm coming.' But nothing, Sammy. He's given me nothing—which says a lot."

"I don't think you should give up. I'm sure he has a good reason he hasn't contacted you."

"Yeah; her name's Marika," Morgan shot back.

"Baloney! Justin would still have the decency to end your relationship. No . . ." She thought for a moment. "There's some reason he hasn't called. Like some natural disaster or something."

"Hey, I don't care if his house burned down," Morgan said. "There still has to be someone who has a phone in that town."

"Maybe he's tried to call since you've been in the hospital."

"I've checked."

"Does he have your new number?"

"I e-mailed it to him and left it on his voice-mail."

"Well, I don't know why he hasn't contacted you, then," Samantha responded with a tone of confused frustration. "But I do know this, you have to go to that restaurant today."

"I can't just get up and walk out of the hospital. The doctor hasn't even released me yet. My parents weren't even planning on coming to pick me up until I called them."

"I can take you home, and I can go find the doctor and get him to come and release you."

"No, Samantha."

"Listen to me, Morgan." Samantha planted her feet firmly and pointed her finger at Morgan. "You are not going to go through the rest of your life wondering, 'What if?' I've watched you grow into a strong, independent woman. I've admired the way you've made big changes in your life and taken chances to go after your dreams and stand up for yourself and what's important to you and, well . . . I'm just not going to let you miss this chance to make another dream come true. Now get dressed while I go find your doctor."

"But—"

"Clothes!" Samantha ordered. "I'll be right back."

Samantha left the room and Morgan stared at the door for several moments. She didn't know what to do. She was convinced he wouldn't be there, but part of her desperately wanted to go, just in case. But having him not show would tear her heart in two.

It would also bring the closure she needed to hopefully move on.

Samantha was right. She had to go. She had to know or she'd wonder for the rest of her life.

She was in the bathroom putting on her makeup when Samantha barreled into the room.

"The doctor will be here any minute. I'm going to pack your things. We have just enough time." Samantha spoke in hyper speed. "Aren't you excited?"

"Scared is more like it." Morgan paused with her mascara wand in midair. "What if he doesn't show up?" Tears stung her eyes, but she didn't want to cry and smudge her mascara, so she waved her hand in front of her face, trying to convince her tears to stop.

"What if he does?" Samantha handed her a tissue.

"I'm starting to feel nauseated," Morgan told her.

"It's probably the tapioca. Now hurry up. I'll finish packing."

They had all of Morgan's things piled into a chair and were ready to go just as the doctor arrived.

"If you experience any discomfort or unusual pain, I want you to call me," he ordered.

Morgan nodded, excited that she was finally getting out of the hospital.

"I want you to take it easy and not engage in anything strenuous for the next week," he instructed. "If you get lightheaded or feel weak, that means you're overdoing it and you need to rest."

"I understand," she told him.

Satisfied, the doctor gave Morgan permission to leave along with a charge to schedule a follow-up appointment in two weeks.

Full of nervous excitement, Morgan took one last look at her hospital room, then was on her way.

Their next stop: Gauchos Brazilian Barbecue.

ॐ ॐ ॐ

"I can't believe I'm doing this," Morgan said as they pulled out of the hospital parking lot. "What about Marika?"

"What about her?" Samantha said. "I was talking to a lady I work with who had a son go to Brazil on his mission. She told me that twice he had to be moved from the city where he served to another part of the mission because parents kept trying to line him up with their daughters."

"Why would they do a thing like that to a missionary?"

"Because it's a way to get their daughters to America and give them a better life."

"I don't believe you. Are you sure?" Morgan had no idea things like that happened to missionaries.

"Absolutely. I can give you her number if you want to call her yourself."

"I don't want to call her. But what are you saying, anyway?"

"I'm saying he baptized Marika. She's obviously beautiful. Her parents are very poor. Getting Justin to marry their daughter is a way for her to go to America to give her a better life. Maybe they even want to get to America eventually. Who knows?"

"You really think so?"

"It's a possibility. I mean, he's never even said anything to you about her."

"True, but he might just be hiding it from me or trying to spare my feelings. I don't know."

"Either way, you have to do this, or you'll always wonder."

"I know, you've already said that. And that's what Rhonda said too."

"Hey, if you have the guts to call off a wedding, you have the guts to go sit in a restaurant for a few minutes and see if Justin shows up."

"What if he doesn't?"

"Then order some lunch."

"Are you sure you won't come in with me?"

"Morgan, I'll be out in the parking lot. We'll stay on the phone until he shows up. Oh, and one more thing; Trevor said to tell you to give Justin a swift kick in the rear for not calling him."

Morgan didn't answer. She couldn't even imagine having him actually show up. What would she say? How would she act? So much had happened since they last talked. Would it be awkward? Would everything be different?

There was only one way to find out.

She would be there at 12:55, and she would wait until a quarter after the hour.

Twenty minutes. That was all he had.

Chapter Twenty-Four

―

The sign for the restaurant was partially concealed by a large sycamore tree. They drove right past it, and since it was a one-way street, they had to drive around the block, which was actually four or five blocks put together. Morgan's nerves were nearly shot.

They searched for a place to park, which, of course, didn't exist near the restaurant, so Samantha drove farther down the street until she found a small alley with room to park.

With a hug for luck, Morgan left Samantha in the car and stepped out into the blustery day. The sky was overcast and there was a hint of rain in the air. She was glad she'd worn a sweater; she'd been to the city enough to know how unpredictable the weather could be.

With a limp in her step, she walked down the sidewalk scanning every inch ahead of her, searching cars, windows, doorways—anything—just to see if there was any sign at all of Justin. But she found nothing to lead her to believe he was actually inside waiting for her.

She nearly flew out of her skin when her cell phone rang. She wasn't used to the new ring on the phone, and it completely startled her.

"I'm just outside the restaurant," she told Samantha.

"Can you see him?"

"No, nothing. I don't think he's in there."

"Keep your phone on while you walk in, so I can hear your reaction, just in case he's in there."

"Oh, all right," Morgan said curtly, as the tension of the moment started an ache at the back of her skull. She wished she didn't care; she wished she could be cool and collected, but the fact of the matter was that she was nearly beside herself with anxious excitement. With all of her heart she hoped he was there. There was so much to catch up on, so much to share, so many questions that needed to be answered.

A bell on the door tinkled as she walked inside. Wonderful, rich aromas of barbecued meat on the grill filled the room. Her mouth watered.

"Good afternoon, miss," the host greeted her. He was a handsome young man wearing a wonderfully crafted gaucho outfit with shiny black leather riding boots, wide-legged dark gray pants tucked inside the boots, a stark white shirt with billowy sleeves, and a wide, black leather belt. With his beautiful dark skin color and coal-black eyes, he could have posed for a Brazilian travel brochure.

"Would you like to be seated, or are you waiting for someone?"

"Actually, I was wondering if he was already here. Has a man been seated who mentioned he was waiting for someone?"

"No, miss," the young man answered. "You're welcome to look in the dining room just to make sure, though."

"Go look! Go look!" Samantha said loudly over the phone.

Morgan smiled and shoved her phone into her purse, then walked over to the dining room entrance and peeked inside. He wasn't there.

"Maybe you would like to wait at a table? I could bring you something to drink," the host offered.

Nodding, Morgan followed him to a table in the corner, then requested a different one that allowed her to see the front door.

She took her seat, ordered her drink, then got on the phone and updated Samantha while she found a spot for her purse, scarf, and sweater.

"I'm an idiot," she said to her friend. "He's not coming."

"What time is it?"

"Eight minutes after."

"You have to give him longer than twenty minutes. What if he's caught in traffic?"

"All right, I'll stay until one thirty. But I'm not feeling well."

"Really? Or are you just saying that to have an excuse to leave?"

"I'm not lying, Sammy."

"Okay, okay. Just hang on for a few more minutes. Maybe you need something to eat. The food there is great. Try the buffalo meat."

"Ooh, yuck. That's not going to help."

"No, it's good. Try everything."

"Okay, I'll call you back in a minute."

A different man brought her drink and introduced himself as her waiter, Geremias. He also brought her some warm, fragrant rolls and butter. She hadn't had an appetite, but the delicious aromas in the restaurant drove her taste buds wild.

Picking up some sort of corn muffin, she took a bite of the sweet, moist bread that melted right along with the butter. She couldn't prevent the "mmm" that escaped her lips.

She polished off the muffin and started on a roll. She wouldn't need a meal; she could get plenty full just on the breads.

After checking the time on her watch, she decided to order something for both her and Samantha to take with them on the drive back to Sacramento. It was one thirty on the dot.

The waiter took her order and brought her out another corn muffin, which was a nice gesture. He probably figured out she'd been stood up and felt sorry for her, which was fine because she felt sorry for herself.

Hitting redial on her phone, she called Samantha again.

"I'm leaving."

"But it's only one thirty."

"Not in Brazil, which is where he is. I'm an idiot. I wondered if he'd come, and he didn't. So now I know."

"Don't leave."

"I'll leave my name and number, just in case he shows up. That way he'll know I was here and can call if he wants to reach me. Okay?"

"Okay. But it's not as romantic that way."

"Romance is highly overrated," Morgan said.

"Did you get our food?"

"Yes. I can't stop eating the corn muffins."

"Those things are to die for. Get some extra for me."

"Anything else?"

"Get some of that marinated, mozzerella cheese salad. It's really good."

"Okay," Morgan said as her deflating hopes sank to the ground.

"I'm sorry it didn't work out, Morgan."

"Yeah, me too. But thanks for being here with me."

As she hung up, she looked around one last time. The lively music and colorful Brazilian decor made the restaurant inviting and fun. She would have to remember this place. Maybe she'd come back someday—if the reminder wasn't too painful.

"Here's your meal, miss," he waiter said as he presented her with two different bags filled with containers of food.

He carried the bags to the cashier for her, then wished her a wonderful day.

She thanked him for his kindness and made sure to give him a generous tip. He'd done all he could to make her meal pleasant under the circumstances.

"I wonder if I could leave a message for someone," she said to the cashier. "I was supposed to meet someone here, but he never showed up."

The cashier spoke only broken English but seemed to comprehend what she was saying. She wrote her name and cell phone number on a piece of paper, then put Justin's name on the outside and handed it to him. "If this man," she pointed to Justin's name, "comes here, you give this to him. Okay?"

The man nodded. "Okay."

Slipping on her sweater, she grabbed the two bags in her right hand and headed for the exit as she dialed the phone to tell Samantha to pick her up in front.

This wasn't the way she wanted it to end with Justin. They'd been close enough that she deserved a phone call, or at the very least an e-mail. But nothing. He'd forgotten about her. *Just like the old saying, "Out of sight, out of mind,"* she thought.

Pushing through the heavy door, she stepped outside as droplets of rain started to fall.

"Just in time," she said, looking up at the dark clouds in the sky and hoping to make it to the car before the clouds broke.

Leaning against the side of the building, Morgan steadied herself as a wave of dizziness blurred her vision and weakened her knees.

Clutching the bags tightly in her hands, she willed Samantha to pull up to the curb so she could get inside and sit down.

Breaking into a cold sweat, Morgan braced herself and pulled in several deep breaths to steady herself, but she felt her strength draining. Just then Samantha's car pulled up, a bright yellow taxicab pulling in right behind it. But as Morgan took a step toward the car, her knees buckled and down she went.

❦ ❦ ❦

"Where am I?" Morgan mumbled, keeping her eyes closed.

"Everything's okay, Morgan," Samantha assured her.

"What happened?" she asked, feeling her strength slowly returning.

"You fainted. You're back at the hospital. But the doctor checked you and said you're fine."

Morgan relaxed, knowing everything was okay. She still felt weak and tired.

"I dreamed about Justin," she told her friend, keeping her eyes closed, wishing she didn't have to wake up yet.

"You did?"

"Yeah, I dreamed he finally showed up. It seemed so real. It was so good to be with him again," Morgan told her. "Too bad it was just a dream."

"Maybe your dream can come true," Samantha said.

Morgan smiled and slowly opened her eyes. "Sounds like you're the one dreaming."

"But it is true," another voice said.

She knew that voice but didn't dare look. Was this all still a dream?

"I'm here, Morgan," he said again.

"Justin?" she whispered, as a knot formed in her throat.

He stepped up next to her bed and took her hand.

"Is it really you?" She stared at his face.

He chuckled. "It's really me. How are you feeling?"

Happiness filled her until she thought she'd burst. "I feel great now. How did you find me?"

"My taxi pulled up just as you fainted. You scared me to death," he told her. "I was glad Samantha was there to explain what was going on."

"Dr. Mortensen wasn't happy to see us come back so soon. You're lucky he didn't put you back in the hospital," Samantha explained.

"But he was pretty cool about everything after I told him what was going on."

Morgan looked at Justin's face, searching his eyes, trying to believe he was actually there.

He smiled.

"I'm so glad you came," she said.

He looked as if he hadn't shaved in a week and like he'd slept in his clothes for at least that long.

"I was glad to see you there too."

They gazed at each other for several seconds, as if trying to convince themselves that they weren't dreaming. Then, as if drawn together by a magnet, Justin leaned down and gave her a gentle hug.

They held onto each other as if their lives depended on it. Morgan wanted to laugh for joy. He was here and she was in his arms, and it felt wonderful! She also wanted to ask him all the questions that had plagued her and kept her up at night. Why hadn't he called? Why hadn't he e-mailed? But she pushed all of that to the back of her mind. For the moment, none of that mattered.

"I'm sorry I was late," he said as he released his hold on her. "I had a hard time getting the flights I needed. I tried to call you and Sammy, but I couldn't get through. I tried your cell phone but the number had been changed. I thought you were trying to avoid me and didn't want to talk to me. But I had to believe you would be here," he said, taking one of her hands in his.

There was no denying the feelings they shared. She felt it in her heart and saw it in his eyes.

"I'm so glad you came," she said softly as tears threatened.

"I would've swum through shark-infested waters to get there today."

They hugged again.

"Your hair smells the same, but you look even prettier than I remembered," Justin whispered. "I've dreamed of this day for weeks. I don't ever want to let you go."

Morgan couldn't believe what she was hearing. She'd wanted this meeting to be wonderful, but she didn't dare dream it could be like this.

"I wasn't sure you would come," she said. "I didn't know what to think, but I had to come. I had to know."

"I prayed all the way from Brazil that you'd be here, then when I landed in San Francisco, I came straight from the airport. My bags are still there because I didn't have time to go get them. I was afraid I'd miss you. And then, when I got out of the taxi . . ."

They pulled back so they could look into each other's faces.

"I can't imagine what you thought," Morgan said with a laugh, holding her ribs with one hand.

"It completely freaked me out," he admitted. "I didn't know what to think." He took her hand and kissed her knuckles. "I'm just happy you're okay. You are okay, aren't you?"

"I couldn't be better," she said, knowing that having him there was all that mattered. Their gazes connected, making Morgan's heart thump wildly in her chest. He looked wonderful. His skin was darkly tanned and his hair a bit longer and tousled from his long plane ride, but his smile was still the same, and in his eyes she still saw the look that warmed her heart in Cancún and rekindled that warmth now.

"What happened to you?" she asked. "I tried to contact you too, but I couldn't get through on your phone and my e-mails got returned."

"I can't imagine what you were thinking," Justin said. "This last month has been completely crazy. I told you about the damage we had from the storm?"

"Yes, you sent me a picture."

"Then my house burned down and everything was destroyed— my cell phone, my computer, and all my travel documents."

Samantha and Morgan exchanged looks of amazement.

"Your house burned down?" Morgan said.

"It was a pain to have to replace everything, especially since we were so far away from civilization. Most of the main roads were impassable. The bridge to Santa Maria had been washed away. It took a week to get power back to the city after the storm, and longer than that to get a new phone. I lived in the church for a while. But all I kept thinking was I had to get out of there and get back to you. And when I finally did get to a phone I couldn't get through to anyone. You guys have some kind of solicitor block on your phone—it doesn't allow calls from outside the country through either."

"It doesn't?" Morgan asked.

He shook his head. "Believe me, I tried. I tried everything to get through to you."

"That is so romantic," Samantha said dreamily.

"How did you finally get to an airport?" Morgan asked.

He chuckled. "I rode everything from a donkey to an old van with a cardboard roof. I nearly lost my life on the back of a motorcycle on the freeway outside of Rio, and I shared a bus with a dozen drug dealers from the slums. The only reason they didn't rob and kill me right there was the fact that I hadn't showered or shaved for over a week and looked like I barely had enough money for bus fare."

Morgan shook her head with amazement.

"But it was my friend, Marika, who helped me the most. I owe her one."

"Marika?"

"Yeah, I told you about her. She's the one I baptized while I was down there. I've known her family since I was on my mission. She's like a little sister to me."

Sister? Morgan was relieved to hear his definition of his relationship with Marika.

"I was having a hard time replacing my visa and passport in time to catch my plane, and she just happened to be dating the son of a government official. It was through her connection to him that I made it on the plane in time, or I wouldn't be here right now."

"I hope I can thank her for helping you someday," she told him. "I can't believe you had to go through so much to get here."

"Morgan, the thought of seeing you again was the only thing that kept me going. I've dreamt about you, thought about you, and carried your picture with me everywhere I went. But I didn't care what I had to go through to see you. I had to be here because . . . I love you."

Tears welled up in Morgan's eyes and her bottom lip trembled. Suddenly, everything she had been through, all the time that had passed, all the challenges that she'd overcome, every bit of it was worth it just to hear those three words.

"I love you too," she replied.

They pulled each other into an embrace, cementing their expressions of love. Being in his arms felt right and then, taking another look into his eyes, she knew she'd made the right decision to wait for Justin.

❦ ❦ ❦

"So," Justin said, as he laced his fingers through Morgan's.

"So," Morgan echoed, giving him a smile, still amazed that he was there with her right now.

They were sitting together on the couch in her parents' living room. Morgan was going to stay with her parents while she recovered, and Justin would stay in her apartment while he was in town.

The meeting with her parents had gone even better than she'd hoped. Her father was warm and friendly, and, to Morgan's delight, so was her mother. But then, who couldn't like Justin? He was just too cute and too nice not to like.

But Morgan was grateful for some private time with him. Her feelings for him hadn't changed at all, but she wondered where they would go now.

"That sure was a nice meal your mom made. She's a good cook."

"Thanks."

"Can you cook like her?"

"Well, I haven't had as much practice, but she's taught me how to make a lot of different things. Why?"

He shrugged, a shy grin filling his face. Morgan's heartbeat sped up.

Morgan nodded, wondering which of them was going to introduce the topic of their relationship. She wished she had spoken sooner, because his next question was one she'd wanted to avoid.

"I was also wondering about . . ." he paused, making Morgan's stomach curdle.

Uh-oh, here it comes.

"I mean, I've gathered from some of the comments from Samantha and your parents that you've had a pretty serious relationship with someone."

Morgan groaned inwardly. She knew that sooner or later she needed to tell him about Manny, but she'd hoped it would be later rather than sooner.

"Is there anything I should know?" he asked. "I mean, how serious is it?"

Morgan drew in a deep breath, then expelled it slowly, allowing herself a moment to gather her thoughts. Then, for the next hour, she told him all about Manny, and how her experiences in Cancún had changed what she wanted out of life. Morgan smiled shyly as she also confessed how worried she'd been about Marika and Justin's feelings for her while he was gone. In the course of the conversation, she also had a chance to honestly explain concerns she had over Justin's work and how it would affect the potential of their relationship to grow.

After a few moments of silence when she'd finished, Justin slowly said, "I've never felt this way about anyone in my life. I've dated some wonderful girls, but none of them was as wonderful as you. And I can't imagine living my life without you."

Morgan continued to smile as tears of joy filled her eyes and spilled onto her cheeks.

"I was thinking that I should move here, to Sacramento, so we can spend time together. What do you think?"

She couldn't speak, so she nodded her head.

"We have something very special, something real, and I want to do everything I can to give us a chance to see where things go from here," he continued.

Morgan nodded again, his words echoing every thought she had—she just wanted to hear his feelings, knowing that he knew hers.

"You can go to school and I can do my work from here. I'll have to fly to New York occasionally, and I hope you'll come with me. I think it's time you meet my parents too."

Her heart began to soar, along with her dreams that were becoming a reality.

"So, what do you think?" he asked.

"I think it sounds wonderful. I think you're wonderful," she said.

He leaned toward her, cupping her chin in his hand. "I think you're pretty wonderful too." He kissed her softly on the forehead. "Thanks for not giving up on us." He kissed her on the tip of her nose.

"You're . . ."

He kissed her briefly on the lips.

". . . welcome," she managed to say before he kissed her one more time.

Chapter Twenty-Five

Six Months Later

Holding hands sixty feet beneath the surface of the water, Justin and Morgan began a slow ascent. The dive had been amazing, and they'd captured every moment using their underwater video camera, a wedding present to each other.

Coming back to Cancún for their honeymoon seemed only fitting. They'd gotten married on the day after Valentine's Day, which was a much more romantic day to them, since it was the day they'd met each other exactly one year earlier.

Their six-month reuniting and engagement had been filled with wonderful experiences of getting to know each other and deepening their love. The more time they spent together, the more their relationship grew. This time, for Morgan, there were no doubts, no sleepless nights. She couldn't imagine life without Justin, and he couldn't imagine life without her.

She'd moved back home with her family, and Justin had moved into her apartment. He'd managed to do most of his work from Sacramento, which allowed them time together and time for Morgan's family to get to know Justin and fall in love with him as much as she had. Her mother had learned all his favorite foods and cooked up a storm for him every time he'd come over. Justin and her father shared a passion for golf and had spent many early-morning hours on the course together.

She, in turn, had traveled to New York with him as often as possible when he went back on business. It gave her a chance to get to know his parents. They had accepted the engagement with some reservation, but Morgan was confident that their relationship would grow more comfortable. His mother also loved art, and together, she and Morgan visited the Metropolitan Museum of Art and other museums and galleries. And even though Morgan had never thought of herself as a great chess player, she could give Justin's father—who loved chess—a challenging game, and had even managed to win several times. Theirs was a very different life from the one her family lived in Sacramento, but Morgan had found she loved the pace of Manhattan and the energy of the big city.

And for Morgan, planning her wedding this time had been a lot different from the first time she'd done it. This time she'd been the driving force behind making reservations and appointments to meet with florists, caterers, and directors of reception centers. And it was her mother who had had a hard time keeping up with her. Together they'd had a great time planning the wedding and reception in Sacramento.

Going to the temple to get sealed to Justin for time and all eternity had been the crowning moment in Morgan's life. There hadn't been a dry eye in the room as they were sealed, and as Morgan had gazed into the mirrors in the sealing room, she was able to see the Lord's hand in helping her through all her trials and challenges.

Patience and faith, she'd thought. *That's all it took.*

Things had worked out for Manny too. From what Morgan had heard, he'd begun dating the realtor who'd sold him the mobile home, and within two months they were engaged. By Christmas they were married, and their honeymoon had been in Branson, of course.

On the way back to shore, with Justin's arm wrapped around her, Morgan realized paradise wasn't a place on the map, somewhere you could visit but had to leave behind; it was something you felt inside, something that stayed with you forever. She knew this, because here with Justin she'd truly found paradise.

"So," Justin said. "After dinner, do you want to check out the karaoke lounge again?"

"Are you kidding? We can't miss disco night!"

Justin laughed and kissed her on the forehead. "You're a nut, you know that? I have a feeling I'm going to have my work cut out for me trying to keep up with you."

"Hey!" she feigned offense. "You're the Dr. Frankenstein who created this monster. You *have* to keep up with me."

"You're about the prettiest monster I've ever met," he said, kissing her lips this time.

"I bet you say that to all the girls."

"Nope, just you. You're my girl."

"I sure am," she said, snuggling closer to her husband. "So, tell me more about Brazil. I want to know everything I can before we go."

"Well," he said. "With you it'll be an adventure." Then he winked and leaned in for one more kiss. When they pulled apart, Morgan sighed contentedly.

"Ah, paradise," she said.

And Justin laughed.

ABOUT THE AUTHOR

In the fourth grade, Michele Ashman Bell was considered a daydreamer by her teacher, and was told on her report card that, "She has a vivid imagination and would probably do well with creative writing." Her imagination, combined with a passion for reading, has enabled Michele to live up to her teacher's prediction. She loves writing books that inspire and edify while entertaining.

Michele grew up in St. George, Utah, where she met her husband at Dixie College before they both served missions—his to Pennsylvania, and hers to Frankfurt, Germany. Seven months after they returned, they were married, and are now the proud parents of four children: Weston, Kendyl, Andrea, and Rachel.

A favorite pastime of Michele's is supporting her children in all of their activities, traveling both in and outside the United States with her husband and family, and doing research for her books. She also recently became scuba certified. Aside from being a busy wife and mother, Michele is an aerobics instructor at the Life Centre Athletic Club near her home, and she currently teaches young-adult Sunday School and Relief Society once a month.

Michele is the best-selling author of several books and a Christmas booklet, and has also written children's stories for the *Friend* magazine.

Michele enjoys corresponding with her readers, who can write to her care of Covenant Communications, P.O. Box 416, American Fork, UT, 84003-0416, or e-mail her via Covenant at info@covenant-lds.com.